CHRISTMAS IN NORTH BEND

WENDI ZWADUK

Christmas in North Bend
ISBN # 978-1-83943-761-8
©Copyright Wendi Zwaduk 2021
Cover Art by Fiona Jayde ©Copyright November 2021
Interior text design by Claire Siemaszkiewicz
Totally Bound Publishing

Totally Bound Publishing books by Wendi Zwaduk

Single Books
Learning How to Bend
Must Be Doing Something Right
My Immortal
You'll Think of Me
Tangled Up
Careless Whisper
Please Remember Me
What Might Have Been
Ever Fallen In Love
Someone Like You
Love Remembers
When You're With Me
Sunshine of Your Love
Firelit Magic
Her Man
My Favorite Mistake
Silk and Decadence
Bound by Desire
Runaway Royal
Christmas in North Bend

Love Lessons
Drawn Together
Written Together
Together Again
Dancing Together

The Refuge
Running with the Wicked
Resisting the Wicked
Serving the Wicked

Clandestine Classics
The Phantom of the Opera

Anthologies
Treble: Savin' Me
Switch: Still the One
Bound to the Billionaire: Play to Him
Whip It Up: Honey and Decadence
Lasso Lovin': Tying One On
Wild After Dark: Taken In
Boots, Chaps and Cowboy Hats: Between Us
Three's a Charm: A Sinful Tune
Sensory Limits: Just You and Me

Seasonal Collections
Heart Attack: Over My Head
Haunted By You: Miss Me Baby
Wanton Witches: Candlelit Magic
Jolly Rogered: Ruined by the Pirate
Naughty or Nice?: Wrapped in Red and Green

CHRISTMAS IN NORTH BEND

Dedication

For everyone who loves Christmas
and Christmas stories
For my Lucky Ducks
For JPZ, the best Christmas present ever

Chapter One

Alex West stood in the middle of the concourse at Cleveland Hopkins airport and toyed with the handle of his bag. His assistant, Jill Gosk, fiddled with her phone and growled. The people on the plane had been irritated by the lateness of the flight and the snow delaying their landing a few minutes. He didn't mind. Christmas, even seven days away, was the time to slow down and spend precious hours with family and friends — not stress over things he couldn't control.

"What's the matter?" He noticed a dusting of snow on the windowsill and wished he were out in the cold. He loved Christmas in Ohio, even if he hadn't spent much time in the state in a few years. "Jill?"

"The car should be ready so all we have to do is retrieve your bags from the claims area. According to my app, the bags are down there." Jill glanced about. "This is a tiny airport."

"It's not LAX, but it works." He pointed to the corridor. "Let's get the luggage." He nudged her forward. "I don't know what I'd do without you. Girl, you save my butt almost every day." He grinned and fell into step beside her. "How's Nick?"

She blushed. "I—I didn't think you knew about him."

"He called to tell me you were together," Alex said. "I told him I was happy for you. I'm glad you found each other." He rode the escalator to the ground floor. The sound of Christmas carols echoed in the air, along with the din of conversation. He watched the people moving about. There were stories in these folks. Stories about love lost, love found, people reconnecting and the joy of Christmas. He chuckled to himself. He could use these bits and pieces for his own upcoming writing. The book wouldn't write itself and he needed the right push to get started.

"Here. Our bags are in carousel C." Jill marched up to the revolving belt filled with luggage. "Keep your eyes peeled."

"Sure will." Alex sighed. He trusted Jill with his schedule and his business dealings. She knew how to get him from point A to point B without issue. He slid his gaze over the array of bags. "Either I'm wrong, or I don't see mine." He pointed to her lavender suitcase. "There's yours."

She nodded and grabbed her bags from the belt. "Got them. Yours should be along." She checked her phone again and turned the screen around. "See? The app says they're here."

"Right, but they're on the second time through and mine aren't there. I've kept an eye out." He glanced over her shoulder at the phone. "The app is wrong."

"It can't be." She massaged her temple. "They have to be here."

He'd learned not to let minor setbacks get to him. Being a writer meant having a thick skin. Just because one person didn't like his work didn't mean a myriad of others agreed. Besides, who could be upset at Christmas? "It's okay. We'll go to the lost luggage department." He guided her and her bag away from the carousel. "My bags are probably halfway to Chicago."

"I'm so sorry, RR."

She'd used his pen name. He shouldn't be annoyed, but he'd rather be referred to by his given name in this instance. "Don't sweat it. We're on the way to my parents and I'm sure I can borrow some of my father's clothes until my luggage gets here — if we didn't simply go to the wrong carousel." He'd bet the bags were on the wrong plane, but he saw no reason to get upset. "It's going to be all right." He strode up to the counter.

The woman at the desk smiled, but before he could speak, Jill stepped forward.

"Hi. I booked the flight for Mr. Taylor and we've arrived, but his luggage hasn't. I have the information on the app and everything." Jill held up her phone. "See?"

The woman smiled again. "Let me check your information." She paused. "RR Taylor? As in the author RR Taylor?"

"That's me." He offered his hand. "I'm heading over to North Bend for Christmas with my family and to do a book signing the day after tomorrow. If you're available, you should stop in."

"I'm working all week," the attendant said. "But it's great to meet you. I've read all your books. I loved *Crispin in New York*."

"Thank you. If you have a piece of paper, I'll autograph it for you." He waited for her to give him something to write on, then signed the page with a special note for her. "There. Enjoy."

"Thank you." The attendant beamed. "Wow." She tucked the paper into her front pocket. "I wish I had better news for you concerning your bags. According to my tracking system, your luggage was rerouted to New York and will be back in two days. We can call you when it's at the terminal."

"No," Jill said. "He needs his clothes."

"I'll get by." He placed his hand on Jill's arm and turned his attention to the attendant. "Thank you. Where can I leave my information?" Not having his clothes or the presents he'd brought for his family wasn't ideal, but he had little choice.

"I've got it on file with your baggage and flight numbers," the attendant said. "I'll be in touch."

"Thank you. I hope I have my luggage before Christmas. If I don't, then I don't. I hope you have a Merry Christmas, too." He nudged Jill. "We should go."

"I messed up," Jill said. "This is bad."

"You didn't mess up." He nodded to the sign directing them to the car rental counter. "Why don't you check on the car?"

"Oh yeah." She darted away with her phone.

Alex sighed. Jill was a sweet woman, but so highly strung. He thanked the cosmos she'd come into his orbit to help with his promotional needs, but he could use a break from her. He followed behind her, but at a bit of a distance. One of his plans wasn't going so well. Time to check on another of his schemes. He sent a text to Nick.

Are you at the hotel? She's upset about my luggage being lost. Might need to be extra sweet to her. Do you have everything you need for tonight?

Alex didn't wait for a response and instead tucked his phone into his jacket pocket. He hurried after Jill. He'd worked with her boyfriend to facilitate Nick's proposal that night. Jill would be happy, Nick would have the woman he loved and Alex would have a break.

Jill stopped walking and her shoulders slumped. Her brow crinkled. She still had her phone to her ear. "You don't understand. I reserved the car a month ago. We need that vehicle. I don't care if it's the holidays. We have places to be. No, I don't want...my client is leaving. Hold on." She stopped Alex. "Wait."

"Take a breath. It's Christmas. Everyone is on the edge and you getting upset isn't helping. The more you and I flip out, the more upset everyone else will be." He pointed to the rental counter. "Let's check on the car in person."

"I'll handle it." Jill pushed past him. "Wait over there."

He should argue with her, but he'd just given his speech on being calm. Disputing wouldn't get him anywhere. Part of him didn't mind taking his time while getting to North Bend, but the rest of him wanted to unite Jill with Nick. Then she'd relax. Good thing Alex had flown Nick in ahead of time and had him installed in the hotel in North Bend.

Alex waited by the bank of windows and stared out at the planes on the tarmac. His thoughts wandered. Why had he stayed away from North Bend for so long? He loved the snow and quiet of Ohio and appreciated the small-town feel of his home base, but his apartment in Los Angeles had everything he needed. His favorite restaurants were within walking distance and while he didn't want for anything entertainment-wise, he missed his friends in North Bend. The people he'd grown up and come of age with. He had so many fond memories of the town. Plus...there was Molly.

He held his bag tighter. Before he'd left town, he had to see Molly. They'd been so tight. He'd once thought he'd marry her. He'd never forget the blue of her eyes, the softness of her hair or the way she blushed when she smiled. They'd been the best of friends and she'd been his first girlfriend. *First lots of things.* Then they'd gone their separate ways. When they'd been together, he'd told her everything. She'd confided in him when she'd flunked her driving test and when she'd thought he wanted to fix her up with their mutual friend Tony. She hadn't been in love with Tony — she'd loved Alex.

Flashes of his years with Molly came to mind — volunteering at the Santa Barn, secret Santa shopping and all those visits to the library... He'd heard about her opening the bookstore and vowed he'd sign books at the shop.

Wouldn't she be surprised when she saw him? Was she single? He'd forgotten to ask his mother about Molly's relationship status when he'd planned his trip back to Ohio. But wouldn't his mother have mentioned Molly being married? Wouldn't Molly have invited him to the wedding — if she'd gotten hitched?

Jill stomped up to him. "Okay. So, here's the problem. We must have a car, but we can't have two like I wanted. Just one, so we have to share."

"I thought that was the plan." It had been when he'd canceled her vehicle. She didn't need a separate car if Nick had one and they'd be together.

"This isn't right. Your luggage is missing, we've only got one car... What else can go wrong?" Jill asked.

"The luggage will come back and the car situation is fine."

"Oh no." Jill pinched the bridge of her nose. "It's snowing."

"I've driven in snow."

"It's cold."

"Ohio is cold," Alex said. He stared at her. "You're holding something back. What's the rest of the issue?"

"I miss Nick. It's Christmas and I'm not with the one I love." She sighed. "I need some sleep and a few hours to regroup. I hate being this grouchy."

"You're stressed. It happens." He grasped her shoulder. "Don't worry about it. You never know — Nick might be waiting at the hotel."

"Fat chance." She sank onto the closest chair. "You don't understand. I'm being pouty, and I hate it. The thing is, I thought I could do this job, but I feel like I'm failing. I'm sorry."

"Stress is a pain in the neck." He sat beside her and took the keys from her. "Take a few moments to recover. While I'm driving us to North Bend, why don't you call Nick? That'll make you feel better."

"Ugh. That's the other part of this. I tried to call him, but I can't get an answer."

He checked his phone. The LED light flashed green, meaning he had a new text. He retrieved the message from Nick.

Here and ready for the surprise. I can't wait.

Good. Nick was in place. Alex tucked his phone in his pocket again. "Well, why not try again? He might have been temporarily engaged." *Drat.* He should've chosen a different word. "Just call him."

Jill stared at him. "How can you be so calm? Is it because you're going to see Molly over Christmas?"

"Maybe." *Not really.* Thinking about seeing his friend excited him. He hasn't spent time with her in forever. He missed their friendship. Plus, he wanted to know why they'd drifted apart.

"Well, she seems nice." Jill stood. "I feel better. Thanks for letting me freak out."

He joined her and started toward the doors leading to the row of rental cars. "You're welcome."

"How long is the drive to North Bend?" She fell into step beside him. "It's far away from here, isn't it?"

"About an hour and a half." He stopped at the parking slot containing the SUV. "This is what we have?"

"The dark blue behemoth. It was the only one not rented out." Jill tried the passenger-side door. "It's not the compact one, but it'll do."

"See? That's the Christmas spirit." He climbed behind the wheel of the SUV. "Here's to the next leg of our journey. You'll have plenty of room to stretch out and it would appear there's satellite radio, so your favorite channels are on here, too."

"Something is finally normal," Jill said. "Yes."

"As for you doing your job, don't worry. I wouldn't be in Ohio without you." He could, but she needed the reassurance. "It's Christmas. We start being jolly as of right now. We won't let work get us upset and won't worry about the signing. The spirit of the season is around us and we're going to have fun." If he had his way, Jill and Nick would be engaged that night and he'd have the next book started. Merry Christmas.

* * * *

Two hours later, Alex drove past the North Bend city limits sign. He rolled down the main drag. The town now had three gas stations instead of one, the hotel had grown—which he'd learned when he'd helped Nick book the suite—and there was now a big box store just over the city line. Still, North Bend had a small-town feel. Every business in town was either on Main Street or Church Street—crisscrossing at the center of town. Tinsel and lights decorated each lamp post, an inflatable Santa and thirty-foot pine tree towered in the town square and a row of evergreen trees stood sentry duty in front of the hardware store. Every pole and sign featured lights and garland. He'd forgotten just how pretty the town could be—like a Christmas card come to life.

Alex sighed. The Christmas spirit he'd longed for swirled around him. He parked in front of the hotel under the awning.

"Why are we here?" Jill asked. "We're staying with your parents, aren't we?" She paused. "Aren't we?"

"You're staying here. I thought you might want a break from me and deserved some pampering. I've made all the arrangements for you to be here while I'm at my parents' house." He shifted in his seat. "You work hard. Consider this my Christmas present to you." Nick had a lot to do with her being there, but Alex wasn't about to let her know that yet. The surprise was Nick's to disclose.

"How will I get around?"

Drat. He had to think of something quick. Something besides Nick had a car for them to use. "I'll stop by my parents' house and borrow one of their vehicles to get around. I'll drop this one off here and use that one."

"Don't you need me close?" she asked.

"It's Christmas and this is one signing. I can fly solo for a while."

"You've mentioned the Christmas thing," Jill said.

"Enjoy this gift. You don't have to deal with me for a while. Isn't that worth something?" He sure hoped Nick was in the lobby waiting for her.

"You did this all by yourself? You never make plans."

"I let you set up the signing schedule, but I can handle going out on my own. I've done it before—I used to control my entire schedule before you came along." He nodded to the door. "Go. I'm a call away if you need me." If the plans were still in place, she'd get her Christmas wish of engagement to Nick, and Alex would have time to explore North Bend.

"I'm not wild about this plan, but I'll go. Call me if you need anything." She left the car, then, with his help, retrieved her bags from the rear of the SUV.

"You'll have a good time," Alex said. "Promise."

"I'll be at the signing. I won't miss it," Jill said.

"I know, and I appreciate your diligence. I've got this." He hugged her, then waved. "Merry Christmas."

"I'll see you before Christmas," she muttered. She stole glances at him as she made her way into the hotel.

Nick stood in the lobby and held roses. If Alex wasn't mistaken, he heard Jill shriek. He watched her embrace Nick. Alex tended to strike out in love, but he appreciated seeing two people fall for each other. Molly had once told him he loved love. Maybe. If nothing else, he'd helped make Nick and Jill's Christmas desire come true.

He left his post beside the vehicle and slid into the driver's seat. He drummed on the steering wheel. Christmas, as well as love, was a strange thing. Some people weren't thrilled by the change of season and chill in the air. Some fell into depression. Others found excitement and fulfillment in the electricity in the air. He embraced the joy of Christmas.

He pulled away from the hotel and started down Main Street. Alex stopped at the traffic light and noticed the bookstore. He'd seen the images of the store on the webpage, but the real view was better. Books arranged as letters served as the signage for the establishment. Christmas lights ringed each window and a Christmas tree hulked on the sidewalk in front.

Alex would bet Molly had the shelves packed with great books. Part of him wanted to visit and check out the place, but the rest of him refrained. He'd be there tomorrow. The signing wasn't for another day and a half. Right now, he needed to get to his parents' house.

He drove through the housing development on the east end of town on the way to his childhood home. There were Christmas lights everywhere. All the area needed now was fresh snow. He almost wanted to break out in a carol or two.

He parked in his parents' driveway, then schlepped his carry-on bag into the house. Despite the lights and decorations on every conceivable surface of the home, the place wasn't the same. No chaos, no people…and no dog. Without those, he felt lost. He couldn't chastise his parents on their lack of a dog—he didn't have one either. He wanted one. He needed a companion.

Alex sank onto one of the stools at the bar. How could a guy with a great life and what he'd always wanted for a career consider changing most of it after one night back in his home town? Because he'd never gotten North Bend out of his system or forgotten Molly. Because his carefully crafted life wasn't as bright as he wanted everyone to think and he didn't have any words for the next book. He hated writer's block, but he couldn't concentrate.

The night he'd broken things off with Molly came to mind. She hadn't argued with him when he'd said he'd call her later. *Famous last words…* He'd broken up with her to follow his dream. He'd thought he was doing the best for them both, but he'd been a jerk. Now he'd come back and wanted her to be nice to him? *Huh. She should tell me to get lost.*

He paused. The house was too silent. Where was everyone? He fiddled with his phone and called his mother. Maybe she'd give him a better idea of what to do and where the heck she and his father were. After two rings, she answered.

"Hi sweetheart. You're home? Already?" she asked.

"I'm at the house. You went a little berserk with the lights and garland, didn't you? I don't remember this much glitter when I was a kid," he said. "It's like walking into a gingerbread house."

"Oh, it's just a few things," she said and laughed. "Did you bring a girlfriend with you? There's food in the fridge and plenty of wood in the bin. We anticipated you'd be hungry."

"Thanks. I appreciate you thinking of me." He sounded so formal. This was his mother. He didn't have to walk on pins and needles with her. "I'm on my own—no girlfriend—so there's more than enough to eat." He pinched the bridge of his nose. "You don't have to worry about me, Mom."

"It's my job to worry," his mother said. "Have you visited Molly?"

"I'll get there," he said. "Will you be home for the signing?"

"Sure. I know it seems like we forgot about you, but this is the big anniversary. Forty years. Can you imagine being with someone for more than half your life?" She laughed again. "Your father planned a dinner tonight with the Pfafs, then we're off to see the new action movie. I don't know what it's called. We're staying in Erie for one more night, then we'll be home in the morning and at the signing. I won't miss this. My son signing books in my local bookstore. My son, the brilliant author."

Brilliant author? His mother knew how to pump his ego.

Alex left the phone on the bar and glanced over at the fridge. Cooking wasn't his forte. He excelled at burning things and ordering takeout. But he had to eat.

He shrugged out of his sport coat, then crossed the room to the closet. Ages ago, he'd left his leather jacket in there. "Please, Mom, tell me you didn't donate my coat." He opened the door and found the jacket. "Score! Thanks, Mom." He donned the garment and breathed in the scent of the leather.

Life wasn't exactly how he'd planned, but not all that bad, either. The time on the plane and worrying about getting to North Bend had caught up with him. He needed a few hours' sleep. Since he had the house to himself, he might as well catch a few winks. If he was going to win Molly back, he had to be on top form.

Chapter Two

Molly adjusted the sign in the front of her bookstore and sighed. Six days until Christmas and she had a book signing scheduled for the following afternoon. Was she crazy? So close to Christmas and she'd accepted RR Taylor's inquiry to sign at her store. She'd seen the name RR Taylor a hundred times. She had the author's books on a prominent shelf and at least one copy was sold per day. Tomorrow, RR Taylor, the author of thirteen spy novels, would be in her store signing copies of his latest book. She should've been happy. The buzz about the author's — she thought the person was a man, but she'd been wrong before — appearance lit up the town of North Bend.

Then why wasn't she happy? She had no idea who the actual person behind RR Taylor was and she should know. She was the bookseller. The information and behind the scenes stuff should've been her angle. Instead, she was just as in the dark as the fans talking about the books. Every time she looked for RR Taylor online, she found stock photos and generic descriptions. No fan photos, lifestyle pictures or anything.

"I see the appearance has been mentioned in the paper." Niecy, Molly's close friend and co-worker, rustled the newspaper. "They talked about the store in glowing terms and we've got everyone talking."

"Do we?" She gazed over at the article. The paper hadn't been able to find a photograph of the author either and had used the most recent book cover instead. She smiled. "Your brother wrote the article. It should be good. He's the best writer on the paper."

"And I might have bugged him until he mentioned it." Niecy folded up the paper. "How much more Christmas decorating do you want to do? We always go overboard." She arranged a strand of garland. "Did you get those glass ornaments you were ogling over at Fynn's Hardware?"

"No. It wasn't in the budget." She folded her arms. Molly loved Christmas and decking the store out in as much green and red as she could find, but considering the recent economic downturn in North Bend, she had to put her money back into the store. "I'll get them later."

"I'll ask Fynn to hold a set back," Niecy said. "I'm sure it won't be a problem. They know you'll come in for them and probably get a few other things, too." She smiled, then tapped the paper on the bookshelf. "Everything should be ready for the Christmas party tonight, too."

"Oh good." She leaned on the pillar and fought the urge to massage her temples. "I must be losing my mind. How could I schedule the staff Christmas party the day before an author signing?"

"Because we didn't know RR Taylor would be coming in. Whoever he or she is, they didn't bother to tell us they were booking the date until two weeks ago." Niecy shook her head. "I'm shocked we've been able to get the word out."

"Me, too." She rested her hand on her hip. "Remember last month, when we had Rachael West here?"

"I do."

"I didn't think she'd get nearly that much publicity, but she not only got attention, but she managed to pack the store. For an indie author, she did a great job." She wished more authors would put the extra effort in to promote. The more the author worked, the better he or she tended to look, and be more reachable, too.

"I liked Rachael. She was sweet." Niecy nodded. "I have to go."

"No problem." Molly sneezed. *Drat.* Her nose tingled. Was she getting sick? No, no, no. She didn't have time to be sick. She met Niecy's gaze. "I'm fine."

"Are you sure? That sounded like you're not at one hundred percent. Want me to check your temp?" Niecy held up her hand. "I will."

"I know you will, but I'm fine. It was just a sneeze." She knew better. She'd sneezed three times before and the scent of the books wasn't getting to her. No, she'd get some and vitamin C. The sniffle wouldn't get the better of her.

"I've got my eye on you." Niecy walked away, leaving Molly to her thoughts.

Molly wished sometimes that she could be more like her best friend. Niecy stood at least six inches taller than Molly's five-foot-two-inches and her blonde hair always looked great. Even bad hair days were photo-worthy. Molly struggled to use her flat iron without burning herself. *Oh well.* She wasn't going to get any taller and one of these days she'd learn how to do her hair and makeup without mishap.

Molly focused on rearranging the garland, then swept her gaze over the large Christmas tree in the middle of the store. The lights twinkled and sent a rainbow of color over the main room. One day she wanted to add glitter-covered snowflakes hanging from the ceiling, and make it look like snow was about to fall on the tree.

She'd put so much of her time and money into the store. The place was her second home. When people walked into Turn the Page, she wanted them to feel like they'd come home, too. She'd added couches and oversized chairs for patrons to use for reading or sipping coffee from the adjacent store.

Molly fixed the display of RR Taylor books, then turned on her heel. When she spied the front doors, she paused.

A woman with black hair down to her shoulders strode into the store and right up to the Christmas tree. She caressed one of the glitter-encrusted book ornaments.

Molly made her way over to the woman. "Hi, I'm Molly. Welcome to Turn the Page. May I help you?"

"You're Molly?" The woman's blue eyes glittered. She pressed her lips together for a moment, then spoke. "You're the one I talked to on the phone, aren't you?" She grinned. "It's great to put a face to the name."

"I'm the owner of Turn the Page and I speak to plenty of people. Did you need help?" Molly crinkled her nose as another sneeze built. *Drat.* She didn't want to sneeze on the woman. "Are you in search of literary ornaments?" She didn't remember talking to this lady, but that didn't mean much. "Are you shopping for a book geek?"

"No, I just thought these were pretty." The woman rested her hand on her hip. Her blood-red nails sparkled in the light. "I'm here with my fiancé. We're scoping out the space for the RR Taylor signing. RR Taylor brings many fans, and I wanted to make sure there was enough room." She strode over to the main staircase. "I love this staircase. It's beautiful. Is it original to the store?"

Molly swallowed her confusion. She'd dealt with many authors and a few prima donnas, but nothing like this woman. She gathered her confidence. *Time to be professional.* "Well, the stairs are original. I fell in love with the intricate carving on the railing. As for the signing, the table will be back here. If you'll follow me, I'll show you. The plan is for the fans to zigzag through the store. That way, they may see another title or two that they'd like, and the hope is for them to buy a few items." She strode to the back of the store to the second RR Taylor display. "We'll have the table here. The line will start here." She glanced over her shoulder. The woman wasn't behind her. "Ma'am?"

She retraced her steps and located the woman by the tree. A man stood beside her and both held different ornaments from the display.

"These are beautiful," the woman said. Her bracelets jangled as she spoke. "We should ask if they're made here in town by a local author and have some made for RR."

"I agree," the man said. "Maybe have a few made for the street team and something smaller for the hardcore fans from the social media page."

The woman turned to Molly. "Are these made around here?"

"Yes. I have a friend who is co-owner of the arts and crafts workshop. She made a dozen for me but sells similar ornaments at her store. I'm sure if you ask about them, she'd craft special versions for you." Molly laced her fingers together. "She'll be pleased to have the work."

"Perfect." The woman offered her hand. "I'm sorry, I've been so rude. My name is Jill Gosk—soon to be Marshall. I'm the promotional assistant for RR Taylor. This is my fiancé, Nick. Like I said, we've spoken on the phone."

"Of course. It's a pleasure to meet you." Molly shook hands with Jill, then Nick. "You're engaged. That's wonderful."

"Yes. We did last night." Jill flashed the ring. "Between RR and Nick, I've gotten my Christmas wish."

"Wonderful and congratulations." Molly admired the diamond bauble. She'd wanted a ring like that, but having no prospects for dates…she wasn't going to get a ring any time soon. Most guys were put off by her devotion to her job and civic duties. She'd built her business from the ground up and was proud of what she'd accomplished. When she found a man who shared her pride, she'd marry him.

"There's the Santa himself." Jill waved. "RR, meet Molly."

"I already know her, like I told you."

Molly paused. She knew that voice. She turned her attention to the speaker. As soon as she saw him, her knees buckled for a split-second. "Alex?" How was her high-school boyfriend standing beside her? He'd gone to California and gotten on with his life. The last she knew, he'd gotten married and was a stay-at-home dad—at least that was the rumor. Wait, had Jill just called him RR? Her heart skipped a beat and she bit back a whimper. Her ex, the man she'd loved so much, was in her store.

"Hi, Molly." Alex grinned. The dimple in his right cheek deepened. He'd grown his sandy brown hair out and a lock of hair flopped over his forehead. His green eyes glittered and the sport coat showcased the strength in his body. He clutched the strap of his knapsack. His cologne wafted around her. He even smelled good. A girl could only take so much, and he was the whole package.

"What are you doing here?" Molly opened her arms. She couldn't not hug him. "I haven't seen you in years. Wow." The moment she snagged him, she missed being held in his strong embrace. Memories rushed into her brain—the nights cuddling together at the football games, hours spent in his truck talking about everything and nothing, afternoons at the pond and the school dances. He'd been her first love and the man she'd never forgotten. Damn it. She'd never gotten over him. She wanted answers, but her heart still belonged to him.

"I'm thrilled to see you, too." He rubbed her biceps. "You haven't changed."

She tensed. Hadn't changed? *Good grief.* She didn't look at thing like she had in school. Her hips were thicker and her hair darker. She had a few more miles under her belt, too. She glanced down at her attire. Now she knew what he meant—of all the days to wear her sequined bespectacled Christmas cat sweater, she had to pick today. "Normally, I'd have a blouse with a dog on it, but I liked the cat. I mean, you have to dress for the season."

"That sweater is so you." He laughed, and the throaty sound warmed her to her core. "I saw one like that at the store and almost picked it up, but I don't wear cat sweaters."

"They aren't for everyone." She laughed and relaxed a bit. "What brings you to Turn the Page?"

"Well, I heard you owned the store and since Jill just mentioned I'm going to be here tomorrow..." He folded his arms and widened his stance. "I heard you host authors, too."

"I do on both accounts," Molly said. Where was he going with this?

"Since this is my hometown, and this is the local bookstore, I had to come here for my signing." Alex flipped the lock of hair off his forehead. "I picked many of the locations for the signing and this is the last one. It's the best one."

"Oh." She pieced through what he'd said. *He picked the locations. His hometown.* Well, yeah, she knew he was from North Bend. He'd been her boyfriend. But what did he mean by *his signing*? "Wait." She tipped her head. "You're..." *No way.*

"I'm RR Taylor." Alex nodded. "Didn't Jill mention that? She's over the moon with her engagement, so I'm guessing it slipped her mind."

She frowned, then picked at the corner of the bookshelf. "You?" She remembered how he loved writing—sci-fi stuff—but she'd never read anything by RR Taylor. Maybe he'd added science fiction to the action stories. "You weren't into espionage and action themes before."

"I know." He grinned. "*I* wrote sci-fi. *RR* doesn't. I hated writing to what the market wanted, but I love the characters. It's a good trade-off. I work on a couple of epic saga kinds of stories in my spare time, but my editor likes to remind me they won't make any money."

"I seem to remember one of our English teachers saying no matter what you write, as long as you put your heart into it and believe in yourself, the work will find the right audience," Molly said. "I tend to agree with her."

"That's the same advice that's propelled me up to this point." Alex smiled. "I wanted to sign here. I'm so glad I pitched a fit to get in before Christmas. This is a cute little store."

"Turn the Page doesn't look all that big on the outside, but we've got the non-fiction in the basement level and used books on the second floor. Our selection is widely regarded, and we handle the tri-county area," Molly said. "We're a hidden gem."

"I agree," Alex said. "North Bend needed a solid bookstore. So many other bookstores are going out of business."

Jill tapped Alex's arm. "Nick and I will be outside. We spotted some adorable ornaments in the window at the hardware store and I'm dying to find the artist who created these book ornaments."

"Two blocks north. You can't miss the storefront. It's *bright* blue. I mean bright blue." Molly waved. "Thanks for stopping by. See you tomorrow."

"Thank you," Jill called. She and Nick left her alone with Alex.

Molly focused on Alex. "Well, tomorrow, you're signing books here. We've been planning this for weeks and there are a lot of people expected to show up." She waved to the back of the store. "Here. I'll show you the signing area and tell you about the plan." She coughed. Why'd she have to have a tickle in her throat now? Because of him?

"Perfect." Alex kept up with her. "If you don't mind, I'll leave a couple of first editions with you. Use them for raffles or prizes or something." He whistled. "I've never gone to a signing where the owner is so hands-on and thorough."

"My store, my reputation." She gestured to the table. She might not have the fanciest set-up or the most exciting store, but she knew how to do book signings. "You'll be here. I'll have the chairs set up for the audience." She cleared her throat. The tickle was back. *Crud.* Despite her attempts to keep the cough at bay, she couldn't stop. "Sorry."

"Tis the season. Don't worry about it."

Coughing in front of the author, no matter how much she wanted to stop, wasn't professional. "I also meant sorry about the layout. I'd set the chairs up tonight, but we've scheduled our staff Christmas party tonight. Delia—I don't know if you remember her from school—but she and I have a dual party for the folks who work at her coffee shop and for here."

"Tonight?" Alex sat on the edge of the table. "Interesting."

"Normally, I don't have signings this close to Christmas, but Jill was so nice, and I agree with them that it'll be good exposure. I wish I'd known you were RR, so I could've promoted the local-author angle, but it's okay. Every time I looked you up, I couldn't find anything other than stock pictures. It's like you don't want anyone to see you, yet you're here in public. If you want to keep your profile low, this isn't the way to do it." She coughed again, then pointed to the display. "Sorry. I'll get the chairs up and it'll be great tomorrow morning. I've got plenty of copies of your books in the stock room and we've had to replace the ones on the shelves at least every third day. We have a policy of allowing attendees to bring their own books, too, but we have a special bag for them."

"Smart." Alex directed her to the edge of the store. "Are you sure you're okay?"

"I'm fine. It's a cold." She waved. "Don't get too close. I'm sure it's nothing and I'll get medicine in me when we close." She rubbed the back of her hand across her forehead. She did feel a little warm. "The problem with owning your own business is when you're sick, you don't get a sick day. The staff keeps Turn the Page going, but I can't miss work. Once you go, I'll get some water. I'll be fine."

"Get water now." Alex glanced about. "Where's the office?"

"Over here, I promise. It's nothing." She allowed him to escort her to the small room at the back of the store. "Colds happen this time of year. Between working here and keeping the store afloat, plus my volunteer work with the Santa Barn and the animal shelter, it takes a lot out of me. I donated a bunch of time and books to the Santa Barn last night. I'm probably paying for being out in the cold."

"Santa Barn? I haven't heard that name in forever, but I'd thought about it on the drive here. They still have that?" Alex closed her office door, then sat on the edge of her desk. "Sit. Rest."

"Oh thanks." She collapsed on her chair. "This feels better than it should."

"Don't tell me you're fine. I know that look. You're a little red and worn-down." He nodded and folded his arms. "Where's the water?"

"Here." She swiveled around to the dorm fridge and withdrew a bottle. "I knew you'd push."

"That's what I'm good at." He turned the folding chair around and sat backward on it. "The Santa Barn. Wow." He rested his arms on the chair. "Do you remember volunteering to be elves when we were in high school?"

She stared at Alex. If she didn't know better, she'd have thought he was a model. He knew how to sit and maximize his looks. "I remember I volunteered to be an elf. You tagged along and groused the first night." Still, the memories of working at the Santa Barn were some of her favorites. She'd hated the costume back then, but he'd always looked good. Being a runner in high school kept him trim. Girls had shown up to see the hot elf. She'd been the extra.

"What made you want to keep volunteering? You've got a big heart. I guess it's part of who you are," Alex said. "Is that it?"

A *big heart*. He hadn't forgotten that detail about her. She fought the sigh. The tickle returned to her throat. She swigged some of the water. Not much of a help, but a little. "Eleven years ago, the Santa Barn was smashed by a tornado. Your mom probably mentioned it. Anyway, when the village rebuilt it, they made the barn a bit bigger. I didn't realize how big the need is here in North Bend. We try hard, but with the steel mill closed, most families have a hard time making ends meet. Having a bigger barn meant more room for donations so we could help more families."

"The mill closed?"

"Last year. Don't you talk to your mother?" she asked. She downed more of the water. The tickle wasn't going anywhere. "The Boosters ask the local businesses to contribute at the Santa Barn. I give books and my time. If they have specific requests for books, I make sure to fill them. Niecy and I played elves two years ago." She shrugged. "It's fun to see the joy on the faces of the kids when they get their wish. It makes my day."

"I bet." His eyes sparkled. He didn't say anything else, but he had an odd look on his face.

"What? Am I turning red?" She touched her cheeks. The warmth hadn't gone anywhere. "I hope I don't make you sick."

"You're not fine, but it's not a problem," Alex said. "I'll live and if I get sick, it happens." He nodded to her desk. "Your party is tonight?" He slid his phone from inside his sport coat and swiped across the screen, then met her gaze.

"It is."

"Mind if I drop by?"

"No." She tipped her head. "I can't be that exciting." She paused. "The muscle in your jaw is tight. Are you okay?"

"I'm fine." He laughed. "I planned this trip so I could spend Christmas with my folks. I don't talk to them as much as I should. Since Alyssa had her first baby, Mom is obsessed with her grandkids. My books aren't as exciting — not compared to a kid, I guess. She'd probably like for me to settle down and give her grandkids, too."

"She likes children." She paused. "According to the RR biography, you're single. That's why you don't have kids?" Part of her hadn't given up on him returning to North Bend to give them a second chance. She missed him more than she'd wanted to admit.

"You'd be right. I keep the biography rather vague, but it's true. I'm single." He swept his gaze over her. "So, the thing with the party and my wanting to attend is I'm on my own tonight. Mom and Dad went to Erie last night for a romantic weekend. Alyssa isn't coming to Ohio this year because she's pregnant with baby number two. I guess you're not supposed to travel when you're almost nine months along. I don't know.

I've never been pregnant." Alex blushed. "I'm guessing you didn't want to know all that."

"You're fine." She smiled. "Your folks like Erie. It's their anniversary, isn't it?"

"Fortieth, yeah." He brightened. "You knew?"

"They had their twentieth when we were in high school. Since it's been roughly twenty years since we graduated, I assumed it would be the fortieth." She glanced over at her phone. *No notifications. Good.* "You're welcome to come to the party. It's not super exciting, but we have fun."

"Thanks, and I will be there. I might be in one of Dad's sweaters, but you won't miss me," Alex said. "When I flew in, my luggage went to New York. At least my laptop, notebook, wallet and phone were in my carry-on. I'd be lost without them."

"I bet." She dug around in her desk. "Your dad is a snappy dresser, you know. I'll bet you can rock one of his sweaters."

"I missed how you see the bright side of disasters."

"Well, it's Christmas. Someone's luggage had to get lost, but if it must be anyone, it's you because you have a way out. I'd hate to be someone who really needed their clothes and had no back-up plan."

"Exactly." He sat on the edge of her desk. "So tonight...can I bring anything?"

"Nah. Delia selected a caterer for the food tonight and the DJ I hired will bring his own stuff. We just show up at nine and have fun," Molly said. She'd intended on making the party as easy as possible.

"Would you mind if I gave you a lift home?" he asked. "So, we can hang out longer?"

"I live on the third floor of this building." She grinned. "I go upstairs and I'm home."

"Get out." He laced his hands together. "Are you serious?"

"Yeah. I'm in debt up to my eyeballs, but I worked with the bank to acquire the entire building. All three floors, the basement and the warehouse portion are mine. The utilities are expensive, but I don't have to worry about a commute or wasting gas driving here. It's great." Pride swelled within her. She'd taken on a lot, but the hassle had been worth the rewards. "I can walk to the grocery store, hardware, library, gym and most anywhere else. If I need to drive, I can, but it's not vital."

"You amaze me."

"How?" She wasn't that exciting. Just a businesswoman determined to make her bookstore shine. "It's good promotion to be seen around town and I like visiting my friends who own the different establishments. How is that so amazing? It's kind of boring." She chuckled. "Maybe very boring."

"When we were in school, I knew you'd do something awesome. You always followed your heart. I wanted to do great things, but I was afraid if I did something different, I'd fail. You never seem to have had that problem." He rubbed her arm. "Now you're here, where you belong, and you've created all this. You're a champion for North Bend and kind of famous. Didn't our yearbook have something about you saying you wanted to be surrounded by books?"

"It did, and I am, so that works out." She snatched the bottle from the desk, then finished the water. "I'm sure you're getting tired of being here and the day has probably caught up with you, so I'll see you later?"

"You will." He offered his arm. "Coming here energized me. I've missed North Bend." He paused.

"But you're giving me the feeling you want to get rid of me."

"I don't want to cough in front of you again." She took his arm. Sparks shot from her forearm to her heart. She'd thought she'd forgotten about her attraction to him, but the moment she touched him, the memories hit her all over again. "Alex?"

"Yeah?" He stopped short. "What?"

"Why did you leave? The first time?" She stared at him. "You dumped me at college. I had almost no one to confide in and it hurt. You cut me deep." She'd never really gotten over the break.

"I was a dumb kid." He closed the door and remained in the office with her. "I thought it would be easier if we didn't try to do a long-distance relationship. They never work and you deserved better than a fledgling writer with no direction."

"I guess not." She fought back the tickle in her throat. "Is that the truth? I kept hoping you'd change your mind and call me or you'd show up and tell me it was all a joke." Her heart broke all over again as she thought about him and their relationship.

"I made a mistake back then, but I won't do it again." He held the office door for her. "I'm glad I saw you and came to the store."

"You're a people person. You love being in public." She knew him too well. He thrived in the spotlight. "You want a place to be the center of attention." And he hadn't really answered her questions.

"That, too, but I'm glad you were here. I think of the good times and how much I miss North Bend." Alex rubbed her arm, then let go. "Being here has invigorated me—like I said. I know I made mistakes, but I'm ready to fix them. You know?"

"Maybe." She nudged him. "Go. We'll wear you out tomorrow at the signing. If you're serious about attending, the festivities start at nine."

"I'm looking forward to the signing *and* the party. See you in a few hours." He waved, then strode out of the store. He'd wandered through the room like he knew the place. The man could act comfortable anywhere.

She hesitated by the sales counter. The things he'd said remained in her mind. He was glad to be back in North Bend. *Wonderful.* She liked having him in town. The only problem? She doubted her heart would be able to handle him leaving again. He'd moved on with his life. Maybe having him around for the next day or two would help to exorcise him from her mind. Maybe.

Chapter Three

Molly strode into the bookshop and paused as Niecy bounded up to her.

"There you are." Niecy narrowed her eyes. "Why did I just see the handsomest man walk out of this store? Tell me he's single and you got his phone number."

"That's Alex and no, I don't have his number." Molly massaged her temples. "I'm not looking to date anyone, remember?"

"You did talk to Mr. Hottie, right? Don't I know Mr. Hottie?" Niecy paused. "Did you say Alex? Is that Mr. Hottie?"

"You know Alex—err, Mr. Hottie, but you don't realize it." She lowered her voice to a whisper. "That's RR Taylor...aka the Alex from high school."

"Oh my goodness. Are you serious?" Niecy clasped both hands in front of her mouth to stifle the squeal. "The super-hot guy is... Does he think he's Davin McCleod? I mean he writes him very realistically. Does he do the stunts to test them out?"

"I don't know, but I'm sure if you ask him tomorrow, he'll tell you. I'm guessing if you ask at the party tonight, he'll be open to debate," Molly said. "I need to grab something for my headache."

"You're not getting any better. But then having your high school ex here would be an awkward thing, I suppose." Niecy tapped Molly's arm. "He's coming tonight? You're sick."

"Yes." Trust Niecy to notice the obvious. "I don't have time to be sick, but I can't cancel the party tonight." She darted into her office. "It'll be okay. Let me get something for this cold and I'll be brand-new by nine."

"Deal." Niecy shut the office door. "Why does RR Taylor—I mean *Alex*—want to come to the party? Because he loves the bookstore or a certain owner?"

She sank onto her chair. A fit of coughs overwhelmed her. Once she caught her breath and got more water into her system, she sighed. "He's a friend of mine and he's alone tonight. He asked if he could join us at the party and I said sure."

"Because you don't say no that often. You've donated tons of books and hours of work with the Santa Barn, you've got that literacy program in conjunction with the library and you're practically on the chamber of commerce board. You need to stop stretching yourself so thin." Niecy sat on the chair Alex had recently abandoned. "Unless you have someone to slow down for. Does Alex have a girlfriend?"

Oh boy. "He claims he's single."

"That's perfect." Niecy crinkled her nose. "The way he looked at you I thought maybe you hadn't extinguished that old flame."

"He's an *old* boyfriend." *There.* She'd said it. "Remember? I just told you his legal name."

"I just can't wrap my head around the Alex you've told me about a hundred times being RR Taylor." Niecy gasped. "When did you date RR, err, Alex? Why didn't you tell me before now that RR was Alex?"

"Niecy." She opened the bottle of aspirin. "It's not like it came up in conversation. Besides, I just told you and you already forgot."

"When I think of you with a guy, I think of you with Doug." Niecy tapped the chair back. "You deserved better than Doug."

"I know," Molly said. "That was a mistake."

"Who? Alex? Or Doug."

"Both."

Niecy's eyes widened. "Alex doesn't strike me as a waste of time. He seemed pretty cool, although I didn't talk to him."

"I'm surprised. You're the unofficial social director of the store." Molly downed more of the water. "I dated Alex back in high school and our first year of college. We split when he went to California. I came back here after college and we lost touch. As for why he's back, he says he wanted to sign in his home town of North Bend." She shrugged. "If he brings in business, I'm not complaining."

"You're a sweet lady."

She shrugged again. "His parents will be happy to see him. You know them — the Wests."

"You like him," Niecy said. She laughed. "You never got over him."

"Niecy." She hated to admit her friend was right.

"You do. You're in deep."

"No." Maybe. But the timing wasn't right. He was a famous author and should have an equally glamorous woman on his arm — not a bookstore owner in small-town Ohio. For all she knew, he had a girl back in California.

"You're lying." Niecy grinned. "To me and yourself."

"No."

"Then what?"

"He dumped me. Even though he could've emailed, he cut off all communication. It's plain we've both moved on, so that's that." Saying the words out loud hurt. Her heart ached and her stomach soured. She'd once wanted a future with him. She'd thought he was the one.

"You're getting hung up on looks and that's not like you," Niecy said.

"You're right. I own a bookstore. I'm a member of the community and I've done a lot for this town," Molly said. She'd had enough of wallowing in the past. She needed to embrace right now and her accomplishments. "Thanks for the reminder."

"You're welcome." Niecy folded her arms. "Still, there was electricity between you and Alex."

"I did mention he dumped me, right? Beyond that, he lives in San Diego and I'm not leaving North Bend. He's not offering to date me and if he was, I'd turn him down," Molly said. "It wouldn't work."

"You say all that, but I don't buy it."

"You never do." Which was probably why she and Niecy were friends, but still.

"I don't buy it because I love you and want you to be happy. You're content here in North Bend. You've got a good life, but you're lonely. Doug was okay to pass the time, but you knew he wasn't long-term. You need more than your job here and your civic work. Part of you has always wanted Alex to come back. Am I right?"

"You've been watching too many of those rom-coms." Molly polished off the rest of the water and leaned back in her chair. "We're good as friends. We had our chance and it's over. I should move forward." But Niecy was right — she'd never gotten over Alex. She deserved closure if nothing else.

"You're sick and still on your feet, so to speak. Not because the store will fold if you're not here or even so you can be at the signing tomorrow. You might be feeling icky, but there's a sparkle in your eye that hasn't been there in forever." Niecy stood and turned the chair around. "Take a break. Get some meds and water, then lie down for half an hour. I've got the fort held down. Recoup so you'll be good for the party."

"Fine." She folded her arms and rested her head on her desk. A nap did sound good. "See you in ten."

"Thirty minutes would be better."

Whatever. Once her headache dissipated, she'd be great. She'd worry about the signing, the party and Alex later.

* * * *

Alex drove across town and took in the sights of North Bend. Every house had some sort of Christmas lights decorating the lawn — unlike his condominium complex in San Diego. The landlord insisted on each unit looking exactly like the others. No lawn ornaments, no lawn furniture…no Christmas lights. He hadn't thought about how boring his place looked until he drove down the main drag of North Bend.

He loved the festive feel in his home town. Part of him missed his apartment. That was his home — the place he wrote and ran the trails to keep in shape, but North Bend had a certain charm.

Alex headed to the drive-through at the edge of town for a cup of coffee and a burger. Once he had food and a drink, he returned home. He had a few hours to kill and wanted information. He set out his food on the bar in the kitchen. When he'd lived at home, he'd secreted a carton in his closet. Was it still there? He snagged a bite of his burger, then wandered down to his former bedroom.

Alex dug around in the closet until he located the container. "I knew no one would look for this." He withdrew the shoebox, then carried it to the bar. During his high school career, he'd kept various mementos and photographs. He settled on the bar stool and opened the lid.

Each item held special memories. He placed a wilted boutonniere on the bar. He'd worn the flowers during the last prom he'd attended with Molly. They'd danced to every song together and he'd never wanted the night to end. He spotted a medal from one of his cross country meets. He'd worked so hard to make it to state during his senior year. Molly had been his staunchest cheerleader.

His thoughts wandered back to when he and Molly had ended their relationship. He remembered the night like it had happened yesterday. He spotted the letter from JK Dobbins. Once he'd decided to become a writer, he'd coveted the chance to write at the Dobbins compound. Anyone who wanted to be the best writer possible applied to attend one of Dobbins' writing courses at his mansion. No matter what Alex had done at the time, he hadn't been able to land a spot in one of the classes.

He'd wanted to discuss with Molly his depression over not being able to further his career. But she had her life at college and wasn't even in the same state.

He'd thought she wouldn't want the complication of him being so far away. He'd assumed a clean break wouldn't hurt as much as dragging out the relationship. He'd driven all night to get to her at the college and break up face-to-face. She'd been so strong when he'd dumped her, but he remembered the look in her eyes. Instead of trying to reconnect with her in any way, he'd forged ahead with his life. He'd moved to California and followed his writing dream.

He hadn't forgotten Molly. Many of his heroines resembled her and shared her personality. He'd opened and left in draft form so many emails he wanted to send Molly. But no words, even for a writer, seemed appropriate. How could he apologize for making the biggest mistake of his life by walking away from her? He'd thought he was being a gentleman. He'd done what he considered to be respectful—he loved her, so he'd let her go in the hopes she'd come back to him. Then there was his fear of commitment. How could a guy be so lucky to already have during his high school years the woman he wanted forever? It didn't seem possible.

He pushed the items aside and finished his burger. His coffee had cooled. He sipped the tepid brew, then fiddled with his phone. He should check his texts and emails. The screen lit up before he could retrieve the messages. Incoming call from his mother. "Hi, Mom."

"Hi, honey," his mother said. "Are you settling in all right? Your father and I feel bad you're alone, but we're having fun in Erie."

"Don't worry about me. I'm keeping entertained." He toyed with the medal. "I'm taking a trip down Memory Lane. I found a bunch of my stuff I left in the closet."

"I wondered if you'd go looking for that old shoebox."

"Oh?" He snorted, then sipped his coffee. "You knew it was there?"

"That's why it hasn't moved. I know every inch of that house," his mother said. "Is that all you're planning tonight? To look through a box?"

"No, I'm considering going to a party at the bookstore tonight." He tapped the medal on the bar. "Thought it might be fun."

"You are? That's fantastic. Are you going to chat with Molly? Maybe you can be friends again."

Was that excitement in his mother's voice? "I'll do my best." He'd like to have the friendship intact again, too.

"Then you've seen her already? Good."

"I have."

"Is she doing okay?"

What was that all about? He toyed with the paper insulator on the coffee cup. "Yeah, she seemed fine. I think she's getting a cold, but she's no worse for wear otherwise."

"Did you take her soup?"

He sagged in his seat. "I hadn't thought about that until now, but smart idea. I'll pick some up at the diner. They make better soup than I ever could." He'd surprise her with it at the party that night.

"Molly will appreciate the company and the soup. She spends so much time at the store and since she and Doug split, she could use a friend," his mother said.

"She's got friends, I'm sure." He paused. "Doug? As in my arch rival, Doug the slug Gerber? Molly had better taste than him, didn't she?"

"She did and yes, she's got Delia and Niecy, but you two had such a tight bond. Alex, you're her best friend."

"I *was* her best friend, but I've been gone a long time." He shuddered as he thought about her ex. Doug had been the guy who'd dated everyone in high school. According to the rumors, he'd gotten at least two girls pregnant and had been tossed out of the football games for smoking. He wasn't exactly a bad boy, but not someone Alex wanted Molly connected to. Alex groaned. He'd left. How could he expect Molly to have kept to herself? He had needs. So, did she.

His mother laughed, then sighed. "Alex, I always thought you and Molly would find a way back to each other."

"Mom." He'd hoped Molly might want to be friends again. He needed her in his life. "Why would she date Doug?"

"There aren't exactly a lot of eligible men in town. Doug asked her out and they hit it off, I guess. They dated for over a year before they split," his mother said.

"But Doug...he never did anything in school other than goof off and date all those girls." *Oh crap.* He'd lowered himself to complaining about Doug. In every popularity poll, he and Doug came out on top — usually tied. Where he'd been a runner, Doug had wrestled. He'd won scholarships and run the yearbook. Doug had charmed the girls.

"Honey, you weren't around. What was Molly supposed to do?" his mother asked. "Wait?"

Yes. "No." His inner romantic wasn't ready to let her go — even if they'd never be more than friends.

"Well, then don't get upset."

"Sorry," he said. "Have fun and I'll see you tomorrow."

"I will. You have some fun, too." She hung up and left him in silence.

Well, crud. He'd missed so much by being in California. He balled the paper from his burger. He wanted to show kindness, but he didn't know how to cook more than the basics, which meant…takeout.

* * * *

Forty-five minutes later, Alex parked across the street from the bookstore. He locked the car and headed into the building. Instead of stopping to chat with the workers, he wound his way back to the office. He left the bag from the diner on Molly's desk. Where was she?

According to his calculations, the party wouldn't start for another hour. One of the workers rushed past him.

"Hi." Alex ducked in front of her. "Where's Molly? I have a delivery."

"You must be with the caterer. She's in the warehouse. Go through that door and don't fall off the loading dock." The girl hurried away from him.

"Okay," he muttered. He followed her directions and stepped into the warehouse. He spotted someone sitting on the loading dock. He'd know her form anywhere—even from behind. Even twenty years on, she resonated in his soul. She'd pulled her hair off her shoulders into a ponytail and the lights on her sweater blinked. The bulky cotton did nothing for her figure, but he liked her unique sense of style.

"Molly?" Alex called. "What are you doing out here?"

"I'm waiting for Niecy to find the boot." Molly stood. She stuffed her hands into her back pockets and grinned. "Every year, we put the boot away and every year we forget the super safe spot we put it."

"You put the boot in the safest, best spot." He chuckled. "Want help?" She hadn't lost her sense of humor.

"Can't hurt." She tipped her head. "Do you know where we put it?"

"Not a clue, but I'm good at seeking whatever's hidden," Alex said. "I left something for you in your office."

"What is it?" she asked. She quirked her brow. "It's not something that'll explode, right? Not like that can of pralines that prematurely came apart in my car during our junior year of high school?"

"It's a present for later, and no, it won't blow up." He wriggled his brows. "You'll like it." He winked. "I'm surprised you remembered the pralines." He'd thought the joke was great at the time, but when he'd filled her car with the coiled fake snakes, he regretted the silliness.

"Can't forget gigantic snakes shooting across the interior of my poor car. Mr. Rasmussen thought I'd lost my mind when I screamed." She paused. "I'm shocked you decided to show up. I really thought you were just bluffing."

"I wanted to surprise and see you." He nodded. "I'll explain once we find this illustrious boot."

Molly shook her head. She frowned and took her phone from her pocket. "Darn. I'll be right back. I need to talk to Delia. Something about a wandering caterer." She left the loading dock.

Once Molly had disappeared into the store, he turned his attention to Niecy. "Where are you, Niecy?"

"Over here." She poked her head out from behind a box. "I can't reach the boot, but I found it." Her eyes widened. "Oh my gosh. You're RR Taylor." She rubbed her hands on her jeans legs. "It's a pleasure to meet you. I've read every book. Davin McCleod is my book boyfriend." She blushed. "I'm sure you've heard that before. If I'd have known you were so handsome, I'd have done my hair. I'm planning a trip to the salon tomorrow before the signing."

"I'm glad you like him, and your hair is fine." He shook hands with her. "I'm glad to meet you, too. Now, where is this boot?"

"Up here." She pointed to the shelf. "Just out of reach."

"No sweat." He grasped the item in question. "If you don't mind me asking, what do you use this for? Name exchanges?" He pulled the boot from the shelf. He'd expected the thing to be heavier. Cotton lined the top of the shiny black plastic boot and a glitter buckle decorated the front. "It's interesting."

"When Molly opened the store, we'd do a secret Santa thing, but it got to be a pain because no one had much money. So, Molly decided instead of presents for each other, we'd take the money we'd normally spend for it and donate it to the animal shelter." Niecy held onto the boot. "The goal is to fill it. Most of us bring items for the shelter, too. Molly will take it all over tomorrow after we close."

"She's a smart woman." He marveled at her thoughtfulness. He respected her decision to help others instead of herself at the holidays. "Before we head into the party, you've known her for a long time, right?"

"Molly? Sure." She held the boot tight. "Not as long as you have."

"She told you we dated?" He should've been surprised.

"She knew I'd pester her until I learned the truth, but she might have let the story slip without much prodding." She narrowed her eyes. "What do you want to know?"

"How'd you guess I'd ask?" Other than he lacked grace when it came to information seeking. "I wasn't smooth, was I?"

"Nope." She tipped her head to the side and half-smiled. "What do you want to know?"

"Nothing." He bowed his head. "I didn't have a plan, but I'm a writer. I'm nosy. I want to know about people."

"Especially Molly?" Niecy asked. "I'm guessing you heard about Doug, yes?" She rolled her eyes. "He was horrible. He sells houses now — I think — and wanted to sell the store out from under her. He thought the property would be better for larger retail space. This is North Bend. We don't need larger retail space."

"You're right, you don't." Doug was in real estate? Interesting. At least the guy had a job. "He was that underhanded?"

"Oh yeah," Niecy said. "All he sees are dollar signs. The whole relationship was a lie. He was nice, she thought he'd be a decent enough date, they kept going out because it was something to do — at least it was for her — then he showed his true colors. The guy was good. He strung it out for a year. Sweet words, bought her stuff, knew just what to say, then bam. He'd been working on the sale all that time. All he needed was her signature and for her to cash the check. She saw the contract, called your father about said contract and *boom*. The sale didn't go through and Doug went bye-bye. She's a respected member of the community and everyone likes her. She'd be the president of the chamber of commerce if she so desired, but she wasn't interested."

"Wow." Where he'd opted for a clean break, Doug had seen a way to con Molly. Alex nodded. "That's rough." Not that he'd been any better, but he saw Molly's position in society and respected her.

Niecy paused. "Look, I know you and Molly had a past. I saw how she lit up when she realized who you are. I don't know all the details concerning your past with her, but she must've really loved you."

"I know." He'd loved her, too. Probably still did. No, no probably about it. He loved her. Every cell in his body screamed to beg for her forgiveness.

"She's the best friend I've ever had, and I don't deserve her." She crooked her eyebrow. "Just…if you're not interested in sticking around North Bend or being the other half of what she's started here in town, then say so. Don't play games."

"I won't." He rocked on his feet. "What do you mean you don't deserve her?"

"She gave me a second chance when I was beyond redemption. I made a play for Doug, I didn't show up for work, I lied to her… I was just a bad person. I was ready to give up, but she didn't let me. She's not a saint. She thought she was in love with Doug and almost sold the store. If you ask me, she thought he'd give her a better life than being broke most of the time and having to deal with customers who aren't happy. But she loves the store. She loves the people. She's not perfect, but she's pretty awesome and North Bend wouldn't be the same without her."

"You're right." He sighed. "I'm sorry I wasn't here."

"I want to believe you're going to be a stand-up guy and be friends, but I'm not naïve." She shook her head and started away, then paused. "Just don't be like Doug."

"Niecy."

She stopped, but didn't turn around. "You're not planning on sticking around." She shrugged. "Call it a hunch I've got. Just leave Molly alone. She's been through enough. Be friends, but nothing more."

This time when she walked away, he didn't follow. He stood on the loading dock and stared the boxes of his books. She had a point. He'd been rudderless in his personal life for so long. Was he ready to drop everything in California to come home to North Bend? No. Did he want a platonic relationship with Molly? Definitely.

Alex made his way into the bookstore. He'd observe. Maybe he'd use what he saw for a scene in his next book. He should make some notes. Later. Right now, he wanted no attention on him. The party wasn't about RR Taylor and he didn't even belong there.

Delia and Niecy stood in the middle of the bookstore. Molly waited off to the side. Niecy held up the boot. "I found it!"

Delia applauded. "Wonderful. It's not the Christmas party without it." She stepped out of the way and nudged Molly to the forefront. "Your turn."

Molly chuckled and flipped her hair out of her eyes. "I've only got one announcement, then I'll turn the floor back over to Delia. She's the PR person. Not me."

Alex watched her in awe. Molly didn't think she had any stage presence, but she commanded his attention. No wonder the townsfolks loved her.

"First, this party is for all of you," Molly said. "Without your help and dedication, Delia and I couldn't have the fine shops they are today. You all deserve more than the meager bonus you're getting on

Christmas Eve, but with the market down, it's all we could afford. Still, the bonuses are tad bigger than last year. Why? Because you all rock. Now enjoy the food, drinks and music. Like I said, this night is for you. Merry Christmas and have a ball." She waved, then ducked behind Delia and out of sight.

Alex doubted he'd have a hard time finding her, but still. She'd decided to hide and keep the attention on the workers. At least the store wasn't that big.

Delia clapped her hands. "One thing from me, since Molly said what we wanted to say so well...she's right. You all rock. Now, what's our second Christmas tradition besides bonuses? Filling the boot! Don't forget to add your pennies and nickels. The critters at the shelter can use the supplies you've donated, and the money will go to vet care. And remember, whatever money you put in the boot, Molly and I will personally match it." She turned to Niecy. "Your turn. I have no idea what you wanted to say, but I'm not arguing."

Alex applauded with everyone else. He'd have to donate to the boot, too. The animals were a worthy cause. Maybe he'd ask Molly if she wanted help delivering the mountain of cat food, dog food and litter to the shelter.

Niecy grinned. "This party is for us, but we've got a special guest."

Alex tensed. *Oh no.* He stepped backward and collided with a bookshelf. *Don't mention me. He* wanted to blend in. He hadn't told Niecy that, but still. She didn't have to bring his name up. No... Molly would think he'd intended on crashing the party.

"Our author for tomorrow, I know you love him, RR Taylor, is here for the party," Niecy said. "Don't pester him for autographs or photos tonight, but I'm sure if you ask him tomorrow, he'll stay afterward." She pointed to him. "RR?"

His skin burned. *Damn it.* He had to say something. Alex stepped forward. "Thanks for having me. I'm excited for the signing and to hang out with everyone. I love North Bend and wouldn't be where I am without this town." He caught Molly's gaze. She didn't appear amused. *Drat.* He had to do something to save the moment. "I'm also donating to the boot. Whatever you raise and Delia and Molly match, I'll match the final amount. The animals deserve our love."

Molly's eyes widened and the crowd broke into applause. Delia sidled up to him.

"You don't have to give a ton of money," Delia said. "We only ever get three or four hundred dollars, tops. Our max donation was fifteen hundred dollars last year."

"North Bend's animal shelter can use the money." He shook her hand. "I'm sorry I crashed your party. Not my intention." And he'd spend the rest of the week making it up to them.

"I'm sure you didn't set out to be the center of attention." She shrugged. "Molly isn't going to go along with this. She'll give you an earful."

"Delia." He gritted his teeth. Everyone was so protective of Molly. She was a gem, yes, but didn't he deserve redemption?

"I was there when you broke her heart," Delia said. She turned her back to the crowd. "I remember how long it took to pick up the pieces. She loved you. Not just kind of liked you or maybe thought you were cool, but *loved* you."

"I know." He'd loved Molly, too. His fear of commitment and of being so lucky to have the woman he wanted forever had made him run the other way.

Just like with his writing, he'd thought if he tortured himself, he'd be rewarded. His talent had developed and he'd eked out a solid career. As for his love life...things weren't so great.

"Then you know coming here and stepping in won't win her over, right?" Delia asked. "She'll see right through your generosity. She's a smart businesswoman and won't turn down the money, but she won't trust you, either."

"It's an honest donation."

"I hope so."

"Delia." He sighed again. Gosh, he'd been sighing a lot since he'd come home. "I want to make things right. I never got over Molly, but I forced myself to move on. I had to. I couldn't ignore my life." *Just ignore my love life.*

"Then don't try to impede on hers. You've got a life wherever you live. Stay there. You can be friends with Molly, but don't torture her." Delia rested her hands on her hips. "I'm serious."

"That's a horrible choice," he said. "I have family in North Bend."

"Then I guess you have to do some thinking." Delia turned on her heel and walked away.

A few of the staff approached him for photos. He plastered a smile on his face and acquiesced to each request. Being the sort of celebrity persona gave him time to think. Delia had gotten to the heart of his problem better than he had when he'd pondered what he wanted to do. She did know him and was right to protect Molly. He'd screwed up and had to make things right...but how?

Chapter Four

Fifteen minutes later, Alex smiled for the last photo. He promised to autograph books for the staff after his book signing. They'd worked hard and he'd show his appreciation.

Right now, he wanted to find Molly and apologize — for the break-up, for the years since then and him unintentionally crashing her party. He ducked through the crowd and meandered back to her. He wanted to gather her in his arms. When she'd hugged him, he hadn't wanted to let go.

"Did you need quiet?" he asked. He sat on the cushion of the chair. "I noticed you're away from the crowd."

"This is their bash. I'm just a spectator." She leaned back on the seat. "Do you know it's impossible to get popcorn out of these chairs?"

"Oh yeah?" He hadn't thought about fishing popcorn or anything else out of the crevices of the seat. "They're comfy." He focused on her. She still had the same smile, but sadness in her eyes.

"I know." She grinned and turned to face him. "But lousy for cleaning. We had a movie night and there was popcorn everywhere. Delia thought it was a great idea. I'm still on the fence."

"So, you're not having another movie night?" he asked.

"Are you crazy? It brought in lots of people, so we're having another one for the local kids on New Year's Eve." She laughed. "Trust me, it's something for them to do and does encourage some sales."

"Popcorn and champagne? They're kids, but kudos on keeping them off the streets."

"Thank you. We'll serve popcorn and sparkling cider." She patted his shoulder. "We don't charge for movie night. It's just a nice thing for the kids to do since it's cold out."

"That's both smart and awesome, but you've always had great ideas." Heat seeped from her hand to his shoulder. Her cologne wrapped around him and he bit back a groan. He'd forgotten how intoxicating her perfume could be and how much he missed the scent.

"That was quite a display," she said. "Matching money, eh?"

"Every little bit helps."

"It does." She folded her hands on her lap. "Some might even be impressed by your gesture."

"Not you." He knew that tone of voice. He'd been warned. "Right?"

"I'm not sure how I feel about what you've done."

"You're wary." He met her gaze. Up close he noticed the blue and green flecks in her eyes. A man could get lost in those eyes. He moved to the edge of the chair and faced her. He knew her pose – she'd closed herself off and put up barriers. He hated that she felt the need to keep him at a distance. "You think I'm a jerk who showed up to act like a big shot and impress everyone."

"Maybe." She crossed her legs. "It kind of looks like you wanted attention. I'm a businesswoman and what you did was great press for the store. We look wonderful and benevolent. We've gotten a writer in not only to wow the audience, sign books, but to donate cash, too. On the financial side, I couldn't be happier."

"I didn't tell Niecy to give that speech. I'd planned on being a quiet observer. But I'm happy to donate to the shelter. It's a worthy cause."

"Then thank you," she said, her voice flat. "The animals appreciate the help."

"You hate me," he said. "I know you. I did something wonderful and helped you—without planning to do so—but you see something else. You're putting on a brave face, but beyond being sick, you're sick of me."

"I wouldn't say I'm sick of you." She cocked her head. "I'm under the weather, but I can't leave my post."

"That's true." He wasn't backing down. He wanted to be friends again. "I feel your irritation in waves. You'd rather I drop dead."

"I never said that, but I might not argue."

He didn't know what else to say. He'd messed everything up. "Molly." At least no one was watching them argue. "I just wanted to help."

She glanced around, then lowered her voice again. "The minute you walked in here, you dredged up a lot of the past and feelings I thought I'd put away. Part of me is thrilled because you were my best friend and it felt like the missing part of me has come back. You're still special to me and I want to be friends again." Her voice caught. "But I'm practical. I know how this ends. You aren't going to stick around. You have a life across the country and no real strings to keep you here. Yeah, your parents are in town, but you don't have to come back to North Bend — even for a friend." She shook her head and her eyes shimmered with tears. "So yeah, we can be pals, but not best friends."

His heart broke. "The way I ended things was a mistake."

She wiped a tear from her cheek. "It's in the past. Don't worry about it."

"I will worry." He cared about her. "I made a mess back then."

"Like I said, don't worry about it." She left the chair. "Enjoy the party. I'm going to my office. I've done my civic duty and I need a break." She started away from him.

He hopped to his feet. "Wait. I'll come with."

"And miss your adoring fans?" She frowned. "No. Stay."

"Molly, I came back here for you." That wasn't entirely what he'd meant, but it was too late to take the words back now.

She said nothing and slipped away.

He gritted his teeth. Touching her, feeling her in his arms and getting close had been detrimental to him. The memories came back. The desire, friendship, need and love hadn't died. He wanted his friend again.

He stared at the tree and lights around the store. The thrill of the season and the beauty of the decorations still stirred his soul. This was the time of year to come together and heal old wounds.

Alex made his way to Molly's office. Instead of knocking, he pushed right into the room. Molly stood at her desk and flipped through a book on architecture. "Are you okay?"

"I am. Is this from you?" She pointed at the bag. "Is that the surprise?"

"It is. I brought soup." He grasped the back of the chair opposite her desk. "Why are you hiding back here and looking at architecture? Why don't you eat? It'll warm your soul and make you feel better."

"I needed a break. The noise got to me and I wasn't sure what to think about you." Molly met his gaze. "Thanks for the soup."

He flexed his fingers on the back of the chair. "Should still be hot. Mom said you could use it. She'd have my hide if I didn't bring you soup."

"Kathy." She shook her head. "Your mom does look out for me." She rounded her desk. "You didn't have to, but thank you and her." She shoved a lock of her hair out of her eyes. "It's funny. For years, I couldn't get you out of my head. Once I did, you came back and now I can't seem to get rid of you."

"I know. You're so darn adorable that I couldn't stay away." He removed his jacket and sat opposite her. "You've done a great job with this store and your party. Everyone out there is having fun." Like he'd said before…he needed to stop repeating himself.

"We try. The gang works so hard through the year. This is the least Delia and I can do." She opened the bag. "Chicken noodle. You're too good." She withdrew the foam container, then the wrapped sandwich. "I'm assuming this is yours?"

"Yep. I wanted a Reuben."

"They make great ones at the diner." She sagged in her chair. "I wish I didn't feel so icky. I'd enjoy the soup and the party so much more."

"Which is why you need to have the soup. We can eat and have some quiet time so you can regroup. The party will still be out there." He unwrapped his sandwich. "Let me take care of you."

"Thanks. I'm too tired to argue, but you don't have to go out of your way. Won't your girlfriend be upset?"

"See, this is how I know you're legit sick. You love to argue with me — except when you're not feeling good." He rested his elbows on his knees. "I'm sorry."

"Colds happen." She dug into the soup. "Thank you for getting this. It's heavenly."

"They cook so much better than I ever could, and I even considered trying." He watched her. She might be seventeen years older than the last time he'd seen her, but she was still adorable. She'd cut her hair, the but the mahogany locks still brushed her shoulders. She hadn't worn as much makeup, and the softer look worked for her. She'd always be adorable.

"You're staring." She paused between bites. "Is that why you're sorry?"

"Nope. I'm a self-avowed stare-er." He laughed. "Isn't that terrible? I'm a writer and I'm still making up strange words. Who uses a word like stare-er?"

"You," she said. "I remember when our English teacher had a fit because you'd used another word that wasn't a word. Didn't she tell you how you wrote fantastic science fiction epics, but your word choices drove her crazy?"

"Oh yes." He nodded. "One of the novellas she told me was garbage got picked up by a small press publisher."

"Fantastic. Is it available for purchase? I'll try to get it in the store." She groaned. "After I finish my dinner. This soup is hitting the spot. Thank you."

"I'm glad." He toyed with his sandwich. He had to be honest with her and get a few things off his chest. This was Christmas—a time to come clean and make amends. The time to be together and love everyone. "I'm sorry I wasn't here."

"Don't apologize. It's in the past."

He couldn't keep the words within him any longer. "Do you ever wonder why I never called you back?" Embarrassment slid around his brain. He'd acted like a jerk when he was younger and wanted nothing more than her forgiveness.

"I've wondered, yeah. Your mother told me you had a wild streak and said you needed to roam." She shrugged. "I knew she'd lied about the wild streak, but there wasn't any point in arguing. You didn't want to talk to me, so I didn't push. I wish I had, but it doesn't matter." She pushed the empty foam cup aside. "Your mother checked on me often."

"She loved you. What about your parents? I went by the house on the way here, but it was dark." He hadn't paid much attention, but he'd wanted to get back to her.

"You didn't know? Dad moved to Portland with Gertie, his new wife." Molly stared at him. "Your folks were at the wedding."

"What?" He had no idea. "Where's your mother?"

"You never heard." She picked at the edge of the cup. "Mom died in a car accident five years ago. A drunk driver went left of center on County Road Twenty-Three." She curled into herself. "She and Dad were having problems and he'd already met Gertie. He'd been stepping out on Mom for a while, but I didn't realize what he'd done. Anyway, the night he ended up telling Mom he wanted to split, and that Gertie was in the picture, Mom drove off in a haze. The other driver never saw her. Mom's death devastated Dad, but not enough to dump Gertie. They sold the house and got married on Valentine's Day. I keep my distance from them and they have their lives across the country. It's not great, but it works. Gertie hates me for not being head over heels for her and I'm not thrilled about my father being married to someone from my graduation class."

She could've knocked him right over. "Honey, I'm sorry. If I'd have known..." His mother had mentioned something about Elise's passing, but he'd written it off as misinformation. He'd been neck-deep in rewrites for book twelve and working on yet another novella for the small press. He hadn't thought he had time for North Bend. Wrong. He should've listened and come back to help his former best friend.

"You can't change what happened." She tossed the soup cup into the trash. "So, what do I need to know about when we split? I heard you'd found someone else." Her voice dropped. "Did you?"

"No." He closed the sandwich paper. He'd eat his dinner later. "I was given the opportunity to work with JK Dobbins in California. Not online or through the mail, but at his writing compound. I couldn't pass it up. Writing with such a big-time author had to be a fluke. I'd never thought it would happen. At the time, I thought it was only fair to you to cut ties. You weren't going to follow me to California. You were still in school and wanted to come back to North Bend. It wasn't fair to make you choose."

"So, you thought it would be easier to split?"

"At the time, I thought it was smart and respectful, but in retrospect, I looked heartless." He hated himself for what he'd done. "All I saw was my opportunity to move beyond this town."

"I see," she said. "You won't believe this, but I don't blame you. I might have done the same thing if I had been in your position. You loved writing and have a talent. You needed to chase every chance you got."

"Molly."

"It's true. It's hard to break into the business. There's a lot of luck and knowing the right people...I've heard the stories. Authors get chatty when they visit. I don't know. Maybe it's my personality or they have grievances they want off their collective chest. But they talk. Many of them aren't where they want to be and wish they could get that one chance to move up. You got that chance and took it. Don't apologize for chasing your dream. You're not wrong."

"I wasn't right." He scooted his chair closer and reached across the desk to touch her hand. When she didn't pull away, he grasped her fingers. "I knew how you felt about me and it scared the hell out of me. We were kids. I was so immature and the idea of staying with one person for the rest of my life freaked me out." He'd never told anyone that. He hadn't wanted to admit he'd failed at anything.

"Why didn't you tell me?"

"I didn't want to hurt you." He knew he'd break her heart and couldn't bear to see her cry. "I was wrong."

"How'd your plan work?" She rolled her eyes and pulled away from him.

"Let me think. I got the life I wanted, but it's not exactly how I'd planned, so yeah, not great." He tipped his head. "I wish I could go back and fix everything."

"You've got a great career and a well-respected position in the literary community," she said. "That's not anything to ignore."

"No." He opened his sandwich to keep his hands busy. "But it's lonely. There aren't many people who understand the hours I keep. I don't write during the same hours every day, but when I do, I need to concentrate." Most of his former girlfriends hadn't understood. They wanted attention when they needed it—not when the characters weren't talking.

"It's a business."

"Yes. I'm unorthodox, but I have to work when the mood strikes." He bit into the Reuben. The bread had turned mushy from him putting off eating his food, but he'd deal.

Molly leaned back in her seat. "Thank you for the soup. Tell your mother I appreciate the gesture and the chicken noodle. It hit the spot."

"I will," he said between bites. He hadn't realized how hungry he was until he started eating. His stomach grumbled.

"My head is pounding and my sinuses hurt." She massaged her temples. "I'm going to text Delia and Niecy. If they'll lock up, I'll get the store ready for the book signing and owe Delia a huge one. I should be in there—it's good PR and, plus, it's just nice—but I can't." She got her phone out. "She'll understand and Niecy owes me."

"I'm sure Delia will be fine with helping." He didn't know about Niecy, but right now he wanted to give her a piece of his mind for making a show of him attending the party. He finished his sandwich, then balled up the paper. "Let me help you."

"You?" She didn't look up from her phone. "How? You need to get home. Isn't your mother waiting for you?"

"Nope. I'm solo until the morning. No one needs me and I want to make sure you get upstairs." He wasn't taking no for an answer.

"I'm not dying." She put the phone down. "It's just a cold."

"Maybe, but it's Christmas and you do so much for everyone else. Let someone take care of you for a change." He couldn't do much, but he'd try to pamper her. He didn't doubt his feelings any longer. Alex West hadn't fallen out of love with Molly. *Not a bit.*

Molly raked her fingers through her hair. Delia had replied already and readily agreed to help. All she had to do was head upstairs and crash — with Alex keeping an eye on her. She wasn't a teenager and they weren't sneaking off to make out. If he kissed her, she'd give him her cold. Not good or sexy. Heck, just by being around her, she'd make him sick.

She locked her desk and gathered up her things in her bag. She tucked the money bag into her satchel, then sighed. Alex hopped up and scooped the bags from her hands. She wasn't that sick. Just icky. But his concern was sweet and arguing with Alex wouldn't do her any good.

"Well?" He tucked her bags under his arm. "I'm not leaving until I know you're in bed."

"Alex." He had to know how bad that sounded. "I didn't think you'd let me off the hook, but still." She'd lost this fight. She left her chair. "Let's go."

He offered his free arm. "Ready?"

"I'm not going to collapse." She brushed him aside. "Let me lock up the office." She turned the lights off and ushered him into the back of the store. "This way." She grasped his arm and bit back a sigh. He still had muscles in all the right places and had to have worked out often. She led him to the private elevator at the back of the building. "You can go. I'm at my front door, so to speak. I'll be fine."

"Nope. Not until you're in the apartment. Wait. This is elevator goes to your apartment?"

"I live above the store."

"Then I'm making sure you get upstairs." He pressed the button for the third floor. "You're pale."

"I'm sick. It happens. Besides, it's the holidays and everyone will get a bug of one type or another before spring. This was my turn. Hopefully, I get rid of it before Christmas Eve." She didn't have time to be ill. She had a job to do and she'd signed up to volunteer. She should be helping, despite her common sense dictating she rest.

"You push yourself too hard." The doors opened and he escorted her into the car. "This is nice." Alex stared at her as the car ascended to the third level. When the car stopped and opened into her apartment, he nodded. "I feel better about this." He paused. "Wow. This is nice. I like how you've got the apartment all attached and that no one can get up to your place without they key," he said. "Makes the commute nonexistent."

"Exactly." She let go of him. Being babied was nice, but wouldn't last. She should be standing on her own. "Thanks. I'll set my alarm for an hour earlier than I'd normally get up and see you tomorrow. Just be here half an hour before the signing for some photos and to make sure we've got the supplies you want. Thank you for your concern and be safe going home."

"I'm sleeping on the couch." He put her bags down, then took off his jacket. "I don't believe you'll actually go to bed. You'll probably shower, then try to sneak downstairs to be super girl and clean up. You need to rest, so I'm standing guard."

"Alex." She stood tall—as tall as she could, despite being almost eight inches shorter than him. "I refused to be bossed around. That's my job."

"Who's bossing you around?" He shrugged. "Okay, so I am. I'm concerned, and I know you. You think the store will collapse if you're not down there. It'll survive for one night. You've got good people down there. They'd tell you the same thing I am—take your meds, get a hot shower and sleep." He removed his shoes. "Go. Once you're in bed and asleep, I'll go."

"No, you won't." He'd hover as long as possible. Back when they'd been together, she would've basked in his attention. "But I'll do what you want."

"Thank you." He sank onto the couch. "I'm waiting."

She left him alone in the living room and headed into her bedroom. She hurried through a shower, thankful for the steam. The heat cleared her sinuses up a bit, making breathing a tad easier. Once she dried off and dressed in her pajamas, she walked back out to the living room in search of her cold meds. Leaving the box in her bag hadn't been smart, but she hadn't expected to have a guest.

Alex sat on the couch, but didn't react to her arrival. He had his elbows on his knees and seemed to be deep in thought.

"Hi," she said. She hadn't wanted to break the silence, but figured she should say something. She spotted what he was looking at—a photo of her with him from high school. The picture had been taken during the Christmas parade. He'd groused about the tinsel she'd wrapped around his band uniform, but had sparkled along the entire parade route.

"Hi." He didn't turn around. Instead, he caressed the edge of the frame. "You've still got this."

"Well, yeah. It's a photo and a reminder of a fun night. Why trash it?" She sank onto the cushion beside him. Her knee bumped his. She fought off a shiver. "I'm not like you—I don't keep my memories in my head."

"I don't." He clutched the frame. "I'd forgotten about this night. We had fun, didn't we?"

"We did." She wanted to rest her hand on his leg or at least wind her hand around his arm. "You gave me a ruby ring that night."

"I did." He smiled. "I saved for a month to buy you that ring." He glanced at her. "Do you still have it?"

"Uh-huh. I keep it in my jewelry box." She tipped her head and watched him. "I used to wear it everywhere. I've had to have the band fixed because I wore it out. Harvey kept warning me to get the stone reset or have it turned into something else because I'd worn the band out so many times." She hadn't wanted to change the ring. Why mess with the memories? "After the last time the band split, I put it away." She'd thought she'd lost him forever and didn't see any reason to be reminded of the love she'd never regain.

"Does it need fixing again?"

"It does."

"I thought it was so expensive." He chuckled. "I begged Harvey to help me pick out the perfect ring. He thought I should've gone smaller, but the moment I saw that ring, I knew it was the one you should have."

"It's beautiful." She missed wearing it. "You picked a good one."

"Thanks." He put his arm around her. "We were a real pair. I miss our talks."

"Me too. No one listens to me quite the way you did." She rested her head on his shoulder. She should pull away, but why bother? Being with him was too cozy. Besides, the meds were starting to kick in and all she wanted to do was be comfortable. "Oh well."

"Not oh well. We were good together for a reason." He stroked her arm. "I love Christmas magic and I think it's trying to tell me something."

She wanted to cling to that magic, but her better judgement screamed for her to keep some separation. "That you should head home? Or if you're insisting on staying, you're sleeping on the couch?" She patted his thigh. "I'm heading to my room. I promise I'll stay there." She stood and wobbled a bit before finding her footing. "See you."

"Wait." He put the photo back on the coffee table, then dragged the blanket off the back of the sofa. "Sit. I'll make you some cocoa."

She sank onto the sofa again and curled up in the blanket. She wasn't sure if she had the stuff to make cocoa, but didn't care. He'd figure it out or give up.

Five minutes later, Alex brought over two coffee cups. "I had to heat up some milk and add chocolate syrup." He sat beside her. "Let the warmth seep into you."

She leaned on him, resting her head on his shoulder. "This is nice."

"It is." He sank down on the cushion. "Remember when we got that huge snowfall right before break when we were in high school? I wanted to go sledding and you freaked out about our midterm exams."

"You showed up on the four-wheeler." She stared at the soft twinkle lights and the bow at the top of her Christmas tree. "I worried so much and you begged me to go with you." She sighed. "I'm glad I did. We had a lot of fun. Did you run into me at the bottom of the hill that last time so we'd have to huddle together for warmth?"

"Of course," he murmured. "The majesty of the snowy afternoon, the chill in the air and the rosiness of your cheeks was too much to ignore."

She sipped the cocoa. She'd fallen in love with him that day. "I still feel terrible about conning you into coming to the college my freshman year. I was so lonely."

"Sweetheart, your parents were splitting and it was your first Christmas away from home. I would've driven across the country to get you. I wanted to be your knight in a beat-up Blazer." He kissed the side of her head. "We sang Christmas songs all the way home."

"We did." When they'd reached her house and her parents weren't there, she and Alex had pretended to be a married couple in their first home. "Do you know I lived for bits and pieces of information on your writing career? Even when we broke up, I cheered the loudest for you to succeed." She wanted him in her life — as friends and to be hers once more.

"Did you?" He chuckled.

"I did." Flashes of her dating life with Alex came to mind — working the lock-ins at the community center, playing games of pick-up baseball in the summer, cheering for him while he competed in the school cross country races, decorating his family home at Christmas...and all those long talks about everything and nothing at the same time. He'd been her rock. Hearing his voice reassured her. She lived for their time together. If she voiced her heart's deepest desire, she could have those times with Alex again.

She closed her eyes. The vanilla in the air, the warmth of the cocoa and the medicine worked on her. Within seconds, she drifted off to sleep.

Her thoughts blurred, and she began to dream. That was the only way she could be awake, yet sleeping. Maybe the meds were messing with her. She opened her eyes and blinked. Where was she? As her surroundings came into focus, she gasped. She stood in front of the Santa Barn. The chill seeped into her bones and she ventured into the structure for warmth.

"Hello?" She held on to the railing and ventured across the foyer. The twinkle lights had been left on and the scent of pine hung in the air. She listened for anyone else in the building but heard nothing. She spied the display where Santa usually sat.

"Oh," she blurted. "Santa?"

He laughed and his belly jiggled. "Did you want Santa magic?"

Santa magic? For what? "Yes. No. Maybe?" Didn't she sound confident? *Oh boy.* Why was she dreaming about Santa Claus? She believed in Santa, but she hadn't given him her wish in years. Not since she'd volunteered at the Barn with Alex. What did she want for Christmas? Nothing, really. She had everything she needed and anything else would be extra. "I don't know."

"You can't lie to Santa." He laughed again. "You wouldn't have dreamed about me if you didn't want the magic." He sobered and stared at her. "What do you want me to bring you for Christmas?" Santa folded his hands on his belly. "I know what your heart desires."

She opened and closed her mouth. He was Santa. Of course, he'd know what she truly wanted for Christmas.

"Why not ask for true love? It's not impossible," he said.

She sucked in a ragged breath. She'd thought he'd say Alex's name. A true love...yeah, she'd like that—someday. "It's not possible."

"Is it?" Santa asked. "Think hard before you tell me what you want for Christmas. Your truest wish and heart's desire."

"I want Alex," she said. She should take the wish back, but couldn't find the words.

"I guess you'll have to wait until Christmas to see if you got your wish. You've got six—no, five days until Christmas." Santa put his finger alongside his nose, then laughed and disappeared.

She blinked. He'd left her alone in the Santa Barn. The nerve of the guy. He'd shown up in her dream, got her to disclose her deepest desire then poofed. "Don't you go. I'm not done. I want Alex for Christmas, but I know better. I can't have him. Don't leave before I fix my wish."

Darkness surrounded her once again. She reached out for anything to give her an idea of where she was, but found nothing. "Hey. Come back. I'm not done. I need to explain. Wait."

"Molly."

She froze. "Santa?"

"Molly? I'm not Santa."

Oh no. She'd said lots of things, but some had been out loud. She opened her eyes. Alex sat beside her on the sofa and touched her arm. His hair stood on end and his shirt was rumpled—like he'd actually slept next to her. He smoothed a lock of her hair out of her eyes. "Are you okay?"

She stared up at him and sighed. "No." *Why lie?* Her thoughts were a mess and her heart ached.

"What's wrong? I put your cocoa on the coffee table when you crashed." He brushed his fingertips across her cheek. The touch was tender, but the laser focus in his eyes spoke volumes. She had his full attention. "Tell me. You asked for Santa?" he asked.

"Don't go caveman on me." She sat up and rested her hands in her lap. "I had a dream that I'd gone to a castle. I think it was Santa's castle," she lied. "Maybe it was the Santa Barn. I'm not sure. Anyway, I talked to Santa."

"About me?" Alex asked. He blushed. "You talk in your sleep."

She'd talked. *Crap.* "You heard everything?"

"I'm sure what I heard wasn't what you dreamed about. Just mutterings." He grasped her hand. "You're still warm."

"I've been under the blankets."

"True."

She stared at him. She did want him for Christmas. She craved her happy ending with Alex. Too bad she couldn't have it. "What time is it?"

"Five in the morning." Alex didn't let go.

"I could've slept for another hour," she said. "I don't have to get up until a quarter after six."

"Why don't you try to catch a few more winks?" He nodded once. "I'll stay with you."

"On the couch?" Why did the idea of him being there both scare and thrill her? "We shouldn't."

"We've been here all night and you've been safe. I'm not taking no for an answer." Alex adjusted her blanket.

She settled beside him and stared at Alex until she couldn't keep her eyes open. She marveled at the sweetness and quiet joy in the moment. Being with him reminded her of all the times they'd snuck off during his last summer in North Bend.

"Remember when we crashed like this in my grandparents' barn? We kept warm during that rainstorm by snuggling in the straw," he murmured.

"I do." She closed her eyes and chuckled. "It was fun."

"We should've caught pneumonia from being out in that storm. I'm glad we were together."

"I am, too." She drifted to sleep. She'd forgotten how nice and safe she felt with him around. She nuzzled the pillow. She used to bury her face against his neck and breathe him in. Did he ever wonder about her the way she'd wondered about him?

"Trust Santa."

She paused, but sleep filled her brain. She wanted to replay what he'd said. Wanted to kiss him and feel his arms around her. She wanted to make love to him again and embrace the feelings she'd never really hidden. Maybe she should trust Santa. Molly fought sleep, but lost the battle. A hundred possibilities filled her mind, but she couldn't get too excited. He would probably change his mind. She gave up battling sleep and decided she'd worry about his feelings later — after she woke up.

Chapter Five

Alex stayed beside her as she went back to sleep. He didn't care if he caught her cold. He had her in his arms and lost his heart all over again. He'd never fallen out of love with her. He'd told her to trust Santa. He wasn't sure why she should or why he'd said it.

He listened to the sound of her breathing. As much as he shouldn't be there, he couldn't not keep an eye on her. He let his mind wander. He could have this every morning if he'd give himself the chance — not sleeping on the chair, but having Molly in his life. He considered what he'd overheard while she talked in her sleep. Molly had asked for him for Christmas. Him! He took comfort in knowing he still mattered to her.

He kissed the side of her head again, loving the softness of her skin. Blood rushed through his body as he touched her. She sighed and curled into him. When she tilted her chin, he nibbled on her jaw. She still tasted as good as he remembered. She shifted in her seat and faced him.

"Alex," she whispered.

She hadn't told him no. He nuzzled her throat and smoothed his palm across her belly. She scooted down in her seat and spread her legs.

Christ, he'd forgotten how responsive she could be. He moved her shirt out of the way and caressed her bare stomach. She held onto his wrist, but didn't push him away.

"Yes?" he asked.

"Yes." She held his palm to her breast. "Alex. More."

If he wasn't careful, he'd lose control. No, she deserved a softer touch and a slower tempo. He stopped short of pinching her nipple. If he was going to make love to her, he wanted to do it when she wasn't sick. He nipped her throat.

"Alex?" She splayed her hand on his chest. "What'd I do?"

"Nothing." He kissed her. "You're wonderful."

"But you..." She stared at him. "You stopped."

"We will make love soon. I owe you a Christmas present." He pushed her knees together and tucked her to his chest. "Sleep."

She nodded and sighed. "I'm holding you to your promise."

He hadn't promised anything out loud, but he'd certainly make love to her soon.

Something beeped. His phone? Hers? He'd better check. Jill and Nick might have finally surfaced from their holiday in the hotel. But she had nothing to tell him that couldn't wait until the signing. If Molly had a text, then he couldn't do much to help her.

Alex twisted enough in his seat to pick their phones up from the side table. The scent of coffee wafted through the air. That had to be the beep he'd heard —

the coffee maker. Still, he checked his phone. No notifications. Good. A little green light pulsed on her phone. He swiped the home screen. If she had a passcode, he'd leave well enough alone. A photo of a comic book hero filled the screen along with the number pad. Locked.

He abandoned the phones on the arm of the sofa, then disengaged from her. He ventured into the kitchen and filled two cups with coffee, then paused. She used to like her coffee with cream—lots of cream. He didn't see any powdered versions on the counter. Maybe she had the fancier refrigerated kind. He hadn't noticed the night before when he'd made cocoa.

"The creamer is in the fridge." Molly shuffled over to the bar. "It's pumpkin spice. I couldn't help myself at Thanksgiving."

"Nothing wrong with liking pumpkin spice." He pushed one cup to her and withdrew her phone. "You're lit up." He busied himself with finding the creamer.

"Lit up?" Molly asked. "Oh, the light on my phone is lit up. I'm still groggy and a little stuffed up, but the good night's sleep helped. I hate to admit this, but I'm glad you pushed."

"My pleasure. I can write and cajole like a champ." He located the creamer, then turned on his heel. "Two shots?"

"Pour until it's mostly creamer." She grinned. "I wish I could wake up."

"Coffee will help." He leaned against the counter and sipped his drink. She stared at her phone and he debated what to say. *Be pushy and pry? Stay cool?"* I saw the light. Hopefully there aren't any disasters you need to handle."

"Huh?" She met his gaze. "What?"

"On your phone. The green light was blinking. I'd planned to bring you coffee in bed and your phone so you could gradually wake up, but you came out here instead."

"Oh." She tapped her fingers on the cup handle. "Your PR person, Jill, emailed me."

"About?"

"Confirming the time. Nothing big."

"Okay then."

She looked up from the phone. "When is your sister due?"

"You'd know better than me. I don't talk to my sister all that often. Why?"

"According to this text from your mother, your parents, along with Alyssa, the baby, the kids and Jeffery are all going to be at the signing."

"They must've been trying to surprise me," he murmured. "I was told Alyssa was staying away for Christmas."

"Surprise?" She picked up the coffee mug. "I'm going to get ready. Let me know what's going on. Don't be upset with your mother. She just wanted to make sure there would be enough places for Alyssa to sit down." She left her phone on the counter and headed out of the room.

"Can I see the text?"

"Sure," she called.

"I need your code," he said.

"Alex."

"I know it's pushy, but I wanted to read the text for myself."

She poked her head around the corner. "It's Alex."

"You have my name as your passcode?"

"The numerical version, but yeah. Unless people know about us, they wouldn't guess that code," she said from the other room. "And it's easy to remember."

He'd argue with her later. He added the code, then located the icon for her texts. The wallpaper on her phone showcased a kind of grungy-looking, but cute dog. The pup appeared to be smiling. Was the dog a pet she'd had in the past? He'd have to ask.

Alex focused on the task at hand and found the text.

Keep it on the DL, but Alyssa, Jeffery and the kids will be at the signing. Alex doesn't know. Hope he's surprised.

His mother had texted his ex. He snorted. He shouldn't be surprised. His mother claimed Molly was the only girl she'd ever wanted him to date. But he'd get to see his sister, his brother-in-law and nephews. *Score.*

Despite his better judgment, Alex closed the text icon and tapped the one for her photos. He listened for her to finishing in the bedroom, but heard nothing. He swiped through the pictures. So many images of dogs, books and one of her with Doug. His stomach churned. Molly and Doug. It wasn't right. He should've been the man with her in front of the waterfall. Why had he given up? Because he'd been scared. He wasn't afraid any longer.

"Are you having fun snooping?" Molly stood beside him and snatched the phone away. "That's mine."

"You don't have anything to hide, right?" he asked. She hadn't said those words specifically, but he'd inferred it from the way she'd acted before.

"No, but I'm not fond of snoopers." She sighed. "You found that picture of Doug."

"I did." His heart ached.

"That was the day he asked me to marry him," Molly murmured.

He nearly choked. *Marry him?* "Molly." Why had she kept the image? "You said no, right?"

"I turned him down, but I kept the picture to remind me of the falls and to not make snap decisions. Lesson learned, despite the beautiful backdrop." Molly sat on the stool beside him. "It's not exactly a regret, but I wish I'd have known more before I got to that point."

"I'm sorry for snooping and for putting you in an awkward position." He raked his fingers through his hair. "My sister is coming home for Christmas. I'm kind of excited."

"Surprise?" She folded her arms on the counter. The blue cable-knit sweater stretched across her chest and showed off her cleavage. "I'll have a chair saved for her so she'll be comfortable."

"Thanks." He abandoned his phone. His first instinct was to kiss her, but he couldn't. She'd push him away. "First, I'm heading with you to the store and helping set up for the signing. I'm here and I'm an able-bodied person. I might as well be useful. Second, I'll head home to change, then I'll arrive forty-five minutes early for the signing and once that's over, I'll try to figure out where my luggage is. The lost baggage lady said she'd contact me, but I've heard nothing."

"You've got no clothes?" She stared at him.

"Yes and no. I borrowed this from my dad, but the clothes I brought with me and the presents for the family are in those bags."

"I'm sorry about the missing bags and presents. That stinks, but I can't help but laugh. You're going to be paraded around for the next five days because your mother is so proud of you. Every family member you've ever known will show up to say hi and the lovely Christmas Eve dinner will be huge." Molly poured her coffee into a thermos. "Fun times. You'll be worn out, but you won't have any choice but to cooperate. I know your mother."

"Yeah, Mom can be forthright and since my sister is in town, we won't stop moving." He sipped the coffee in his cup. "About the dinner, why don't you join us? Tonight, and on Christmas Eve? We can catch up and I'm sure Mom and Dad would love to see you."

"Alex." She screwed the cap onto the thermos. "I don't know."

"What? You're family." And he couldn't handle not having her around.

"I have to run the store. The Christmas season is hectic. My staff is fantastic, but I've got other things to do, too. I volunteer at the Santa Barn and have to take the money and supplies from the party to the animal shelter, plus other stuff."

"Good point, but you shouldn't be alone on Christmas." He should've thought of that. "You're open until eight every night?"

"Nine. This close to Christmas, it's easier to stay open for another hour. We get quite a bit of business that way because people know they can hit the other stores that close earlier, then hit ours." She shrugged. "It's not great for Christmas parties, but it helps my bottom line and since it's been so saggy lately, I'll take what I can get."

"Even Christmas Eve?" he asked. She deserved some time off or at least to herself. She should be with family and the ones she loved, not customers.

"I'll close on Christmas Eve at six. That gives my staff enough time to get home to do whatever it is they do that night. I tend to go over to the animal shelter for a couple hours. I play with the dogs and kitties." She met his gaze and squirmed. "I do close for Christmas and the day after. But right now, I have to get going. The room won't set itself up."

"I said I'd help."

"For your own signing? That's not fair." She left her seat and scooped the thermos into her hands. "Go see your parents, sister and the family. Have some private time with them."

"It's Christmas and I didn't get you anything yet. Consider it a present." He wouldn't take no for an answer.

"You've got to write that check, too."

"For the critters? I know. Count up what was donated and I'll toss in my share." He waggled his fingers. He'd add enough to make the donation substantial. "Come here."

"Alex." She darted away from him. "This isn't right."

"You're my friend. You're tired, not feeling great, and I missed you. I want to give you a hug." He rounded the bar and snagged her in his arms. "I needed this."

"Me, too." She rested her head against his chest. "You're dangerous to me, though."

"I know. You're pretty hazardous to my health, too." He let her go. "I have to be honest. I needed to hug you and know someone cared."

"Your parents care." She stared at him and kept distance between them. "As far as Christmas Eve dinner is concerned, it's for your family. I'm not family."

"Mother would insist."

"Let her."

"She'd want you there instead of being alone." So would he.

"I won't be. I told you I volunteer at the shelter."

"Or will you be seeing Doug?" *Crap*. He shouldn't have said that.

"What?" Her eyes widened. "Did you say…"

"Well?" He wasn't ready to share her. "Doug wasn't right for you."

"I know and I ended the relationship, but that's not your business."

"Tell me you're not going back to him."

"Alex."

"I'm right here."

"What makes you so much better for me?" she asked. "I got the hint. You're trying to tell me I should allow you back into my heart, even if it's just as friends." Molly shook her head. "We can be friends, but that's it."

"Molly." She wasn't supposed to say that.

"I'm serious. You don't have to worry about Doug. He got married last year. As for Christmas Eve, I'm going to visit my mother's grave, then go to the shelter to play with the animals for a couple hours. When I'm done, I'll head home." She zipped away from him. "Maybe you should leave. You've overstayed your welcome and someone is probably worried about you."

"Molly."

She put her boots on and didn't look at him.

"Molly, this got out of control and I'm sorry. I'm sorry I'm hurting you." He grabbed his coat, then stepped into his shoes. "You don't understand."

"Oh, I do." She stood and glared at him. "You waltzed in here and reminded me of how much I cared. You made me feel something, but just like before, you're going to get nervous and leave. You called it a clean break. You have a great life, but you're willing to screw it up for a trip down Memory Lane. Yeah, count me out. How I feel about you is still deep. I still care, but what we had was in the past. Once the signing is over, I don't ever want to see you. We had something and it's gone. I'm not playing games with you."

"Molly." She'd cut him to the marrow. He doubted the sincerity of her words, though. She wouldn't be so angry if she didn't have some love for him somewhere in her heart.

"I gave you everything years ago and when the relationship got too heavy for you, you put up walls. I'm not doing it again. It's Christmas. This should be a time for joy, not me getting my heart broken again." Molly stuffed her keys and phone into her purse, then tucked the thermos in the crook of her arm. "I'm leaving. Close the door when you go." She turned on her heel and left him alone in the middle of her apartment. When she walked out, she slammed the door.

The silence enveloped him. He hated being along, but he'd brought the outburst from Molly on himself. He'd jumped into something he couldn't control and expected things from Molly she couldn't give. He wanted everyone to do what he wanted, but life was all a matter of chance. He controlled everything in his books, but not his life.

He had to make things right with Molly, but she was right. He hated tension and drama except in his books. He made his way down the staircase and willed his thoughts to clear. He needed the walk to his car and the quiet to think. He'd made such a mess. How in the hell could he fix it?

* * * *

Molly busied herself with arranging the conference area for the signing. She moved the garland and mini trees out of the way, then picked up the cups and napkins left over from the party. Her heart sank. She wished she'd have been able to stay for the entire festivities, but she also had hoped the staff could've picked up after themselves a little more.

Alex had been right—she needed a break. Between the meds working and sleep, she did feel better. Now she had the final Christmas push to handle and a signing. She had to make people happy. Not impossible, but easier when she felt her best.

The memory of Alex rubbing her inner wrist came to mind. She'd loved it when he'd massaged her and the fact he'd remembered the sensual spots on her body. Her skin tingled and she longed for his touch again.

What good would that do? Bring the chemistry back. She'd take the chance to make love to him next time. Right now, she had to get back to her duties at the store.

She surveyed the area, then arranged the trees to make the table appear more festive and ordered. Once she had the table set, she re-draped the garland and tinsel. Despite them being an upheaval in her schedule, the signing table and different setup did look nice and would increase business for the day.

Delia strode into the room. "Feeling better?"

"I am." She stretched. "It seems like I've been getting this ready all morning and I'll never be done. I still have to put out the chairs." To be honest, her joints ached a bit from sleeping on the sofa. But she'd had Alex beside her. Why complain?

"The setup looks great, though. I'm sorry I didn't get everything thrown out. People kept leaving cups and paper plates in strange places. I tried to keep up, but I got tired. Niecy picked up the slack, but we missed things." Delia held up the money bag. "We have to get counting so the check will be delivered on time."

"Oh, I thought you'd done it." Molly walked with Delia to her office. "I'm not sure why I assumed that. We always count it together." She pulled her notebook and calculator out of her desk. "Tell me you got sleep, too."

"I did." Delia grinned. "Sounds like you had a quite night. The whole store buzzed after you left."

"What?" She dumped the cash and coins onto her desk. "What are you talking about? I slept and tried to get rid of this cold. My night was very boring." What did her friend know that she didn't? She hadn't blurted to anyone she wanted to sleep with Alex, had she?

"Alex isn't boring. I know he went upstairs with you. No one saw but me, but yeah. I noticed. Niecy assumed you'd left together. When we heard rumors, we reminded the workers you're the boss and to hush. They did." Delia tipped her head. "I know you. Girl, you never got over him. Was he good? Did you fuck?"

"Delia. Watch your language in the store." She separated the bills from the coins. "You're right that I'm not over him, but that doesn't mean I did anything. He was a gentleman." He'd stayed beside her and made her crave him.

"That's a great thing. You've got a second chance with him. Tell me you took it. Tell me romance is a real thing." Delia gathered up the coins. "You're cute together and one of us needs to have a good time."

"Delia," Molly said. "He made sure I went upstairs and we slept." They'd been asleep together. They'd been tangled in the blanket, tight together. If she'd only have felt better, she'd have taken advantage of him being so close. But she'd felt awful and the opportunity to do more than cuddle hadn't presented itself.

"Um...he left just a couple minutes ago."

Molly's heart sank. She'd told him to go, but she'd sort of hoped he'd come downstairs and plead his case once more. She shrugged to hide her concern. "Nothing happened."

"I guess not," Delia said. "When I saw him leave, he looked angry."

"Because I reminded him that we're never going to be anything besides friends." Molly rubbed her forehead, then resumed sorting out the bills. "He walked out of my life and didn't explain until last night. I want to be platonic, but I don't know how to trust him."

"Wait a minute. Neither one of you is the same person you were back in college," Delia said. "If he's not asking for forever, then give him a chance. You're good as friends."

Molly piled each denomination of bill, then tallied up each pile. "Maybe you're right, but it doesn't take the sting from his leaving away."

"Let it go. Focus on right now." Delia paused. "Speaking of now, I'm heading to Vermont on Christmas Eve. Mom finally called. I'm flying out at noon. Trixie's closing for me. I can see if there are last-minute tickets available if you want to come along."

"Nah, I'll be okay. I hope you have fun, though." Molly stacked the coins. "Tell your mom I said hi and Merry Christmas."

"I will."

Molly recounted the bills, then sat back. "Okay. Trade." She jotted down her numbers in the notebook. "See if you come up with the same numbers I did."

While Delia counted the cash, Molly tallied up the coins a second time. Delia tapped the last stack of ones. "I got six hundred and forty-three," Delia said. "And fifteen dollars in change."

"Ditto." Molly figured up the total by hand, then on the calculator. "I come up with a grand total of six hundred, fifty-eight dollars. That's with tossing in the last seventy cents to make a full dollar." She met Delia's gaze. "If we double it, then that's thirteen hundred and sixteen dollars. I'll add the extra four dollars to make it an even twenty."

Delia grinned. "Wow. If Alex doubles that, then the shelter will get over twenty-six hundred bucks. That's a great donation."

"Yeah." She hadn't thought about Alex's contribution. "The crew really came through."

"They did. We've got at least three loads of supplies to take over, too." Delia folded her hands. "If that doesn't help, I don't know what will."

"Agreed." Molly banded the money, then tucked everything into the deposit bag.

"Are you going to adopt Boober finally? You know you want to."

Molly tensed. She loved the scruffy dog but she'd have to leave him home alone a lot. If she brought him to the store, she risked people complaining that he irritated their allergies. Did she want that headache?

"You need to adopt him already. No one else takes him because we swear you will. Stop leaving him in limbo."

"Delia." *Limbo?* That made her sound heartless. "I've been busy and someone is out there ready to adopt him. I don't want to take their opportunity."

"You love him. Take him. We could use Boober as our mascot." Delia grinned again. "We could dress him up in sweaters for the different holidays and people would remember the store because of him. Think of it as a good promotion and goodwill in the community."

"You're right. I should adopt him." She loved the dog and hated that he hadn't been taken home yet.

"Good. Do it." Delia stood. "I'll bring my check over at lunch. Want fresh coffee?"

"I've got the thermos, but sure." She didn't want to have to look at the thermos and think of Alex.

"Okay, I'll bring you a carafe." Delia rapped her knuckles on the desk. "I'll pop over during the signing, too. I've got the feeling you could use the moral support."

"You know I can handle this." She folded her hands on the bag. "I've wrangled authors for years. Just because I know this author better than some of the others doesn't mean I'll let him walk all over me."

"I know." Delia paused. "I spoke to Alex. I thought maybe my sticking my nose in would be enough. I also kind of hoped you'd have a better story this morning."

"Me, too." She couldn't lie. "But I'm glad you're protective." She left her chair and locked the cash in the safe. She walked out to the main room with Delia. "I can use all the protection and support I can get. You're a good friend and I'm glad to have you in my life."

"Likewise." Delia hugged her, then left.

Molly folded her hands in front of her mouth and debated what to do next. In the matter of twenty-four hours, she'd reconnected with her first love, dreamed about Santa Claus and confessed her deepest desire…and verbally committed to adopting Boober. Maybe the true love from Santa was going to be in the form of the dog. It was the safest answer and she'd take it. The chance Santa meant Alex was almost nil. The odds weren't in their favor.

Molly sighed. Once the morning crew arrived, she'd open the store. *Just let me get through today and Christmas.* Alex would go home after that and she could go back to her normal life. Why did being alone sound so yucky, especially during Christmas? Because she hated being single. Because, geez, she'd never fallen out of love with Alex.

Chapter Six

At noon, Molly grabbed the wristbands and headed to the line of fans waiting for RR Taylor. People had started arriving when she'd opened the store. She'd listened to the scuttlebutt going around the staff. Alex was famous — but she knew that. He'd hit the bestseller lists with the thirteenth book and the fans were rabid for the edition. She shouldn't have been shocked. He had a talent with words and a flair for presentation.

She stood at the head of the line with Niecy and clapped her hands.

"People," Niecy shouted. "May we have your attention?"

The store quieted, although a few people continued their discussions.

"Hi." Molly smiled. She'd held hundreds of book signings, but this one made her nervous. "Since you're the first fifty people in line and we don't have the capacity to have three hundred people in the store, we've got wristbands for you. Each one is numbered.

You've gotten here early, so you're guaranteed seats during the question and answer session. With the wristband, you're also guaranteed your spot in line. Anyone outside of the store isn't guaranteed an autograph." But she'd heard Alex would sign until everyone made it through the line. "You're free to roam the store until the Q and A session, but you're welcome to stay where you are." Most people tended to wander the store and make other purchases since they were guaranteed a seat in the Q and A session. She passed the bracelets out to the first fifty people waiting in line in the store.

"Thank you," one woman said. "I've been waiting so long to meet RR." She clutched three books. "I've got all his work."

"Even the collected short stories?" another woman asked. "He published a collection of speculative fiction under the name of Alex West. They aren't as good as his crime stories."

"Oh, I don't have it." She turned to Molly. "Can I get that here?"

"No," Molly said. "It's out of print." Although she'd tried hard to get the used copies she could find. No one wanted to part with them. "Seems it's a hot commodity, though. If you want, I can try to hunt down a copy, but I've had no luck so far."

"Yeah, there aren't many copies," the second woman said. "A single print run was all they did. It didn't sell well and I think it wasn't really him anyway. I think someone claimed to have his help or to be him, but it's not. If it's really his work, he should self-publish it."

"He should," Molly said. She'd browsed the excerpts online. Alex had started some of the stories when they were in college, but she wasn't about to tell the fans that.

A third woman shook her head. "RR had his name mentioned on the cover to help the author sell the book, but the stories weren't what RR fans wanted and they're not up to par, so it didn't sell."

Molly fought the urge to roll her eyes. She smiled, then continued down the line and left the women to their discussion. They were wrong. Alex and RR were the same guy, but he wanted to keep his lives separate. Good for him. Now if he could keep himself separate from her, she'd be even better.

"I'm not leaving my place," a blonde woman said. "I've followed RR to each of his last signings. I'm a super fan."

"Ah." Molly handed her the bracelet. "Well, keep this just in case someone questions you."

"Do I look okay?" the woman asked. "I want to look my best. I know this time he'll notice me."

"You look fine." Molly started away. She should've guessed he'd have groupies. He was handsome and sweet. People should be drawn to him. Unfortunately, she'd been drawn to him, too. She focused on distributing the bracelets until she ran out—right at the door. She stepped outside long enough to check the line. The queue ran the length of the block and disappeared around the corner.

Delia had a cart outside and one of her workers offered coffee to everyone waiting. The girl behind the cart grinned. "I'm keeping everyone warm."

"Good job," Molly said and waved. At least her friend was helping keep the patrons occupied.

Molly headed back into the store and clicked the barricade back into place.

"We won't get in?" a man asked. "I've waited for three hours and I'm being left out?"

"No one will be left out. I just can't have more than fifty people in the store at one time. Fire codes," Molly said. "I've been assured Mr. Taylor will sign for everyone who is in line. You've just got to stay where you are until the line moves and be patient."

"Good. I don't want to have waited for nothing," he said. "I'd be mad."

"I can't say I blame you." Molly pushed the door shut to keep the heat in.

The last person in line in the store, a woman, touched Molly's arm. "I hear RR is private, but someone saw him out jogging this morning." She nodded once. "I saw him out last night. Such a nice man. He stopped and signed books and whatever anyone had. Sweet man."

"I don't think that was him. I've heard RR doesn't mix with readers outside of the bookstores and cons," an elderly man said. "He's very quiet."

Molly stuffed her hands into her pockets and made her way across the store. She didn't want to listen to the *RR Taylor is wonderful* discussion. Not right now.

Niecy blew her hair away from her eyes. "We're sold out of books two, three, five, seven and eight. We've got plenty of the other books, but book thirteen is running low, too. I don't know if we're going to have enough for everyone who comes to the signing."

"We'll survive." She never knew how many books to order. One author might be a big name and do a ton of advertising, yet sell only a handful of copies. Others did the same and sold tons. A few smaller-named authors sold out, while others sold none. If she ordered a lot of copies, then she tended to have to send many of them back.

"Oh, and the bell on the garage dinged. Jesse went back there to check it out." Niecy moved papers out of the way. "He said you've got visitors."

"Okay, I'll head back." Molly left the counter and went to the back of the store. She spotted a woman standing behind the signing table. Molly recognized Jill. "Hi," Molly said. "Can I help you with anything? We're ready for the event."

"Hi." Jill balled her hands and grinned. "This is fantastic. You've got everything he wanted and more. You're so on top of things. I wish every venue paid this much attention to detail."

"It's not my first go at this," Molly said. "If there's anything else you or RR need, just shout."

"Thank you." Jill strode around the table. Her high-heeled shoes clicked on the floor. "You're making my job so much easier. I barely have to be here."

"That's the sign of a good assistant," Molly said. "Working with you has been super easy. Thank you, too."

"I heard you know RR…err…Alex." Jill's eyes lit up. "Did you get to talk to him? His luggage hasn't arrived, so he's not exactly dressed for the signing, but we tried." She paused. "So, did you really go to school with him?"

"I did." Molly surveyed the store, then turned her attention back to Jill. "Just an FYI. This is his home town and people know him as Alex so they'll call him that."

"I figured they would. No worries." Jill nodded to something behind Molly. "Here's the man of the hour and family."

Molly turned. She spotted Kathy, Earl, Alyssa, two little boys and Alyssa's husband, Jeffery. She hadn't expected to see Alyssa and her family so soon — not with her being nearly nine months pregnant. She squared her shoulders. Alex's family wasn't the problem and she could face them. He was another problem, though. "Look at all of you. Merry Christmas."

Alex spotted her first. He rushed over to her. "Sorry. I had no idea the entire clan would be here."

"Molly." Kathy opened her arms and enfolded Molly in a hug. "How are you feeling? You look tired. I'll bring some soup for you later."

"I'm sluggish, but I'll be fine. I promise not to breathe on anyone. No need to make anyone else sick." Molly appreciated her surrogate family. "Promise." She hoped Alex hadn't caught her cold, but she sure wanted to have him in her arms again.

Alyssa waved. "I have a toddler and a kid in kindergarten. If there isn't some sort of sickness going around my house, it's a shock." She laughed, then directed Molly away from the others. "So, you and Alex? You're going to do it again, right? Please?" She touched Molly's arm. "Please say you are."

"There's nothing going on with Alex." Molly half-shrugged. His family didn't need to know she'd cuddled with him the night before.

"I heard he stayed over." Alyssa folded her arms on top of her massive belly. "He's crazy about you."

"But the distance will be a problem so...we just won't."

"Distance?" Alyssa slid her gaze to her brother. "Have you, the woman with the bookstore and an entire section filled with romance novels, never heard of true love? Overcoming obstacles? He is your destiny."

Alex blushed. "You're overstating things, aren't you, Lyss?"

"Destiny is a big deal." Alyssa rolled her eyes. "I will not let you pass up this chance — even if I have to stick my nose into your business every hour of the day."

"You're being overly dramatic." Molly nodded to the door. "We need to get this show rolling. I'll head out there and make the announcement at one. Once I've given the little talk, RR will take over. The fans will be able to ask questions and at two, we'll turn it over to the signing portion." She faced his family. "Make yourself at home."

"Molly." Alex hugged her. "Thank you for being nice to my family...and me."

She steeled herself. He kept being sweet and she refused to give in. "You've got a full house and plenty of people lined up outside. You're more popular than we expected. Should be a great day."

"Sounds wonderful," Kathy said. She touched Molly on the arm. "Will you be joining us for Christmas Eve dinner like you do every year?"

"Oh." *Crap.* She hadn't planned on answering that question tonight and not in front of Alex.

"You said you'd do your own thing." Alex stared at her. "You knew you'd be there all along. Do you go every year?"

She wanted to melt into the floor. She hadn't done anything wrong, but she hated the way he looked at her. Her skin crawled. She'd been invited every year, yet she wished she'd never gone.

"Alex," Earl said. "What's gotten into you?" He directed his son to the side. "You don't treat your friends like that."

Alex continued to glare at her, but the harshness was gone from his gaze. "You're right. I'm sorry."

"Alex, I've had Christmas with your family since my mother died," Molly said. She wasn't ashamed of joining them at Christmas. "Dad never cared and had his new wife, so your parents and sister became my second family. They've been here for me when I've had no one else." Her voice caught. *Crud.* "You're going to be late for your signing. Once I make the announcement, it's all you. Niecy and I will funnel the people, so here we go."

She walked away and tried to compose herself. She was at work and had to act professional.

"Molly." Alyssa snagged her and rubbed Molly's shoulders. "Hey. Don't let him get under your skin like that. He's happy you're being cared for and I'm glad you're the adopted part of our family. You're the sister I never had." She rubbed her belly. "Besides, how can I name the peanut Molly Elizabeth if she doesn't know her Auntie Molly?"

"Alyssa." She hadn't known Alyssa and Jeffery were going to name the baby after her. Tears slipped down her cheeks. "Are you serious?"

"Yeah. Jeff and I already agreed." Alyssa beamed. "She's strong, feisty and full of life—just like you."

"Thank you." She wiped her face and hoped she hadn't screwed up her makeup. She hugged Alyssa. "I'm honored." She swallowed against the lump in her throat. A baby named after her...wow. "I'll talk to you later. I need to introduce your brother."

She left Alyssa in the stockroom and drew a couple of deep breaths, then exhaled. She could do this. She had to. Alex wasn't her best friend or her boyfriend. He was a famous author who had no use for her drama. Besides, it was Christmas — a time for peace, love and understanding. She'd take all the understanding she could get.

* * * *

Alex rubbed his temples. She'd been a part of the family all this time. *His* family. She'd found a way in and he hated being left out, but he didn't mind. She hadn't told him she was close to his parents and sister — not on this level. And they hadn't passed along word one that she'd missed him, too. He should be prepping for his question-and-answer session and focusing. If Jill were there, she'd have him secluded and running through his speech. He gritted his teeth. Where was Jill? Probably off with Nick and staring at her engagement ring. He couldn't blame her. He couldn't focus. Molly had invaded his thoughts.

Alyssa marched up to her brother. She led with her belly and bumped into him when she stopped.

"I have pregnancy brain and even I remember how much Molly meant to you. You told us to take care of her."

"I know," he said. "I just didn't expect... No, I did and I'm overwhelmed." One moment he wanted to see Molly and the next he worried about his next book.

"Did you bring luggage or is it missing?" Alyssa rubbed her stomach. "You're wearing Dad's blazer."

"My luggage went to another airport, but my assistant is supposed to be tracking it down."

"Ah." Alyssa groaned. "Have you ever had a baby do gymnastics on your bladder? Where's the bathroom? I haven't been in here in ages."

Jeffery moved Alyssa to the side where Kathy directed her to the back of the store.

"That baby loves to jump on her bladder," Jeffery said. "The other two did as well."

Alex faced his brother-in-law. "I can see the wheels turning. Whatever you're going to say, say it."

Jeffery stood between Alex and the door. "Are you going to fix this? You know what you did. You know why you're upset."

He groaned. Jeffery knew him too well.

"Let me guess. Your stomach hurts," Jeffery said.

"Yeah." *Not fair.* Jeffery shouldn't be so smart.

"You want to kick something, don't you?" Jeffery asked.

"Maybe." His patience thinned. Of course, he wanted to kick something—himself.

"You hate that Lyss is right...because she *is* right, huh?"

He groaned again. "Yes." *Darn it.*

Jeffery tipped his head. "Molly didn't just show up and demand we pay attention. We were here when everything fell apart. She held herself together pretty well after you left, but then her parents split and her mother passed. Mom noticed Molly was just going through the motions. Molly lost a lot of weight and withdrew into herself. Yeah, she's not perfect, but who is? We welcomed Molly into the family because she needed someone. The woman is the strongest one I know, save for your sister. She kept moving forward when most others would crumble."

"I know," Alex said. He respected Molly even more. When he looked into her eyes, he knew what Christmas was all about—love and being with family. "One question."

"I'm listening."

"Why didn't anyone keep her from Doug?" Alex asked. "At least you could've warned her. You knew how slimy he was and yet no one said 'Maybe you shouldn't date him.'"

"She kept the relationship secret." Jeffery shrugged again. "He's history and he knows if he comes around, I'll clean his clock. He was not a good person for her."

"I doubt I'm much better."

"You're not." Jeffery grinned. "But you're family, so I can't say too much."

"Yeah. You can." And now he needed to face his fears. "I don't know what to do." He cherished his night with her and wanted another. But how?

"Um, yeah you do know." His brother-in-law stepped in close, then clapped him on the shoulder. "It's Christmas and we're supposed to be jolly. Do what makes you happy—like the real kind, not what you think everyone wants you to do."

"Right." He noticed Niecy waving at him. He shook hands with Jeffery. "Here goes nothing." He turned his back on his family, then headed over to the main room of the bookstore. "Molly's right," he muttered. "I've got to give a half-hour talk, then sign." He stopped at the doorway and called to his family. "Feel free to watch or whatever. Once everyone's through the line, I'm gone."

His father nodded and his mother waved. Alyssa smiled. Jeffery draped his arm around Alyssa's shoulders. "Everyone?" he asked. "Interesting."

"If they come, then I sign. It's the least I can do," Alex said.

"Then do your job," his father said. "We'll catch up."

He faced the door and Niecy. She handed him the box of pens and his bag of candy canes. She plunked a Santa hat on his head.

"Gotta be festive," Niecy said.

"Right." He blew out a ragged breath. *Time to be RR, not Alex. Time to shine.*

Throughout his discussion with the fans, he looked for Molly as she circulated through the crowd. Niecy stood at the back with the folks who couldn't get a chair. His parents mingled with the fans and wandered around the store with the grandkids. He clasped his hands together. "Last question, then I'll sign your books."

The blonde who had shown up at all his signings stood. She waved at him. "I have a question. In every one of your books, you have Davin talking about a woman. Ellie? Is she modeled off anyone or is she purely fictitious?"

He could give a bland answer or be honest. "Ellie? Or Regina? Davin is a ladies' man."

"I get the feeling she's based on someone. I see she's become more prominent as the series goes." The blonde smiled and pursed her lips. "Well?"

This was one question he could answer without worry. "Ellie is based on a real person, but I won't give names. I took the elements of that individual, plus those of a few other people to create Ellie. She's a rather perfect character and human beings aren't perfect. They're flawed and make mistakes. You touched on a good point, though. I need to work on Ellie's character to make her more imperfect and relatable." A lot of

Ellie's qualities were based on Molly and his recollections of his best friend.

Alex folded his hands. "If there aren't any other questions, it's time to sign some books." He gestured to the first woman in line. "Who am I making this out to?"

"Shirley." The older woman beamed when he handed her a candy cane. "I've read all your books. Love them."

"Thank you." He scrawled his name on the first page. "I'm glad you're a fan. Merry Christmas."

The next woman in line plunked all thirteen of his titles on the table.

"You're a true fan. Thank you for coming to the signing." He scooted the stack of books over, then handed her a candy cane. "Who am I making these out to?"

"Melanie. I'm a big fan," Melanie said. "Molly ordered all your books for me. Whenever there's a new one, she knows I want a copy."

"She's a good woman." He scribbled his name and a short message in each hardback book.

"I kind of hoped you and Molly would hit it off, RR. She's like the Ellie in your books. Well, she is to me. I know. It's so cliché to think you'd fall for the bookstore owner, but we all love her," Melanie said.

"I'll let her know you said that and no, I don't think it's cliché." He finished signing the last book. "Thank you for coming and Merry Christmas."

"It is a Merry Christmas now." She grinned and collected her books.

He sighed. He'd dealt with long lines, but this one couldn't be long enough to give him a chance to sort out his next move. All he wanted to do was apologize to Molly and make her see he rather liked the cliché —

they belonged together. He needed to be with her again and stir the fire burning between them. She'd given him a chance and he wouldn't squander it this time around. What a wonderful time of the year!

Chapter Seven

Molly traded places with Niecy and manned the line. She wanted to keep the people moving. Between Delia giving them coffee and Alex's desire to sign everything, the event seemed to drag on forever. Everyone seemed to be happy, so she refused to complain.

Jill strolled up to Molly. "I'm so glad you allowed us to sign here. This has been a fabulous event."

"You're welcome. I love to support authors — especially local ones." She turned her attention to the line and making sure everyone who wanted an autograph made it into the store. "Did you need something?"

"Just checking on the signing," Jill said. "Alex doesn't tend to need much help once he gets going, but it doesn't hurt to keep an eye on him."

"I've been here all day and the line seems to be progressing quite well." Molly closed the door and glanced out of the window. No other people were waiting outside. *Good.* She'd gladly welcome anyone else who wanted to visit RR, but she'd rather keep the heat in the store.

"Alex made my Christmas bright. If it wasn't for him, Nick might not have proposed in the same way." Jill toyed with her sleeve and moved her bracelets out of the way. "I'm pinching myself. It's a dream come true."

"He is a romantic," Molly said. "This has already been a Christmas to remember." Alex had helped with the engagement? The man kept surprising her.

"It won't ever be topped." Jill waved at Molly. A gigantic diamond glittered on the ring finger of her left hand. "Nick is my hero and Alex is a gem. Why don't you make a play for him?" Her eyes lit up. "I should so get you together again. Wouldn't that be cute? He helped us and I'm going to help you."

"You don't have to." She hadn't seen that coming. "I've got my hands full with the bookstore and I'm planning on adopting a dog."

"A dog? Oh my gosh, that's adorable." Jill clasped her hands together and squeed. "Nick and I need to get a dog."

"Adopt, don't shop. I volunteer at the shelter here in North Bend and all of the animals are fantastic." Molly counted the people still in line. There had to be three dozen people. Alex would be here for at least another hour, plus however much time he'd dedicated to signing things for the staff.

"Well, I'm going to work on getting you and Alex together." Jill nodded. "He's almost done and I need to plan. See you." She winked, then walked away.

Oh boy... Molly sighed. Jill was a hurricane. No one could stop her.

"Do you mind if I take this chair?" Alyssa collapsed onto the armchair before Molly could answer. "The peanut is active today. She knows I'm upset."

"Why?" Molly waved to Niecy, who brought over a bottle of water. "Thanks," Molly said, then turned her attention to Alyssa. "The baby? Is she driving you crazy? Or is Jeff? He's a guy. They do that." *Alex?* Molly knelt beside the chair. "Don't let Jeff bother you. He loves you and he's just being himself."

"Oh, he's fine. It's everything else. I'm so ready to not be pregnant. I'm tired of being the size of a house." She downed the water. "I'm tired of the hundred trips to the bathroom every day."

"I guess I'm glad I never had a kid," Molly said. She'd lied. She wanted to be a mother, but when the time was right and that never seemed to come. "Sounds scary."

"It can be scary, but it's not, too." Alyssa chuckled. "Each pregnancy has been different, too. The boys were easy until I went into labor. They wanted to hang out as long as possible. The peanut has been active the entire time. I'm worn out."

"Aww. She's trying to keep you on your toes." Molly slid her gaze over to Alex, then back to Alyssa. "FYI, Alex's assistant is trying to get Alex and me together. She's made it her mission."

"Interesting." Alyssa toyed with the bottle cap. "You don't seem thrilled about that prospect. Want to clue me in?"

"I guess Alex helped her and her fiancé, Nick, get engaged." She stared at her friend. "When she said he'd intervened, I wasn't shocked. He's got a big heart."

Alyssa nodded. "He does." She waved her hand. "I'm getting tired. Would you mind if we headed out?

Alex will be here forever and I need the baby to settle down for a little while. She's going to be a gymnast, I just know it. Plus, I'm sure the boys are bored. Would it be okay if Jeff took me back to Mom and Dad's?"

"I don't mind and I'll tell Alex where you've gone. Get some rest and put your feet up." She hugged Alyssa. "See you."

"You're coming over on Christmas Eve for dinner, right?"

Molly wanted to confirm her place at the table, but didn't. "We'll see."

"You'd better come. I'll hunt you down if you don't and you don't want a pregnant woman chasing you. I'm not fast, but I'm persistent." Alyssa waved. She left with Kathy, Earl, Jeffery and the boys.

Molly lingered at the end of the barricade, before dismantling the first few posts. The line was down by half and she didn't need the barriers in the store. She noticed Jill at the table with Alex. He tended to treasure his friendships and Jill must've been special if he'd worked to get her engaged. Molly missed the way Alex hugged her. Would it be wrong to fall into his arms one more time?

Molly carried the posts to the stockroom, then headed to the main doors again. She stopped to adjust the ornaments on the small tree on the table in the middle of the store. When she walked around the table, she spotted Doug.

"Hey, you." He held out his hand. "I heard you got him to come to North Bend, but I had to see for myself. I'm proud of you."

"I landed a big author, yeah." She fidgeted with the ornament. "Did you need something? You don't come to North Bend these days. You're in Cleveland, aren't you?"

"You've got a big-name author in the store, I had to come." Doug folded his arms and widened his stance. "You're still adorable."

"Don't start. I'm not in the mood to let you down," Molly said. "I don't like the empty flattery, either."

Doug stepped around the table and touched her shoulder. "You're pale. Are you all right? Are you catching a cold?"

"It's nothing major, but I've got the sniffles." She put space between them. "I don't want to make you sick." She rubbed her forehead. The dull ache behind her eyes increased and her temperature hadn't gone away. "Go say hi. The line's gone down."

"I will." Doug paused. "You know, ever since I saw his name in the paper I've thought about our past. You and I were never supposed to be together, but you and Alex? Yeah."

"And you know this how?" Molly asked. He made a lot of sense, but still. He hated Alex.

"He used to be my best friend." Doug met her gaze. "I never told you that and I doubt he mentioned it, either. We used to be tight. When we were younger, we were the best of friends. Then he got taller and I got better at football. Instead of admitting we were good at different things and girls would like us because of our strengths, we stopped being tight. You got closer to him and he forgot about me. I kind of didn't mind, but when he acted like a jerk because I dated around, I decided I hated his guts."

"Are you serious?" She'd known both since they were all in preschool. She'd never known they were friends.

"Anyway, I came here to apologize to you. Now that I have a kid, I realize just how attached a person can get to other people and to things. I can't imagine not having Pearl in my life." Doug smiled and his eyes shimmered. "She's my world. Because of the things I've learned about me, I want to say I'm sorry. You deserved better than me. Still do."

She hesitated. He tended not to do anything without an ulterior motive. "Apology accepted."

"Thanks, Molly. Second, I'm in town, so Pearl can meet my mother. It's crazy. Pearl's almost two and she's never met her grandmother." He shook his head. "I'm trying to rectify my mistakes and that was one of them. She loves Gam Gam."

"I'm sure she does."

"So, since I'm in North Bend and currently childless because Mom's got Pearl, I thought I'd come down here and see my former friend and former girlfriend. I've seen you, so I've met goal number two."

"Shouldn't you have seen me first, then apologized?" She laughed. "You're backward."

"My plan is." He shrugged. "It's good to see you smile."

"Thanks." Was she blushing? The tips of her ears burned. Yeah, she had to have been blushing. "Why don't you get in line? If you and Alex were friends, maybe you can mend fences."

"Nah. I saw him. That's enough." Doug turned his attention to her. "Molly, don't settle. Take what you want—what you deserve—this Christmas." He hugged her. "Oh, and don't faint when you see the order I placed with Niecy. She wanted to kill me until she saw the list of books I ordered and the cash in hand once said order was placed. It wasn't small."

"Thanks." She stared at him. "Why would you order something here if you can get it online? I'm guessing we're not the cheapest."

"I bought from you because I wanted to shop small, to help a friend and keep the economy in North Bend chugging along." Doug rocked on his feet. "I tried to ruin this town. Now I want to build it back in — in a small way, but still."

"Thanks." She paused. "Why weren't you this personable when we were together? If you'd have been nicer or at least pretended to care more, we might still be together." Maybe not, but anything was possible.

"Until Pearl, I didn't think I wanted to settle down. Yeah, I married Sally, but she wasn't wanting to stay around, either. Pearl changed my life. I look back on what I've done and the damage in my past and I'm ashamed. I had a great girl and dumped her because she wouldn't part with a piece of property. Now, I've got a daughter and it's Christmas. I see just how people and the wonder of the season are important."

"I turned you down," she corrected.

"True." He dipped his head. "I see RR coming and he looks angry, which means he's not ready to bury the hatchet. I'm going to go, but I'll be on the lookout for that box of books. Merry Christmas, Molly."

She leaned against the table for support and watched Doug dart out of the store. She shook her head. She'd never thought she'd see the day when Doug apologized.

Alex approached, but Niecy stopped him. She directed Alex back to the table. An elderly woman waited for Alex. *To be so famous and wanted...* Molly sighed as he turned on the charm. Just like old times — his smile could melt anyone.

Molly made her way to Alex's table. One fan remained. Alex signed books for the man, plus a few for the staff. His bag of candy canes sat empty on the table. The Santa hat slumped backward on his head and he flexed his fingers.

Molly chuckled. When he put on his RR author persona, he was unstoppable. "Looks like you're done."

"Guess so." Alex left his chair and rounded the table. "Thank you for working with me."

"Glad to have you here." Molly laced her fingers together. "I'll let you know how many copies were sold and how many people made it through the line."

"I appreciate that," Alex said. "Are you carting the items to the pet shelter tonight? Dad's got a truck and I'd be happy to lend a hand packing it up as well as delivering the donations."

Him coming around would give Alex a reason to be with her. He'd probably try to land in bed with her. Was that a bad thing? Molly sighed. No, it wasn't. "Thanks for the offer. I've coordinated with the shelter and since there's so much, they're bringing their truck by to collect the donation. Since we're donating almost twenty-seven hundred dollars, too, they're happy to drive over to collect. I'm guessing the donation will be mentioned in the paper, too. Last I looked at my schedule, they'll be here at seven-thirty. I'm hoping to get some pictures, too. I like chronicling our charity work on the store's website. So, yes, please. We can use all the help we can get."

"Smart." Alex grinned. "I'll have that check to you tomorrow."

"Why don't you take it directly to the shelter? They'd like that and you can get your own recognition.

I bet they'd love to have a photo of you during the donation to put on the wall. RR Taylor gave us money." She folded her arms. "I bet they'll make a plaque for it, too."

"I suppose they would." He didn't say anything for a long time and turned his back on the signing table. "Thank you for letting me sign and being a friend. You're a treasure. I'm sorry things haven't been the best between us. Hopefully we can stay friends. Merry Christmas, Molly."

"Merry Christmas, Alex. You're welcome to sign whenever you want." She waved as Jill joined him. "I heard about your goodwill gesture this holiday season. Good job helping Jill and her fiancé get together."

"It wasn't hard." He blushed. "I knew he wanted to propose and you can't find a more picturesque town than North Bend."

"Yes." Jill fiddled with her phone. "Nick wants to go to dinner. Do you mind if I go?"

"No," he said. "Have fun. It's Christmas."

"Thank you." Jill hugged him then Molly before she walked out of the building.

"She's bubbly." Molly sagged against the bookshelf. "Are you out of here?"

"Not yet." He caged her between his body and the door. "I missed you." He brushed a lock of her hair from her face. "I loved our evening together."

"I did, too." She breathed him in. Up close, his strength became more obvious. She missed being held in his arms, his kiss and hearing his voice.

He tilted his head and brushed his mouth across hers. Oh, God. She'd never be able to stop him if she didn't put the brakes on now. She slid her hands over his chest. He'd grown stronger with time and the feel of him excited her more than it had the night before. She opened to him, tasting him again.

Alex groaned into the kiss and threaded his arm around her. The power of him overwhelmed her. She smoothed her hands under his jacket along his sides to his lower back, then down to his ass. Christ, she loved touching his ass. She fitted her hands into his pockets and squeezed.

He broke the kiss and panted. "Yes, do that again."

She laughed as she grabbed his ass again. "Like it?"

"Love it." He eased one hand along her belly to her chest. He cupped her breast through the knit of her sweater. "Missed this...you...everything."

She leaned into him and closed her eyes. She and Alex could be caught at any second and they'd be turned in to the tabloids, but she didn't care.

"I need you." He bit her bottom lip. "Take me upstairs. I want to strip you and taste every inch."

She wanted to give in. No, she needed to. Voices filtered through her Alex-induced fog. She tensed and nudged him. "We should stop."

"Why?" He nibbled her jaw. "This feels right."

"It is, but not at this moment." She withdrew her hands from his pockets and put space between them. "You're expected by your family. I have work. When you come by for the party...we can take up where we left off."

"You'll make me wait, but I'm not backing down." He paused. "Why don't you come over for Christmas Eve dinner? I'd love to have you there."

"We'll see." She wasn't about to commit to anything else today. "I've got to clean up and get the store in shape for the last-minute Christmas rush, plus meeting with the volunteers from the shelter."

"Okay. Consider what I said." He stepped closer to her until she could feel his breath on her skin. Instead of the kiss she'd expected, he walked away.

A piece of Molly's heart went with Alex as he left. It was Christmas time. She should be happy. Tomorrow, she'd take an hour at lunch and go to the shelter. She wanted love and Boober needed a home. She'd give them both the best Christmas. Part wanted to join Alex and his family for Christmas. The holiday was the time for love and forgiveness. Could she move past the hurt and embrace the friendship she craved?

Chapter Eight

Alex sat in the sunroom at his childhood home and stared out at the snow. He wasn't in the mood for a discussion with Jill, especially not over the phone. He'd rather be back at the store with Molly. The pain in Molly's eyes resonated in his soul. He'd seen her speaking to Doug and though things seemed pleasant, Alex had wanted to protect her. His nephews ran in and out of the room, offering momentary interruptions, but not enough to stop Jill.

"So, the signing," Jill said. "I'm glad it's over, but I think we need to set up another signing there when the next book drops. You've got a lot of fans here."

"I do, but I grew up here, so people know me." He sank onto the couch. "We've debriefed and you're still talking about the signing. Want to tell what you're trying not to say?"

"You know me too well. What if I tried to help you and Molly get together the way you did for me and Nick?" Jill asked. "You're cute as a bug when you're around each other and I'd hate to see you leave North Bend without even trying. I could totally set you up."

He took the Santa hat off and massaged his forehead. "No, Jill. I don't need this part of my life managed. Even if you're doing it as a friend, just...my love life is my own problem. Stop trying to micromanage, okay?"

"But you and Molly...it's...I've never seen two people trying so hard to not be around each other when that's what they want the most."

"You're thinking of you and Nick."

"I like Molly. She's sweet," Jill said. "And you're miserable without her."

"So? I should be writing, not worrying about my love life." Bone-deep weariness hit him hard. He needed to sleep and reset his brain. He should be working on his book, but the words weren't there. According to his editor, he needed to turn in the fourteenth novel by January. Without the outline even done, the book wasn't anywhere close to being formed.

"Will you let me *try* to set something up?"

"No." He gripped the phone. "Leave it alone. I need to go and you should be doing whatever newly engaged couples do two days into their engagement." He hung up without giving her the chance to argue.

His mother stood in the doorway. "Are you okay? A woman from the airlines dropped off your luggage today. I signed for them and put everything in your room."

"Thank you." He stretched his legs and turned his phone over. "A lot has happened, and I feel like I'm on the outside looking in at my life."

"Why?" She sat on the creaky armchair. "Did Alyssa yell at you? She's pregnant. Don't take anything she says personally."

"That's not it." He stared out of the window at the Christmas lights on the neighbor's trees. His head ached. The foam of the cake box crackled in his hands. "I had a different idea of what this Christmas would be. I thought if I came back to North Bend, I'd get closure. Instead, nothing is how I expected."

"Because of Molly?" Kathy asked.

"Yes. I look at her and think about all the ways I've barreled along with my plans and didn't consider hers."

"She loves North Bend," Kath said. "You used to love this town, too."

"I doubt she would've left for me, though." Not that he'd asked her. Man, he needed to grow some courage and find out how his ex truly felt.

"Molly thought the world of you and would've followed you anywhere because she believed in you." His mother picked at the fraying fabric on the arm of the chair. "When you love someone, you have to learn to adapt. I had to learn to live with your father's tools being everywhere and his need to make everything. It's a balancing act of what can you accept and what you can't live with."

"Mom." She'd given him a lot to think about.

"You walked out on Molly without giving her a chance. A second chance is staring you in the face." Her forehead crinkled. "How do you feel?"

"I'm not sure about anything."

"Then that's something to consider." She tapped the cushioned chair arm. "You've got a few days until

Christmas to figure yourself out. It would appear you need those days."

"You're right." He sighed and picked up his phone. "Thanks, Mom."

"I'm here when you need me and even when you don't. I love you." She hugged him. "You'll always be my favorite son."

"I'm your only son and I love you, too." Alex shucked his coat, then headed to his bedroom. He had his clothes and the gifts in hand. Things were starting to work out. Maybe the Christmas magic hadn't evaporated around him. What did he want for Christmas? For Molly to forgive him for being thickheaded and allow them to be friends again…she'd invited him back into her life. With a little luck and a lot of work, he'd have his Christmas wish.

* * * *

The next day Alex woke at eight in the morning—later than his usual wake-up time, but he hadn't set his alarm. Back home, he'd have had the alarm on and his day scheduled. Most of the time he didn't stick to the schedule, but when the muse decided to cooperate, he listened. He should get a run in, but wasn't in the mood. *Four days until Christmas.* The decent night's sleep had helped, but once he remembered his to-do list and his looming deadline for the outline of his next book, the uneasiness returned. But he had two entire days to finish his Christmas shopping. If he talked to his editor, he might be able to buy another month to finish the outline. She liked him. She'd work with him. He hadn't asked her for a continuance before and tended to turn everything else in early. That had to count for something, right?

But the words weren't there. None of them. Maybe a walk or finishing his shopping would help. *Can't hurt.* He dressed and left the house before anyone seemed to notice. *Good.* He hadn't wanted any help shopping. He'd rather go on this hunt all by himself. He drove into town and spotted the Santa Barn. He hadn't been there in ages. Molly had mentioned the place was different. Whoever had renovated the barn had enlarged it. A lot of kids could stand in line to visit with Santa. When he'd volunteered with Molly, only about thirty people could stand in the line within the building. The rest waited outside in the roped-off area. He didn't see the maze or pylons to make the temporary barricades.

Instead of heading to the first store like he'd planned, he pulled into the Santa Barn parking lot. The place wasn't open for another couple of hours. No matter. He wasn't ready to head inside yet. He stared at the barn. He had some fond memories of the place — the old version. Hours spent with Molly, helping parents pick up gifts for their children, stacking coats and food for the various pantries…and not having to think about himself. He could be with her, do something good and lose his heart. Molly knew how to buoy his spirits then and even now.

An idea came to mind. She'd done so much for others. Maybe it was time for someone to do something nice for her. He pulled his notebook from his pocket and jotted down a note for later. Once the Santa Barn opened, he'd return.

He headed down the main drag of North Bend. High school students were building snowmen in front of the band shell. More students worked a stand and sold cookies and hot cocoa. A group of carolers stood in front of the bank in the center of town. Music filled the air. He parked in front of the hardware store. Every year he'd sworn he'd get his father a fancy hammer and one of the retro tool chests. Would the hardware store even have the tool chests any longer? He'd never know until he went inside.

Alex strode into the hardware store. Fynn stood behind the counter. He hadn't seen his cross-country pal in ages. Probably since they graduated. Alex waved. "Fynn!"

"Alex West. You're home." Fynn rested his hands on the wooden surface. "I never thought I'd see you in North Bend ever again. Wow."

Alex shook his head. A little thicker in the middle and now wearing glasses, Fynn still looked a lot like he had in high school. Still smiling and happy — probably without a care in the world.

"How are you?" Fynn asked. "You're really here?"

"That seems to be the thing everyone says." Alex wandered down the aisle to the counter. "Did I leave that big of an impression?"

"You just had wings on you long before you left." Fynn shook hands with him. "Have you talked to Molly?"

"That seems to be the go-to second question." Alex laughed. "I have. I signed books at her store yesterday. I'm guessing you saw the line."

"I did. I don't read very much unless it's a how-to manual. My wife, Kelsi, swears I should read a novel or two." He nodded. "Remember Kelsi?"

"Vaguely. She was two years behind us in school, right? Ran cross country with us and competed in track. I thought she was state bound in the hurdles."

"She was. She took fifteenth overall in hurdles at state during her senior year. We started dating after I graduated. One day after practice, she came to the store looking for a part-time job. Between Kelsi and I, we helped Father since Mom passed. We were a strange little team. Dad kept telling me not to hook up with Kels, but things happened." He grinned and folded his arms. "Dating, then marrying her has been the best thing to happen to me, aside from taking over the store and having our girls."

"Plural? You're a dad?" Life had passed him by. He'd wanted to be a father, but the time hadn't been right before. If the time wasn't right, then the girl wasn't either. Now he was looking down the barrel of forty and had only his career to show for his time. Part of him wished he had a family to go along with his job. "How many?"

"Three. They all look like Kelsi and I'm glad. I'm nothing great to look at — sometimes I wonder why she even married me. Guess she decided I was the best of North Bend at the time." He chuckled again. "What about you? Did you sweep into town to rescue Molly? To take what was always yours to begin with? She never forgot you."

He bit back a wince. Everyone seemed to want to bring up Molly. Who was he kidding? He liked knowing she still cared — even if she didn't want to admit it. "Just to sign books. I'm not with Molly." Although every cell in his body wanted to go for coffee and let nature take its course.

"Really? I would've thought you'd come in to buy the ornaments Molly's been wanting. She keeps saying she'll buy them, then doesn't. I know money's tight and I've considered sending them to the store as a secret Santa kind of present. That woman does so much for North Bend. She's the best promotions person the town's ever had." Fynn snorted. "But you're not here for her. You don't see what's right under your nose, do you?"

"I see it, but there's seeing and there's her letting me in." He focused on one detail. Ornaments. He'd have to see what baubles Molly wanted. "She doesn't want more than friendship."

"Wow. I thought for sure you'd get together the moment you came to town." Fynn cleared his throat. "So, you're here. What can I help you with?"

Finishing my Christmas shopping, that's what. "I remember seeing a tool chest here when we were in school. I'm sure it's probably out of favor, but it was old-looking. I think it was called retro, but I could be wrong. Dad said he'd love to have one of those tool chests and I wanted to get him one. I'm going to assume you either don't know what I'm talking about or if you do, that you don't have those any longer. Still, it's worth a shot to ask. Oh, and I want a hammer. One of the top-of-the-line ones."

Fynn frowned, then knocked on the counter with his knuckles. "I know what hammer you're wanting. Your father kept telling me he wanted it, but the price was too high."

"Then that's what I want to get for him." He followed Fynn to the display. He spotted the one Fynn described. "This one."

"Good deal." Fynn rested his hands on his hips. "I think I know what tool chest you mean. We've only ever sold three of them. Dad thought the look would be a big selling point. I never saw the draw." He gestured to the back of the store. "I've got the remaining three in the stock room. The company wouldn't take them back and I can't get rid of them."

He stayed at the doorway and waited for Fynn to return with the tool chest. Hopefully, it was the right one. Part of him kind of wanted to get the thing anyway, just because Fynn had gone to the hassle of looking for it.

"What about this one?" Fynn called. He appeared from behind a stack of boxes and held up another box. "I never took this one out of the packaging."

Alex inspected the pictures. He remembered looking at the tool chest twenty years ago. "Yes. This one. Actually, I'll take two. One for my brother-in-law, too."

Fynn's eyes widened. "If you'd have asked me yesterday if I'd ever sell these, I would've laughed." He carried both boxes to the front of the store. "Alex, you've made my day."

"Good. That's what I wanted to do—spread some Christmas cheer." He put the hammer on the counter. "Where are the ornaments Molly wanted?"

Fynn looked up from the register. "Um, they're the blown glass ones that look like they're from the fifties. It's a set of three."

"Good. I'll take two boxes of those as well. One set for Molly and one for my mother." Alex pulled his wallet from his back pocket. "Would you be willing to deliver the ornaments to Molly?"

"Sure." Fynn rang up the total. "Thanks for the business."

"You're welcome. I knew North Bend had a lot of hidden gems, but I forgot just how great this place can be." He handed over his credit card, then signed the slip. "Thank you for helping me make my Christmas special."

"Sure." Fynn bagged up the items. He adjusted his glasses. "At first, I wasn't sure about you. In school you used to be hard to handle and I thought that's how you'd be now. I knew you were famous-ish. But you're more down-to-earth than I expected. I don't know if that's who you really are, but I hope so. I'd like to be friends again." He handed Alex a piece of paper with a poinsettia on it. "Write a note for the ornaments. Might as well, then she doesn't think it's not worth opening."

"Smart idea." Alex grinned. "You're a good friend. I'm sorry I took so long to realize that." He jotted down a note on the page, then read through what he'd penned. "When we were in school, I wrote a note to Molly and it was the most awkwardly worded note. I tried to make it rhyme and it was horrible." He added another line. "Let's see if she figures out who these are from."

Fynn snorted. "I know you can write, but yeah, that's horrible. If she doesn't make the connection, I'll be surprised."

"Molly's on top of things. I'm sure she will," Alex said. "Thanks for delivering those ornaments and Merry Christmas." He missed this—the quaintness of the town and the way everyone came together.

"Hey, Alex?"

He stopped and turned.

"Have you ever thought about coming back to North Bend?" Fynn asked.

"All the time, but I'm happy in California."

"The town isn't the same without you." Fynn waved. "See you."

"Thanks." Alex left the store with his bag. He wanted to be the laid-back guy Fynn talked about and saw no reason why he couldn't. He put the bag in the trunk of the car, then put the ornaments on the back seat to keep them from getting crushed. He clapped his hands. Where should he go next?

Alex stopped next at the grocery store, but before he went inside, he stood on the stoop and dialed the number to the Santa Barn.

"Merry Christmas from the Santa Barn. Santa's busy in the workshop, but I'm happy to take your call. How can I help you?" the girl said.

"I have a question," Alex said. "When I worked at the barn years ago, sometimes they'd rent out the main room for parties. Is that still one of the practices?"

"We do, but are you wanting to use the barn before or after Christmas?"

"Before if possible." If his idea was going to work, he needed things to start moving now. "Name the hours you've got open."

"Nothing really," she said. "But we're closing at six the day after tomorrow. You're welcome to use the main room tomorrow night after six. Will that work? If so, you need to put down a deposit. Can you come in today and do that?"

"Yes, and yes. I'll be there shortly. Thank you." His spirits soared. "Really, thanks."

"What name would you like to hold the reservation with?" she asked. "I'll pencil you in."

"West and I should be there within the next two hours. Thank you," Alex said. "You've made my day."

"You're welcome." She hung up, leaving him in silence.

Alex grinned and listened to the Christmas music playing from the speakers at the grocery store. For the first time in a long while, he lost himself in the gentle lull of O Christmas Tree.

Kirk stepped out of the store and waved. "Alex! Come inside where it's warmer."

Alex kept grinning and headed into the establishment. He met Kirk by the meat counter. "How are you?"

"Doing well," Kirk said. "I didn't get a chance to visit yesterday at Molly's. I love your books."

"You do? Thanks." He clapped his friend on the back. "I had so many people come through the line. I might not have remembered you if you'd been there."

"You can't forget me." Kirk laughed. The sound echoed through the store. "What can I do for you? Did you need to take something to Molly?"

"I don't know about her needing anything. I was wondering if you'd like to help me. I've got the germ of a plan in my mind and I don't even know if it'll work, but I'd like to do something special for Christmas. I know it's crunch time and you're probably slammed, but...this will be a great thing." Alex nodded to the counter. "Can we talk?"

"Sure." Kirk's eyes lit up. "It's close to Christmas, so there isn't much time, but what are you thinking?"

"Santa Barn. It's always been a special place for my family. Christmas Eve is always a busy time there, but when I called they said they aren't using the main room on the twenty-third after six. I want to throw a dinner for the people who work there and my family. What do you think?"

"We can make something happen." Kirk nodded. "Talk to Glenn and Desiree. Find out how many people you're thinking of including and I'll work up a price."

"Deal. I'm heading there next."

"We'll make it something great. Your parents, sister and brother-in-law will be amazed." Kirk pointed to the counter. "See you after a while."

"You bet. Thank you."

Alex strode out of the store, then climbed behind the wheel of the car. His Christmas spirit increased. Now that he had a plan, no matter how oddball and he wanted to see it through. He drove across town to the Santa Barn for a personal appearance. A couple of cars were parked in the lot. Maybe he could get in long enough to ask a few questions. He stopped, then headed up to the building. He noted the hours.

"The Santa Barn's open?" He stared at the placard. "Already?" He checked his watch. "I assumed you wouldn't allow visitors until after two."

"It's almost Christmas. We get a lot of last-minute requests—like yours about using the barn." Desiree hugged him. "It's good to see you, Alex. I'm glad you called."

"Good to see you, too," he said. "You've taken a lot on." He swept his gaze over her. Where her husband seemed to spend the entire month of December and most of November decked out in his Santa gear, Desiree wore a red gown embellished with fur. "You're Mrs. Claus."

"Well, when you get to spread Christmas cheer, you do the best you can with your job. I've got the assets to be the jolly old elf's wife and since I'm married to him...I'm game. I don't mind. The smiles and laughter are worth the itchy costume." She escorted him into the building. "Are you here to ask Santa for something for Christmas?"

"I wanted to talk to Glenn when he's got a free moment." Alex nodded. "I'd like to do something special and I'll need a little help."

"I'll ask him. Give me a few moments." Desiree paused. "I'm glad you're here. Are you available later tonight? I know it's short notice, but we can use the help and it will grease the wheels for your party the day after tomorrow."

Was she bargaining with him? She didn't even know what he wanted. "I'm game, but what did you have in mind?"

"We need an elf. The high school concert is tonight and our volunteers aren't going to be available. Would you want to come back and be an elf?" she asked.

He didn't have to think about it. "Yes."

"That makes my heart happy." She hugged him again. "Okay, one crisis averted. I'll let Glenn know you're the one who called and we'll sort out the deposit."

Alex wandered around the barn. While the children in line discussed with Santa what they wanted for Christmas, he toured the barn. So many things had changed since he'd been there last. The new owners had installed a beverage bar, a cookie stand, ornament station and a place to take silly photos. The upgrades definitely made the place more festive. But for all the changes, there were still some things that weren't different. The time-worn wreath still decorated the space above the main doors. He'd helped Molly add the ornaments to the wreath when they were in high school. Ribbon and tinsel had been draped across the rafters. Maybe it wasn't the same from years ago, but they'd matched up the colors to make the décor look old. He loved the ambiance. Santa's chair appeared to be the same one from before, but with a new coat of paint and refurbished red velvet.

Alex spotted the Giving Tree. Most of the tags, placed by members of the community to encourage others to be secret Santas for local families, were gone. A few remained. He rubbed his chin. If he went around town and visited a few of the stores again, he might be able to fulfill the rest of the wishes on the tree. He tugged the rest of the tags down and stuffed them in his pocket. He'd fulfill the requests that afternoon.

"You took the rest of the tags. I hope you're good for the wishes."

Alex knew that voice. He turned. "Coach Hipsher. You're volunteering? I thought you were the head elf. Shouldn't you be running a 10k somewhere?"

"Alex." Coach grinned and slapped Alex's shoulder. "Look at you." He laughed. "We had a Santa run yesterday over in Sparta. I came in seventh overall. You should've been there. Would've been some great competition."

"You're slipping." His coach had been the fastest guy in the county since his days in high school. He expected more than a hundred percent from his runners. Alex appreciated his devotion to the sport.

"My creaky joints don't like the runs, but I love 'em." Coach widened his stance and folded his arms. "Are you running?"

"Of course. It's always a perfect, wonderful, great and awesome day for a run—just like you said—except for today since I had a couple of Mom's blueberry pancakes." He rubbed his belly. "I'll let it settle and run at lunch."

"Smart. I saw a guy who looks like you on social media. Better tell that guy to give your face back," Coach said. "Or make sure you're getting paid for it."

"That's me." He grinned. Why did admitting he was semi-famous now embarrass him? "I'm an author and I did a signing at Molly's."

"No kidding. And you're still running? Got to work out those ideas while you're pounding pavement, eh?" Coach laughed. "Nice."

"I do work out plot problems that way." He hadn't thought about his methods, but Coach was right.

"I'm proud of you. Congrats." Coach slapped Alex on the back. "Guess I should've stopped in and talked to the real author I know."

"I've used your coaching to help with my writing," Alex said. "You used to tell me every day not to accept less than my best and chewed me out when I didn't perform. It's helped."

"Good," Coach said. "Are you here with your sister and Molly? I saw them around town together."

He paused. Coach would have to mention Molly. "I'm here on my own accord. I guess my folks and my sister's family are planning on visiting tomorrow before the crowd arrives and I've got a surprise going the day after." He wished Molly were there. Then he'd have his family complete. "Molly's working."

"I'm glad you're together. She leveled you."

"I'm not with her," he admitted. He should've turned things around by now, but he'd have to wait for the magic of Christmas to do its work first.

"Oh, sorry." Coach blushed. "I just assumed…well, enjoy the Barn."

The Barn... Alex paused again. An idea filed his head. "Actually, I'm waiting for a quick minute with Santa."

"You know he's Mr. Martin," Coach said.

"Yeah. Desiree spotted me outside and gave me the lowdown. What they've done with the Barn is fantastic."

"Then I'll go back to manning the crowd and leave to you to your plans. I hope you have a good Christmas. Ask Santa for something you deserve." Coach shook Alex's hand and left.

"Thanks. Merry Christmas." Alex wandered around the Barn and pieced through his idea. The more he thought about it, the more he liked what he wanted to do.

Alex read over the wall where the visitors signed after stopping at the Barn.

"Alex West." Glenn Martin strode over to him. He'd removed his beard and hat. "Look at you. All grown up and important. Have you been a good boy this year?"

"Not really." Now it was Alex's turn to blush. "Bad explains it pretty well." He had to admit, not only did Mr. Martin evoke the spirit of Santa, he sure could lay the guilt on thick. Did he ever come out of character?

"Well, you've got time to do a few good deeds." Glenn chuckled. He changed the tone of his voice and sighed. "I've been Santa for so long that I forget to break character. My wife swears I'm not me again until January." He shook his head. "So, I hear you wanted to talk to me and you cleaned the rest of the tags off the Giving Tree."

"I do want to see you and I did take the tags." He held up the wad of requests. "I need your help."

"Want me to take a few of those off your hands?"

"Nah, I can handle them." He folded his arms and widened his stance. "I've got a bunch of stops to make to fulfill these wishes and I should drop a check off at the animal shelter. I promised the staff at Molly's store that I'd double their donation after Delia and Molly matched whatever they collected. I never got the money to the shelter, so I'm delivering it myself."

"You heard Molly got a dog? He's now the official mascot of Turn the Page. She picked Boober up last night. That pup makes me laugh. He's so full of energy around Molly, but protective. Everyone thought he was…" Glenn shrugged. "He didn't seem social and everyone thought there was something wrong with him. He just needed Molly. He's her constant companion, I've heard."

Her true love at Christmas. Alex forced a smile. The *dog* was her love… Would she have room to love him, too? "Was he the dog she's been thinking about adopting?

"Yeah. When she came to the Barn last night to pick up her costume, she had him with her. I guess they stayed open a little longer so she could get him," Glenn said.

"Sweet." The more he thought about the dog, the more he liked what he'd heard. He'd always wanted a dog, but never got around to adopting one.

"So, what's the problem?"

"I want to give someone an awesome Christmas and I need Santa to help me," Alex said.

"Do I know this person?"

"You do," Alex said. "All of them. I'm thinking a family dinner the day after tomorrow after the Barn closes. I know it won't be Christmas Eve, but you can't have everything, right? I'll help clean up afterwards and I've got a deal going with Kirk to provide the food. I'd like you to be there, too. What do you think?"

"Then you're the one who wanted to have the party on the twenty-third. I see. You want to create a Christmas memory? That's wonderful. I don't normally open the Barn up to parties — we're usually too busy, but you were promised the date and I love this idea." Glenn toyed with the elastic on his beard. "We miss you in North Bend."

Funny how everyone kept mentioning that. "I've missed North Bend, too. Everyone here is wonderful. They know each other and keep an eye out. It feels like home." Home in so many ways. Although part of him wished he'd never left, he still believed he had to leave to realize what he'd had all along. Now he could properly treasure his blessings.

"Then why not stay here?"

"I've asked myself that a hundred times since I've been back." Alex stuffed his hands into his pockets. He had no good answer. "Maybe I should stick around."

"You'll figure it out," Glenn said. "I'll help you, but if you can bring the donations here by five and have everything cleaned up by ten on the twenty-third, that would be best. That way we can get the stuff to those who deserve the smiles for Christmas and you can have your party."

"You bet, but it's our party. I'm inviting you, Desiree, Fynn and his family, Kirk...maybe I'll open it up to the town."

"You never cease to amaze me. If you and Molly were a team, you'd be dangerous." Glenn laughed. "I hear you're volunteering tonight. Can you be here at five?"

"With my elf costume on."

Glenn waved. "Merry Christmas."

Alex strode out of the Barn. He hadn't asked for Molly for Christmas, but he'd set the plan in motion to get the most important gift of his life.

Chapter Nine

Alex headed out to the car. If he was going to move on with his life, he needed to give Kirk the green light on the party. First, he needed to stop Jill from her master plan to get him together with Molly. If she didn't love him, then they both deserved to move on.

He sent Jill a text.

Don't push Molly. The way I left things wasn't nice and you pushing won't help. I can do this on my own.

He drove back to the grocery store and spoke with Kirk. When he returned to the car, his phone rang. *Jill.*

"Hi," he said. "What's wrong?"

"You really want me to stop pushing you and Molly together?" Jill sighed. "Why?"

"When we split, I cut things clean, but it wasn't nice. She's on the verge of allowing me to be friends with her again and I'm worried that if you push, she'll put up walls."

"You're not giving yourself enough credit. You're quite smooth when you try and if you let me do a little nudging, you'll have your dream girl by Christmas."

"Don't get excited." He had some plans, but he couldn't guarantee Molly would give him a second chance. After she saw what he'd done to get into her good graces, she might never talk to him again—or she'd admit she loved him, too.

"I'll back off, but I can't be trusted to not push just a little on Christmas Eve. You're meant for each other. Everyone can see it," Jill said. "I'll talk to you later."

"Yeah." He hung up, then drove over to Molly's store. Maybe he was crazy, but he needed to see Molly. Maybe he'd bump into her. He headed into the bookstore. On first check, he didn't notice her. He wandered over to the display of his books, then pulled the pen from his pocket. He autographed the rest of the books and kept an eye out for Molly.

"What are you doing?" Molly put her hand on his arm. "Oh, you're signing them. Thank you."

The warmth of her touch filled his soul. "I thought I'd come back and leave a surprise in the books. This way anyone who didn't make it yesterday can have a signed copy."

"Would you mind if we labeled them as signed?" She half-smiled. "I know it's forward and you want this to be a surprise."

"I'd be hurt if you didn't." He could gaze into her eyes forever and not get tired.

"I'll make up a sign." She let go, but didn't walk away. "You came in here to be benevolent?"

"To spread some Christmas cheer and to touch base with my friend." He grinned, wondering if she'd caught on to his wording. "What if someone wished for a copy of my book and couldn't imagine getting a signed one? I wanted to add an extra surprise. Don't you like to get autographed books?"

"I love first editions." She blushed. "Then thank you. My customers will appreciate it. Merry Christmas. I've got to get back to work…friend."

She'd noticed. Hallelujah. "I'm not going anywhere. Well, I'm leaving the store. I've got to be somewhere, but I'm sticking around North Bend until after the holidays." Talk about a spur-of-the-moment decision. He trusted his gut. She'd given him an opening and he wanted a few inches more. "I'm sure we'll bump into each other again." He squeezed her fingers. "Merry Christmas."

"Yeah." Her forehead crinkled and she half-waved.

Alex couldn't hide his smile. He loved being unpredictable. When he wandered out of the store, photographers intercepted him. He blinked against the flashes and cursed his bad luck. Each of the pictures probably had him making silly faces. He stopped. One of the reporters stuck her audio recorder in his face.

"Is it true the famous author RR Taylor is back in North Bend to stay?" she asked. "Rumor has it you're planning on buying a home and putting down roots."

The reporter knew more than he did. He'd just decided to stick around for a few days after Christmas. Alex smiled and switched into his author persona. "I'm here for the holidays. My family lives in North Bend and I'm happy to be here." If this was Jill's idea of pushing him and Molly together, she'd failed. This kind of publicity wasn't what Molly wanted.

A male reporter stood beside him. "We've heard you're stumped with your next book. Are you considering setting the book here in North Bend?"

"I've got notes, but, as with my other books, I don't like to give spoilers. I'd rather let the book write itself. If the characters are sparked by North Bend, then that's how it might go." Did he make sense? He hoped so.

"How about some photos? We'd love to feature you in the paper," one of the photographers said. "Should be in the entertainment section the day after Christmas."

"Sure." He didn't have much choice. He stood in front of the Christmas tree and smiled. One of the reporters produced a copy of his book. He held the copy as the photographers captured his image. Out of the corner of his eye, he spotted Jill and Nick waving. At least they were both there.

"Are we good?" Alex asked. "I'm meeting someone."

"The rumor is you're here for a secret love?" The male reporter held up his recorder. "According to sources, she's here in North Bend, too. Is that true?"

"I'm not at liberty to discuss that information." A secret love? "I'm required at the coffee shop. Thank you. Merry Christmas." Alex waved, then headed into the shop.

"You're popular." The corner of Jill's mouth quirked into a smile. "You seemed to be enjoying the attention."

"It's interesting. I'm not that popular at home," Alex said. "I'm glad you're both here." He had a few things he wanted to say.

"You don't like that I got them involved, do you?" Jill twisted the ring around her finger. "Alex, you have to get it into your head…you and Molly are destined."

"Will you stop? The more you push, the more I want to dig in my heels," he said. "I finally got her to call me her friend. Yes, I would love a date with her, but come on. She's a smart cookie. She won't like being cornered into anything."

Jill's smile fell. "I wasn't trying to do that."

"I told you he gets it. He knows you want everyone to be deliriously happy like you are." He nodded to Nick. "But cajoling won't get anyone anywhere in this situation."

"I know," Jill murmured. "It's Christmas and I'm tired of seeing Alex cranky. I'll bet one good kiss and his muse will come back. I see Molly being the jumpstart to so much."

Alex sighed. He took the empty chair. "I'd like to take part in this discussion, since I'm the topic."

"Sorry," she said. "I just thought if you had a secret romance and word got out about it…it'd help sell books and you wouldn't be lonely."

"Jill." Alex stared at her. "My personal life shouldn't be a motivator to sell books."

Jill folded her arms. "I know, but I see why you and Molly liked each other. She's adorable and you're handsome. She's smart, funny and right on point with her business. You're free-spirited, and with your writing you need someone who understands the hours you keep. She would. She already does. Besides, the electricity in the room is off the charts."

"Maybe, but there are a lot of years between her and I. We're friends now," Alex said. "If she even thought I'd just talked to those reporters to get in good with her, she'd have a fit."

Nick shrugged. "He's right."

"Thanks." Alex turned his attention back to Jill. "Molly is one of my oldest, dearest friends and now she's finally on speaking terms with me. My family can't help but want her and me to be together. My sister wants Molly in the West clan. This trip was for the signing, but so I could reconnect with Molly." He rubbed his forehead. "I've done that. The rest is just for the sheer fun of Christmas." He hadn't forgotten his plan to bring Molly around at Christmas. He'd have to *tell* her she'd been invited, but still. He'd get there.

"Alex." She grabbed his shoulders. "You love Molly and she loves you. It's so obvious." She pinched her lips together in a frown. "Don't get mad about the reporters. I'll tell Molly the truth—it was all my idea and she won't hate you. I know she won't."

He didn't know what to think. "Tell her that, but...I have a trick up my sleeve." He hadn't wanted to bring Jill in on his surprise, but she might have some good ideas, too. "I set up a dinner situation. I want to get my family and a few people from the community together."

"Including Molly?" Jill asked. Her eyes lit up. "That's a good start. Is any of this situation romantic?"

"Yes."

Jill paused. "What do you need me to do?"

"First, explain to her that you're pushy and trying to get us together, since it's the truth. Second, back off. I mean it. Let me do this—not for publicity, but because I might happen to agree on the destiny thing."

"Wow," Nick said. "You're getting romantic in your old age."

"We're the same age." Alex rolled his eyes. "But thanks."

"I don't like being left out," Jill said. "But, I understand. You've got my help."

"It's crazy. I loved Molly and I made a mistake by walking away, but I got where I am now. I don't regret my past, just how I broke things off with her." Alex stuffed his hands into his pockets. "The more I'm around her, the more I can't imagine not having her in my life. That's crazy, right? That's too soon. Has to be."

"When love hits, nothing is too soon." Nick shrugged. "Take it from one who knows."

Jill didn't speak right away. Instead she chewed on her bottom lip and stared at him. Part of Alex wanted to question her, but the rest of him opted not to push. Still, he wondered what went through her mind. Jill sighed and narrowed her eyes. "I'm saying this once. It's Christmas. Drama and the holidays are inevitable. Foolish things like me getting a little too exuberant about creating couples...it happens. Don't forget your loved ones — even if they drive you crazy. Don't give up on someone who makes you happy. The miles and years apart won't matter if being with them is what's meant to be. Sometimes, those people are all you've got. For Christmas, there's no place like home — wherever home may be — with the people you love."

Alex kept quiet. His assistant had made a lot of sense. "Then it's a good thing I'm in North Bend. I need to recharge and come together with the ones I love. Thanks for the advice."

"Any time."

"When are you and Nick flying back to California?"

"Tomorrow," Nick said. "I'd like for my family to spend time with my fiancée this Christmas."

"And I can't wait to be more than just the girlfriend," Jill said. "Think about what I told you."

"I will." He chuckled. "Enjoy the bonuses I gave you and Merry Christmas. I'll see you when I get back."

"Merry Christmas, Alex. Remember what I said." Jill curled her arm around Nick's and left Alex in the coffee shop.

Alex scrubbed both hands over his face and debated his next move. He hadn't finished his Christmas list for his family and still needed to tackle the ones on the tags from the Santa Barn. At least he had his love life kind of sorted out. Jill wasn't pushing in and he could move at Molly's pace. Instead of rushing to Molly to explain, he opted to let Jill do the talking. He headed over to the second-hand store. His mother liked retro items, such as cookware and jewelry. He strolled through the establishment. If anything caught his eye, he'd inspect further.

"May I help you?"

He glanced over his shoulder. He knew that voice. "Mrs. Sandoval."

She rearranged the knickknacks. "Do I know you?"

He grinned. "Alex West. You used to shoo me out of the store when I was a kid." He faced her. "I grew up."

Her eyes widened. "Alex? I thought you looked familiar." She touched his arm and laughed. "Your mother was in here the other day. If I'd known you were home... It's a pleasure to have you back."

"I'm surprised she didn't tell you I signed books yesterday at Molly's store," he said. "You still love to read, don't you? I'm RR Taylor."

"You? Well, I never." She gestured to the back of the store to the book display. "We've got two of your books in stock. I'll have to grab them for myself. I only read on my tablet, but if they're by a North Bend-er, then I have to have them."

"I'll autograph them when I'm done shopping." He held up his finger and pointed. "What do you have in blocks and building stuff? Alyssa's boys love to build." The might like something besides the books he'd bought while still in California.

"I just got a set of building logs. Brand new and never opened. I've got a couple of sets that are open, but practically new. Checked them over yesterday." She nodded. "Toy aisle. I've got a couple of necklaces your mother might like. She was eyeing the faux emerald one. Said it was costume jewelry from the 60s. I'll pull it out of the case for you."

"Thanks. I'll be up to the counter in a bit." He wandered over to the toys and spotted the building sets she'd mentioned. His nephews would love them. His sister had an affinity for second-hand over new and the boys wouldn't care where the toys came from as long as they could play with them. He tucked both boxes under his arm. He spotted the record section, but resisted the urge to hunt for Victrola records. If he did, he'd never leave the store.

Alex wandered past the cookware section, then up to the counter.

"You're quite the shopper." Mrs. Sandoval pulled a plastic bag from under the counter. "I picked up those books. Did you want to look at the necklace?"

"Sure do."

She withdrew the display board from the glass case. "This one." She adjusted the necklaces. "Molly liked the blue one. Have you spoken to Molly?" She paused. "I'm sorry. You must've talked to her — you were at her store."

"I was there and yes, I spoke to her. She hasn't been feeling all that great. She's got a cold. I'll bring her more soup later." *Or treat her to some after our shift at the Santa Barn.* "I believe she's donating her time over at the Santa Barn, too."

"I noticed a twinkle in your eye and the spring in her step." She bagged up the blocks. "Did you want any of the necklaces?"

"Yes. This blue one, the emerald one and the pearls. Molly had a navy sweater on yesterday and the pearls would look great with it." He spotted a music box with cat and dog figurines in the upright glass case. The animals reminded him of Molly. "I'll take the music box, too."

"Let me make sure it works. I'd hate to sell you something that's broken." She plucked the music box from the shelf and twisted the knob. "It wasn't working the other day." Strains of *O Come All Ye Faithful* emulated from the ceramic figurines. "Guess I was wrong. I'll find a box."

"Thanks." He marveled at his haul. He'd found so many great things in North Bend. Why would anyone want to go anywhere else? He'd have to go to the big box store for some of the items on the tags, but no problem. He stared out of the front window at the town square. There was a story in North Bend. All he had to do was find the words and get to writing.

"Here we go." Mrs. Sandoval boxed the figurine, then the jewelry. She tapped the keyboard on the register. "You're up to fifty-seven dollars."

"Great." He handed over the money. "Thank you."

"Here are the books." She opened both to the title pages. "It's exciting to have an author in North Bend."

He scrawled his name, then paused. "Do you want these made out to you, or leave them with just my autograph?"

"To me." She bagged up the rest of his items. "I'll treasure them."

"I'm honored." He jotted down a note in each book, then pushed both to her. "Enjoy."

"I will."

Alex gathered up his bags. A thought occurred to him. "Is Heather's place the only salon in town?"

"Yes. The other one closed when the girl accidentally dyed Mrs. Burns' hair purple." She shrugged. "I liked the purple. It went with her complexion. Anyway, that girl closed her shop. Why? Your hair looks fine."

"I thought I'd buy a gift card for my mother and Molly. She's been feeling down. She might like a day at the salon," Alex said. He didn't want to be too forward, but she deserved some pampering at the holidays.

"In addition to the jewelry?" Mrs. Sandoval asked. "Are you planning on getting back with her?"

"Maybe. I'm not expecting anything." If Molly would give him at least one date, he'd know where he stood with her. "If she'll go out with me, then fine. If not, then she can use the salon time however she wants."

"I've got faith." Mrs. Sandoval waved. "Merry Christmas."

"Merry Christmas to you, too." Alex took the bags out to the car, then whipped his phone out. He dialed the number on the front of Delia's coffee shop.

"Hello?"

He didn't recognize the voice. "May I speak to the owner?"

"Delia? Sure. Just a moment." The other end of the line crackled and he heard hushed voices before the line cleared again.

"This is Delia. How may I help you?" she asked.

"It's Alex." He leaned against the fender and crossed his ankles. Fresh snow began to fall. "If I buy a certificate for Molly to get her hair done, will you make sure she gets there?"

"Are you crazy?" Delia asked. "I mean, Molly would love that, but what are you trying to do? Weren't you just in my shop?"

"I was because I'm trying to visit the various establishments in North Bend to give them business. I'm buying Christmas presents." He tucked his free hand into his pocket. "What do you think about the salon day? Think she'd like it?"

"You're crazy." She sighed. "But I think she'd love a day at the salon. If you can set it all up, I'll nudge her in the right direction."

"Thank you. I appreciate the help."

"Wait."

"Yes?" If she mentioned destiny or how he belonged with Molly, he'd swear the whole town was conspiring against him. He leaned against the fender. "Delia?"

"Just...I like you. Not romantic, but I like you. I thought I hated you for splitting with Molly, but I've had second thoughts," Delia said. "The thing is, you're almost trying too hard."

"Am I?" He hadn't looked at the situation that way and since Delia didn't know about the dinner he'd planned, he wondered how she'd come to her conclusion.

She sighed. "You're clueless, aren't you?"

"No?" Was he? He frowned. "Delia."

"Anyone with a pulse can see you're pining after Molly. You've fallen for her just like everyone else," Delia said. "You want her to like you as much as you do her, but forcing the situation won't help. Prove to her you're the same guy you were when she loved you but more mature. She needs a guy who can be strong beside her. She's a force to reckon with and a pillar of this community. If you do something you'll regret, you won't have only me or even her to deal with. This town loves its bookstore owner."

He spotted Molly in her store. His heart lightened, and he wanted to rush in to speak to her. Instead, he stayed put. "I understand." Molly had put her heart and soul into her store and making North Bend a better place. He respected her more than ever. "Message received. I'll phone you later. I need to finish shopping."

"Works for me. See you." She hung up.

Alex tipped his face to the sky. Snow dusted his cheeks. His life wasn't perfect, but his plan was coming into place. Coming back to North Bend sure felt like the best decision he'd made in a long time. Once he finished shopping for the items on the tags, he'd get to writing. The magic of Christmas bubbled within him. He'd fallen in love. He hoped Molly felt the same way.

Chapter Ten

At four-thirty, Molly put Niecy in charge, then ducked into her office.

"Going to the Santa Barn?" Niecy asked. "Why don't you wait a moment. You've got a delivery. Why don't you open it before you leave?"

"Niecy." She accepted the box. "From the hardware store? I didn't order anything."

"Don't ask me. Fynn brought it over a little bit ago." Niecy leaned on the doorframe. "Maybe it's a present from a secret Santa."

"Unless someone at the store decided to buy me a gift—looking at you, Niecy—then I don't have a secret Santa." She untied the twine and removed the paper. "There's a note." She opened the card. *Sometimes Santa comes early. Sometimes he's a little late. This gift is for you. I hope you think it's great.* She frowned. "Whoever wrote the card isn't great with words."

"Then it's not Alex." Niecy chuckled. "Open it."

"It's funny. I remember a note kind of like this and it was from Alex." The tips of her ears burned. "He'd tried so hard to make the poem rhyme. It wasn't very good, but I didn't have the heart to tell him that." As much as she wanted to consider he might be the one to send her the surprise gift, she knew better. He probably didn't even remember the silly note or trying so hard to impress her.

"I'm guaranteeing this isn't from Alex. That boy was just outside talking to the media. I've never seen that many photographers in my life."

"Yeah, Jill, his assistant, told me about that. She wanted publicity for him and the store. I won't turn it down. The more press I can get and positive at that, I'll take it." Molly touched the edge of the box. "Think this might be from Jill? Like a thank you?" The note made no sense if it was from Jill, but who was she to question?

"I don't know." Niecy crossed the room and plopped onto the other chair. "You'd better open it. I'm dying from anticipation."

Molly removed the paper and gasped. "The ornaments." She met Niecy's gaze. "I wonder who told Fynn I wanted them. Did you?"

"Not me. I was going to go later and tell him to hold some back, but I did tell Jill about them when she inquired on the ones we have in the store." Niecy shrugged. "Now I don't have to see Fynn. Whoever wanted to surprise you did and you've got the ornaments. Take them upstairs before you forget where you put them."

"Bossy, aren't you?" Molly tucked the card into her desk drawer, then moved the box off to the side. "I've got to come back to the store after my shift at the Santa Barn. I'll take them upstairs then."

"Good." Niecy followed Molly out of the office and waited as Molly locked the door. "I'll hold down the fort, boss. Have fun and give out those toys."

"I'm working the line until seven, then we'll make sure the wish bags are distributed." Molly put her coat on. "I'll see you at nine or shortly thereafter."

Niecy saluted, then darted in the direction of the registers.

Molly left the store and walked the four blocks down to the Santa Barn. The nip in the air, the lights sparkling and excitement around her buoyed her spirits. She had a secret Santa. Doug? Nah, he had his daughter and a new life. One of her staff members? Probably not. They'd donate to the animal fund instead. Delia? She'd given Molly a pair of gloves and leggings. Niecy? Nah, Niecy couldn't keep secrets, even her own. Oh well. Jill? Possible. She'd find out when the Santa wanted her to know.

She ducked into the Santa Barn through the staff entrance. The sound of children speaking and Christmas music filtered through the air. She changed into the elf costume. The bright green did little for her figure, but who cared? She wasn't there to entice anyone. She pushed the curtain aside and stepped up to the mirror. At least she felt better than she had for the last two days.

"Look at you." Alex stood in the doorway. "If I'd known there would be cute elves, I would've volunteered before now."

She whipped around and faced him. "Alex."

"Hi." He grinned. "Since I'm in town, I thought I'd help out. I'm glad I did."

"You knew I'd be here." She rested her hands on her hips. "Who told you?"

"I remembered how many nights we spent here in these costumes — well, the less exciting versions because these are great — and how much fun it was. I wanted to recreate those memories." He tucked a lock of her hair behind her ear. "What? I'm not allowed to help? But Delia did mention you were volunteering your time tonight."

"Delia would." She shook her head. "This was fun, hanging out with you and having a reason to be together without my parents thinking we were up to no good.'

"My parents said you were a positive influence on me. I'd like to think they were right, but we did get up to no good from time to time." He sighed and folded his arms. The sleeves stretched tight across his arms, accentuating his lean muscle. "How are you feeling?"

"I'm okay. Better than I was. The soup helped." She picked up the basket of candy canes. "We should get to work."

"I'm having soup brought in after our shift." Alex stopped her in the hallway. "Are you mad at me?"

"Why?"

"The photographers. I made a spectacle in front of your store."

"Oh that." She swiped her hand through the air. "Any press is good press. People are coming into the store and sales are up a teensy bit. I'm not knocking the help, so thank you."

"Then I'm glad I chatted up the store." He paused. "You're tense. Are you afraid of me?"

"No." She just didn't want to look him in the eye. The more he wore her down, the more she missed him.

"I'm trying to run into you and you're trying to avoid me." He tipped her gaze. "I'm not going to do anything rotten. Promise. It's Christmas and I'm working for Santa. He frowns on misbehavior."

"I'm here to do a job, not flirt with you."

"Flirt?" He laughed. "Molly. You're taking this too seriously." He put both hands up. "I take that back. You should take your job seriously, but loosen up. Let's have fun."

He kept her on-edge. She needed her confidence. She blew out a ragged breath and forced herself to be cool. "I'm heading out there. You can follow if you want, but I'm getting to work." She brushed past him and went to the head of the line to relieve the high school girl already there.

A hundred memories rushed into Molly's brain. She remembered the times she'd spent volunteering with Alex there at the Barn. Hayrides, car trips to the lake and all those long talks. She'd thought he was the one. She couldn't deny the attraction, but she had no choice. They lived separate lives.

Alex paused beside her for a moment. "Don't avoid me." He took his place behind the camera. "We're working together. It'll look silly if the elves won't talk to each other."

"Alex." She wanted to toss the basket of candy canes at him. "You're right."

"I'm Elf Alex."

She chuckled. "You are." She embraced the Christmas spirit and the fun of being at the barn. "Elf Alex, I'm not avoiding you and I'd love to talk to you."

"There's the smile I wanted to see. We're here to make children happy and spread holiday cheer." Alex winked at her. "Let's have fun and be friends. We can do this."

Molly nodded and her smile widened. "We can."
She got right to work, but having Alex so close frazzled
her. She focused on being Elf Molly and helping to keep
the line moving. She handed out candy canes and when
a child appeared scared, she got down to his or her level
to offer words of support. So many frazzled nerves and
fear, but also excitement. The electricity between them
was palpable.

Molly spotted a little girl and her father joining the
line. The girl didn't seem to mind being there until she
got closer to Santa.

"No," the girl cried. "I can't. No."

Molly abandoned her post at the head of the line and
knelt next to the girl. "What's wrong?"

Dad squeezed the girl's shoulders. "Honey, it's
Santa. You've talked about visiting him since
Halloween." He turned his attention to Molly. "Sorry. I
didn't have a chance to bring her up before now. I know
it's last minute. I'm sorry she's causing a fuss."

"You're not the first to be a little afraid." Molly dried
the girl's tears. "It's perfectly okay to be scared. I
happen to know Santa and he's a very nice guy." She
met the father's gaze. "It'll be okay."

The dad sighed. "If you say so."

Molly held the girl's hand. She'd gotten through to
her. *Good.* "Have you thought about what you wanted
to ask Santa for?"

"I did." The girl hiccupped. "I know."

"Good." Molly stood and checked the line. "Looks
like you're next. If you want, your father can go with
you to see Santa."

"He can?" The girl nodded and held tight to Molly's
hand. "Can you come, too?"

Molly hesitated before answering. "Ah..." She wasn't supposed to go up to the dais, but... "If your father doesn't mind."

"Sure." He smiled. "Any help is welcome help." He made his way up to Santa. The girl relaxed, despite holding Molly's hand.

Molly glanced over her shoulder and caught Alex's gaze. He seemed to be watching her and had an odd smile on his face. She couldn't read him. Was he upset? Irritated? Confused? Jealous? Or was that admiration? She wasn't sure.

The girl hopped onto Santa's lap. "Hi, Santa. This is my friend, Elf Molly, and my dad."

Molly's heart twinged. In another life, she could be the one bringing her daughter to see Santa. She and Alex had talked about having children. But being single, she doubted she'd become a mother any time soon.

"Well, Krista. How are you?" Santa asked. "I'm glad to see you."

"He remembered me, Dad." Krista kicked her feet. "I'm happy to see you, too. I'd like a doll and a bear for Christmas. Dad knows which ones. The doll has red hair and a pink dress. The bear is all the colors of the rainbow."

"Well, I'll add those to my list." Santa laughed. "You keep being good and I'll visit your house on Christmas."

"Thank you, Santa." Krista hopped off Santa's lap. She hugged Molly. "I'm not scared anymore. Thank you."

Molly offered her another candy cane. "You did a great job. Merry Christmas."

The dad didn't walk away. He offered his hand to Molly. "Thank you. I'm glad you were here. I get overwhelmed. We're new to North Bend and I'm still getting used to being a single dad. Parenting is hard."

"You're doing fine." She shook hands with him. "She's a sweet girl. Why don't you take a moment and breathe? She won't be small forever and you'll miss this. Maybe one day she'll decide to be an elf here at the Santa Barn. Or you could volunteer." They always needed help at the Santa Barn. "If you'd like to, just let Mrs. Claus know."

"Maybe. Krista and I just might take you up on that offer." He waved, then walked away.

"There's only two more," Alex said. "We're almost done."

"Oh." She hadn't been paying attention. "Thanks."

Alex remained beside her. "You did a great job averting that crisis." He clapped her on the shoulder. "Good job."

"She was nervous." Molly bowed her head. "She needed someone to say it'd be okay."

"So did her dad," Alex said. "You're a pro at understanding your audience."

"He was overwhelmed." She slid her gaze over Alex and cocked her hip. Was he giving her a hard time? Or secretly happy she'd shown her gumption? "Are you jealous? He wasn't trying anything. He's new in town and doesn't know anyone."

"He was flirting and yes, I'm a little jealous. He couldn't seem to take his eyes off you, but cute elves tend to make things more complicated. I should know. I've had a hard time concentrating. You're so darn adorable in that dress." Alex took his place behind the camera. "Smile."

"Alex." Now who was flirting? She propped her hands on her hips. "Like this?" She offered her best smile. "Or this?" She stuck her tongue out at him.

"You're so bad. Smile again." He twiddled with the camera. "I'd be nervous if I were him. You're an adorable elf and I'm drawn to you, too. I haven't forgotten those kisses in the hallway of your shop."

Cute? Adorable? Drawn to me? The kisses? He had to add to her nervousness, didn't he? She held up a candy cane while mugging for the camera, then ducked away from him.

A rush of people showed up, giving her something else to do besides think about what he'd said. She couldn't help herself. If she didn't avoid him, she'd start giving in. She was there to be an elf. The joy and excitement should've been enough to keep her going. Children were visiting Santa and people dropped off donations for the Giving Tree. That's what she was there for — the magic of the season. She forgot about her irritation with Alex and focused on being the best elf she could be. The spirit of Christmas was too much to overlook.

Once the last family made it through the line, Mr. Martin stretched, then nodded to Molly. "That's it for the night, otherwise we won't be able to get the bags out before nine. Desiree already left. After putting in twelve hours today, I told her to head home so she can rest."

"She deserves it." Molly put the sign out and locked the front doors. When she turned, Alex stood in the foyer doorway.

"Good job tonight," Alex said. "I don't know how you do it. I haven't been around this many crying children since I was a kid. It's so shrill."

"Dealing with kids is a gift," she said. "I treat it like I would the people at the store. Unlike my shoppers, the kids get scared. Santa's a stranger and I think the beard freaks them out." She shrugged. "Are you sticking around for Giving Tree distribution? Mr. Martin and I can use the help. Usually a couple of the high school students are here to assist, but they're at the concert."

"And here I thought you wanted me alone." He grinned. "I thought you wanted to kiss me again."

"You're incorrigible." She laughed. "No, I don't want you alone." Not that she'd let him know anyway. Not right now. She *did* want to try those kisses again.

"You like when I'm a pistol."

She shook her head, but couldn't stop smiling. "Are you helping? We need you."

"I hope so." Alex reached for her and tugged her to his chest. A growl rumbled within him. "You make it hard to say no. Yeah, I'm planning on helping. I'd kind of like to see the faces of some of the people I bought gifts for today."

"Oh. You..." He'd been shopping? She shoved hair out of her eyes to hide the trembling. She should've known he'd be benevolent. "Well, sometimes the people picking up the items aren't the ones who requested them. Sometimes it's family members who want to surprise others. Many times, it's community groups who come in. They try to keep everything as hush-hush as possible. A lot of people don't want charity."

"I hadn't thought about it like that, but it makes more sense."

She detangled from him, needing space between them. "How so?"

"Most of the stuff on those tags — at least the ones I had — were things the people needed. Not things they wanted. Like socks and coats, not toys or anything frivolous. Kind of shocked me, but made me sad, too. I never realized how many people don't have coats."

She stared at him. "You really did shop for those things? Just you?"

"Mom's busy helping my sister. I don't mind. It's nice to shop for someone besides me." Alex took the basket from her. "So, what do we do?"

She tucked her hair behind her ears. Her hat slipped forward. Alex had become a deeper person than she'd remembered. More mature. He'd become more handsome with age. The slight lines around his eyes and flecks of silver in his hair added to his appeal. He'd grown better at kissing and flirting, too. She fixed her hat, then shook her head. Time to focus again. "We turn off most of the lights here in the front and main rooms, then head to the back. The Boosters added a drive-through in the back with an awning. The people drive up and give Mr. Martin their ticket. It corresponds with the number from their tag. He gives us the number and we'll hunt for the right one. He gives the items to them and they have a merry Christmas."

"We're actual elves, so says the tag in this costume." Alex chuckled. "This is so cool."

"It's fun to make sure people who might not have a Christmas get one and get what they can use or want." She picked up the notebook and nodded to the door. "I've got the numbers here, too. Come on." She strode ahead of him. "It's fun to see the people brighten when their wishes are fulfilled." She opened the door to the back room. "Be prepared to run. Sometimes it takes a little bit to find the right bag and some folks get a little antsy."

Alex nodded. "I can run."

"I remember." A memory of Alex in his running shorts and a tight T-shirt came to mind. He'd always struck a handsome pose in those outfits. He looked good in the elf costume, too. She swallowed past the lump in her throat. One time, she'd have cuddled against him while waiting.

"Ready?" Mr. Martin poked his head through the doorway. "We've got a long line."

Alex stood beside Molly and brushed his hand over here backside. "We're ready, Santa."

Molly bit back a groan. Why did Alex have to smell so nice and know how to touch her in the ways that made her thoughts blur?

"Ho, ho, ho," Santa said. "Welcome to my barn. Do you have your ticket? Wonderful. Let me speak to my elves." He handed Molly the piece of paper. "I need the packages for number thirty-four."

"Thanks, Santa." She grabbed Alex's arm and tingles shot through her body. "Here we go. We need bag number thirty-four. Bags one through fifteen are in this row. Sixteen through thirty in this one and thirty-one through fifty over here."

"Got it." Alex returned with the bags. "This one had two."

When he touched her arm, the sparks increased. Just like old times. She shivered, then stepped out of the way as Alex passed the bags through the doorway to Santa.

"We're a good team," Alex said. He waved at the family. "Seeing these people kind of makes me want to pull up stakes and come home."

"It's Christmas. Everyone gets nostalgic this time of year." Molly took the next number. She couldn't deny being a little wistful for the good old days. "I need number eight, please?" She brushed her hand across her cheek. The fever had come back. Because of her recent illness, or Alex? She wasn't sure, but she'd bet he was the reason.

Alex brought over a box. "There's a bag, too. Let me get it." His muscles flexed as he scooped up the bag. "I brought these. Three coats."

"The family has three little girls. Two were his and one was hers. Although both parents are working, it's tight. The mom brings the girls into the store once a month to shop for a book each." She averted her gaze. "The box is probably full of food."

"Oh, then there's two boxes." Alex produced the second one. "This one has the food. That one had toys." He took the items out to Santa, leaving Molly alone in the storage space.

Molly shivered again—this time for the chill, not the way Alex filled out his costume. She kept busy, but the December air managed to wind into the room. An hour later, most of the boxes and bags were gone.

Alex strode up to her. "You're freezing."

"A little."

He snagged her in an embrace. "Sweetheart, you're shaking."

"It happens."

"Then let's go into the other room and get warm," Alex said. "That car was the last one for the night." He captured her in his arms and brushed his nose along hers. "I've got you."

"I know." She tipped her head and gaze into his eyes. The power of the night, the mistletoe and

Christmas spirit overwhelmed her. The kisses in her hallway had been sinful and sweet. She needed more. She pressed her lips to his. A moan resonated in her. Alex rubbed her back and tucked her close to his chest. He opened to her, sliding his tongue along hers. She shouldn't be kissing him again—not here. They could get caught.

Alex slid one hand over her chest, then parted the front of her dress. He eased his fingers past the bodice and rubbed the upper swell of her breast.

"Yes," she murmured between kisses. Blood rushed to her core. The chill didn't bother her and she wished she and Alex were truly alone. She needed him inside her, moving with her and easing the ache he'd left behind. She longed to give in to her deepest desires with Alex. Right now.

"Hey, you two," Mr. Martin asked. "Molly? Alex?"

Molly jerked away from Alex. "Sorry."

Mr. Martin ditched his beard, closed the door and laughed. "I remember being young, too. I'm going to close the gate and change. Why don't you catch your breath in the other room? When I'm done, we can sort the new donations."

"Sure thing." Molly escaped into the main portion of the barn. She needed the quiet and separation from Alex. She'd let her guard down again and nearly let him have his way. She wanted to be with him, but that didn't matter. She'd made a mistake.

Alex joined her. "There were a lot of bags. I thought I bought a lot, but man..."

"The town comes through. We don't have much, but we're willing to help out." She pushed the donations cart from the closet to the main room. "Shouldn't take us long to sort this."

"You're quick," Alex said. "I can't keep up. Slow down." He laughed. "I'll get a complex."

"You're just fine, but I'd like to get home before too late. I've got a dog that probably needs to go out. Besides, keeping busy is good business." She brushed past him and started sorting. "You'll be great. We'll have it sorted and be done so you can go home." *To whomever you're going home to.* She focused on the task at hand. If she kept talking, she'd say something she'd regret.

"Stop." Alex grabbed her hands. "Molly."

She didn't fight him, but didn't look in his eyes, either.

"Molly, stop. You're avoiding me."

She met his gaze. "I'm almost done."

"You're Superwoman, too."

"I have a job to do and I want to do it right. My behavior has nothing to do with avoidance." She wanted to pull away from him, but with the Christmas lights twinkling and the music playing, she couldn't. The crackle of the logs on the fire echoed in her ears and the scent of pine wafted around her. The magic of the evening stirred something within her. She wanted to envelop herself in the warmth of his arms. Instead, she should be pulling away.

"Slow down and enjoy the moment. We've got music, lights and no one else to share the room with for a little while. Dance with me." He turned her around in his arms. "I promise not to pounce on you again."

She swayed with him, but kept some distance. Being with him was too easy and sweet. He held her and inched closer. "This feels good."

"Alex." She needed to keep her wits. They weren't a couple. She'd made a mistake by letting him get beneath her defenses.

"I'm right here." He tilted his head. "I missed this. Missed you."

So did she.

"Okay." Glenn Martin strolled into the room. "Well, I've—oh. Right. Uh…"

Molly jerked and pulled away from Alex. Good thing Mr. Martin had shown up. She yanked her hat off her head and backed up. "I should go."

"Wait up, Molly. I'll walk you out."

Molly escaped to the privacy of the dressing room and changed into her street clothes. No matter how much she told herself she wasn't going to fall for Alex, wasn't going to let him in or kiss him again, she did. Every time. She needed to find her damn sense. Alex wasn't going to stick around North Bend. He was famous. He'd want his freedom again. She patted her pockets for her keys. *Crud.* She'd walked over to the Barn. What time was it? She finished changing, then checked her phone. She had notifications for emails and texts. She swiped through the screens.

Niecy: *Locked the money in your office and closed the store. Didn't think you'd make it back before 9:30. I checked on Boober, too. He's happily chewing on a bone. He was sleeping on the couch when I went upstairs. See you in the morning. Be safe and text me when you get home.*

She sighed. She hadn't looked at the clock—ten minutes to ten. What had she been thinking? Walking home wasn't bad, but so late? She sent a reply to Niecy.

Thanks for closing. I'm leaving now. Thanks for checking on me.

"Molly?" Alex knocked on the door. "Are you ready?"

She tucked her phone into her coat pocket, then donned her coat and hat. "I am." She left the dressing room. "I'll see you. Bye, Mr. Martin."

Mr. Martin waved. "Thanks for the help. Merry Christmas."

"Merry Christmas." She shoved her hands into her pockets and started for the staff door.

"Molly." Alex blocked the door. "I don't see your car out there. How are you getting home? Niecy?"

"I'm walking," she said. "It's only a couple of blocks."

"You know I can't let you. It's not the gentlemanly thing to do." Alex shook his head. "It's below freezing out and it's dark. I'd be happier if you'd let me take you home."

"In what?" she blurted.

"The rental SUV." He blushed, then shrugged. "How else do you think I got around town to shop? Let me drive you home. It'll ease my mind to know you're not walking and that you got home in one piece. Please?"

She didn't have much choice. She needed to get back to empty the safe and check on her dog. "Okay."

"Perfect. Come on." He grasped her hand again. "Did you get your Christmas shopping done?"

"I did. You?"

He opened the car door for her. "Almost. I have to find one more thing, but I've got an idea where I'll get it."

"For anyone special?" She relaxed in her seat. Talking to him was still easy. "Niecy mentioned she'd seen your name in one of the tabloid papers. You're possibly dating a movie star?"

"Now who's jealous?" He settled on the driver's side. "I told you I'm unattached. No movie stars or anyone else."

"Oh. I was just making conversation." She watched the snow fall outside the vehicle. "He needed someone to understand what he was going through. That's our job — to be nice and show the Christmas spirit."

"I admit to being a little jealous. I'd give anything to have a cute elf helping me, but mostly I admired your ability to know what to do. I get out in the wild and I'm dangerous. I'm so used to being alone..." Alex sighed. He pulled out of the lot and onto the main drive. "I saw the way he looked at you and you had no idea. You're smart, pretty and wonderful." He stopped at the traffic light. "I know what we had and that whoever you decide is worthy of your love will be a lucky man. I wish he were me."

"Alex." Did he really mean what he'd said?

He pulled to a stop in front of the store. "I'm sorry, I'm not sorry I overstepped. We had a lot of fun tonight. Made me think of old times and how I'd love to volunteer with you again." He stared at her for a long moment, then sighed. "I was going to wait to bring this over on Christmas, but I can't." He pulled a box from his pocket. "I want to see you open it now."

"Christmas isn't that far off." She hesitated to take the gift. He'd gone to the trouble of wrapping it and adding ribbon. "Thank you, though."

"Open it, Molly." He turned the car off. "Please?"

"You could save this for Christmas."

"I could, but I don't want to," he said. "Promise it won't take long. You'll be able to let your dog out in a moment."

Molly untied the ribbon. The paper came loose and fell on her lap. She opened the lid of the box. Nestled in the cotton was a necklace. She held up the piece of jewelry. "Is this the rhinestone piece from the secondhand store?"

"Yeah." He grinned. "I thought about getting you a brand-new necklace, but I know how you love the vintage stuff. I saw it and thought of you."

"I love it." She met his gaze. "I'm speechless."

"Then I've done my job."

"Thank you." She put the necklace back in the box. "I feel a little silly, though."

"Why?"

"I haven't picked anything out for you," she confessed. "I didn't think you'd still be in town."

"I know, but I don't expect anything in return. I got that for you because I wanted you to have it. The blue stones will look fantastic against your skin." He placed her hand on the box. "You're my friend. I wanted to get you something nice. The necklace is pretty and the kind of thing you like."

Tears burned behind her eyes and her throat ran dry. He kept surprising her in delightful ways. "Thank you, Alex. It's beautiful. I love it."

"Then that's all the gift I need." He paused. "Come here." He helped her onto his lap, straddling him. "Better."

"Alex." She tensed, despite loving being on his lap.

"No one will see us. The window tint is dark and there's no one out on the street." He rubbed along her thighs. "I missed holding you."

Although she wanted to throw herself into his embrace, she slowly slid her arms around his neck. Being this close caused all her synapses to go haywire. She closed her eyes and basked in the sizzles in her veins. "I miss being held."

He kissed her, giving her little chance to think. All she could do was experience him. He slid his hands around her hips to her backside. He squeezed her ass. The bulge in his pants grew. Heat engulfed her. She grinded on him and broke the kiss long enough to catch her breath. He stroked her back, then eased his palms beneath her jacket and sweater.

Her skin tingled. She arched into his touch and moaned. "Alex," she murmured. She loved how he made her feel. Her head swam, but she wouldn't change a moment of their time together.

He hiked her sweater out of the way and caressed her breasts. He flicked her nipples through the fabric of her bra.

She moaned again and bit his bottom lip. The idea of making love in the car seemed scandalous and fun, but she hesitated. When she opened her eyes, she noticed a flash of light. She tensed and pushed her sweater back down. "Did you see that?"

Alex removed his hands from beneath her blouse, but held on to her. "It could've been a short in one of the streetlights. A power surge? I'm sure it's nothing."

"Probably." She laughed to hide her fear of being caught. "We're not kids," she rationalized. "We should take this inside."

"Right now?" He kissed her again. "I want to but you're scared." He paused. "We'll do this when you're ready, but know this—I'm more than ready. I've waited a long time to show you how I feel and be with you again."

She wanted to believe him, but the flash of light had spooked her.

"I'll wait as long as you want," he said. "Promise."

"Thank you." She splayed her hands on his chest. "I should go. Thank you for your help and the necklace."

"You're welcome, sweetheart," he said. "I'll be here until I know you've made it inside. Merry Christmas, Molly. Thanks for working with me tonight and enjoy your gift. You made me realize Christmas isn't the same without the ones you love. Maybe we can do this again sometime."

"I'd like that. Merry Christmas, Alex." Molly left the car and hurried up to the front doors. She unlocked them long enough to dart inside, then locked up again. She waved as he drove out of sight. Her heart swelled and she clutched the jewelry box. His words echoed in her mind. *'Christmas isn't the same without the ones you love.'* He'd purchased a present for her. One he'd picked specifically for her. That had to mean something, right? Or was she holding onto an impossibility?

In the quiet of the store, she faintly heard barking. Boober. Molly snagged the money and her bag from her office, then headed upstairs to her dog. The moment she opened the apartment door, Boober bounded up to her. She tumbled backward and laughed. Despite the other things going wrong in her life, Boober was one of the right ones. He might be a dog, but his love was true — just like she'd asked for in her dream.

Chapter Eleven

Alex drove home and hummed along with the radio. The Christmas music seemed jollier, now that he'd made some inroads with Molly. He'd melted her defenses a bit and the friendship was solid again. He parked in the garage, then headed inside to his bedroom. He crept across the silent house and chuckled to himself. During the day, the place practically jumped. Now that the boys were in bed, they'd probably worn his sister and Jeffery out.

Voices came from his parents' bedroom. He knocked on the door. "I'm home."

"Thanks for letting us know," his mother said. "How was the Santa Barn experience?"

He nudged the door open. His mother and father sat up in bed. The television flickered and he could barely hear the people speaking on the screen. Alex cleared his throat. "It was good. I got to see some of the folks I helped with my donations. By the way, thanks for helping me shop. I never would've gotten everything for those tags without a little help."

"My pleasure." His mother beamed.

"Need anything else?" his father asked. "Did they get enough donations?"

"Based on what Molly and I distributed today, I'd say we're good." Alex shrugged. "I never realized how much need there is in North Bend."

"There is," his mother said. "Molly...I assume you saw her again?"

"She volunteered with me." He put both hands up. "Before I get the lecture, I'm not pushing Molly. I'm simply rediscovering my hometown. That's why I wanted to shop at the stores and help the community. I thought I had to leave to find what I was looking for, but it turns out what I wanted was here all along." Molly was there all along, too. "North Bend doesn't need me, but I need it."

"Then I'm glad you volunteered." His father grinned. "I hear you're planning a dinner."

"You are?" His mother's eyes widened. "Why didn't you tell me?"

"It was sort of spur of the moment." Alex rested his back against the doorframe. "The idea started out as me wanting to take some of the stress off you, Mom." *And getting Molly to come to the feast.* "Then I wanted to include some friends. Kirk and his family, Fynn and his...Heather, Mrs. Sandoval...I thought it would be nice to treat them. This town did a lot for me and it's my turn to give back."

"And Molly?" Earl stared at him. "Did you invite her?"

He tensed. "Yes." *Why lie?*

"What about the clip on the news?" His mother shook her head. "I saw a piece about you being in town and having a secret romance. You'd tell us if you had someone special you wanted to bring around, right?"

"I didn't realize that had made it onto the news, but yes, there's someone. I haven't said anything because I want to be sure the feelings are returned before I make public statements." Alex hooked his thumbs in his belt loops. "I'm not looking for a rebound, but I'm not closing myself off any longer." He glanced at his bedroom door. "I'm going to write. If the light's on, will that bother you? I'll close my door."

"You're fine." Kathy grinned. "See you in the morning. Your sister wants to take the kids sledding, so I'll be up early for that. You're welcome to come along."

"Thanks. I want to see how the writing goes," Alex said. "Night, Mom. Night, Dad."

"Night," his father called.

Alex darted across the hall to his room and closed the door. The urge to write had finally hit. He wouldn't argue. He turned on his laptop, then changed out of his sweater and jeans. He donned his favorite sleep pants and a T-shirt he'd saved from his college days. The laptop pinged with notifications.

He wasn't in the mood to deal with social media or his email. He clicked ignore on all the notifications, then opened his writing folder. "Where was that document?" he mumbled. He scrolled through the list of documents until he found the untitled fourteenth book. Maybe calling each work in progress 'Untitled' wasn't smart, but he kept better track of what he'd started that way.

He pulled his phone from his coat, then placed it in the holder to charge it. He'd snapped a few photos of

Molly at the Santa Barn. He should've left well enough alone, but she'd looked so pretty in the glow of the Christmas lights and she'd posed for him. He sighed. He'd tried so hard to flirt with her and thought she'd returned the sentiment. In some strange way, she'd always be his girl. His true love. He scrolled through the pictures, then darkened the screen. If his plan went the way he wanted, he wouldn't have to look at photos to remember her.

Alex opened the document on the laptop, then his notebook. He'd jotted down notes in between shopping stops. Would he have enough to plot out the book? Probably not, but he'd have a better start. He read through what he'd already written and added a few more notes to his notebook. The story didn't work in its current form. Ellie and Davin wouldn't even see each other until chapter seven. Not good. He scanned through the plot points he'd put in on paper, then added separations to the document.

"If I can get ten thousand words written tonight, I'll be good." He cracked his knuckles. He could almost hear Molly cheering him on like she had when they'd been in school. He tended to write around ten thousand words a day when he focused. Concentrating was the last thing on his mind, but he had a deadline.

When the characters wanted to talk, he could write volumes. When they'd didn't, then he struggled to meet his word goals for the day. He had the germ of the book idea, though, so that was a plus. He could allow Ellie and Davin to grow as characters and find their way to each other faster. He nodded and started typing. Misspelled words and run-on sentences didn't matter. He simply needed to get the story onto the page. He started in Davin's point of view, but the story stalled.

Every time he typed a sentence, he could hear Ellie's voice in his mind.

He gritted his teeth. Why was he forcing this? If he let Ellie start first, he'd be fine. But Ellie tended not to have a major voice in his books. He wrote from Davin's point of view. Until now, Davin had been the one to talk. Ellie seemed to want her version of the events told. Fine. He'd expand his horizons and hers, too.

He typed the words in the notebook into the computer, then let his imagination and the characters run. He hadn't planned on either character going to a bed and breakfast, but before he knew what had happened, Davin and Ellie were in a small town and stranded. Davin had to find out why anyone would want to damage Ellie's car.

Alex grinned to himself. None of the plot he'd typed into the document was in his notes, but he liked the direction better. The computer keys clicked as he typed. The faster he went, the more his heart raced. This was one of the best parts of writing — getting swept up in the characters, action and pacing. He didn't even know what would happen next and he was the one writing it.

Within three hours, he'd made it halfway to his daily goal. He typed the last sentence, then leaned back in his chair. He'd spent so many hours at this desk writing papers in high school. He'd sat there for hours listening to his favorite rock bands and trying to keep his grades up so he could get into college. He'd called Molly countless times from that desk, too. He'd written her love letters, too. He chuckled. Did anyone write love letters any longer? Did she have those notes? He'd have to ask.

An idea popped into his head. Davin wasn't one for talking, but he did like writing. He opened his notebook and jotted down the notes. He tried to keep up with his character, Davin. The people trying to destroy the B&B in his story were corresponding through letters, but disguised to look similar to the one he'd sent Ellie.

He finished writing and pumped both fists. His muse had come back. The words weren't gone—just in hibernation. He couldn't wait to tell Molly. She'd be proud—then she'd ask why he'd told her. *Oh well.* He saved the document, then closed the laptop. He'd worry about his characters later, after a few hours' sleep.

Alex brushed his teeth, then climbed into bed. He gave into the tiredness, happy that he'd not only helped a few people, but found his muse and a direction for the next chapter in his life.

* * * *

Alex woke the next morning and stretched. He had no idea what time it was or how many hours had passed since he'd quit writing for the night. He listened for any movement in the house, but heard nothing. *Good.* He'd be able to get a few more thousand words down. He headed to the kitchen in search of something for breakfast. Would his parents have energy bars or protein shakes? Probably not. Instead of his normal fare for breakfast, he snagged a donut and milk, then headed back to the bedroom.

"How many words will I get in today before the party?" He polished off the donut, then washed his hands and took his place at the desk. At times like this, he wished he had a cat or dog to talk to. Then he wouldn't be talking to himself.

Alex opened the lid of his laptop, then the document. Within moments, he familiarized himself with what he'd written the night before and launched into the next part of the story. If he could get another five thousand words written, he'd go for a run to stretch and get some exercise. By then, he'd need the move.

Four hours later, he'd hit his goal. Perfect. Only another sixty thousand to go. First, he'd get a run in. He changed out of his pajamas and into his running pants and a long-sleeve T-shirt. Good thing he'd packed his running shoes. No way he'd try to go five miles in boots or casual shoes. He headed into the living room to stretch. Once he limbered up, he tucked his phone into his armband. He hated running without music.

Alex strode out to the garage and considered his route. If he remembered his routes from high school, the center of town was just under two and a half miles from his parents' house. If he ran there and back, plus a lap around downtown, he'd meet his five-mile goal. He tapped the music icon on his phone, then closed the garage door and started off. If he happened to need a quick break while downtown and happened to see Molly...he'd thank fate for throwing them together again.

As he ran down the sidewalk, he spotted his mother's car. She stopped alongside him and rolled the window down.

"Where are you going?" Kathy asked. "It's freezing out. Don't tell me you're running in this. You'll catch a cold."

"It's always a perfect, wonderful, great and awesome day for a jog," he said, quoting the line his high school coach had used when he wanted to inspire the runners. "It's good exercise and since I was stuck at my desk writing all morning, I need to move." He pointed to his armband. "I've got my phone if you need to contact me, but I'm going to try to get in five miles."

"Good luck and be safe." She rolled the window up and drove away.

Alex started back off. His muscles ached from not being exercised for the last few days, but within the first mile, he settled in a steady pace. His thoughts turned back to Molly. She used to meet up with him after his cross-country practices at the school. She cheered him on at every race. She'd been his date for the homecoming dances, the prom, and helped him get elected to student council. She'd gone with him on so many trips to the lake and listened to him complain about his various stories. He never should've let her go.

The chilly air burned in his lungs as he sped through the housing development toward the center of town. Part of him wanted to go easy and only run three miles, but if he didn't work hard, he wouldn't have accomplished much.

His footsteps crunched in the snow on the sidewalks. He passed the house where Molly had grown up. Another family lived in the house now. He wondered if they'd put the Christmas tree in the picture window in the back of the home like Molly's family had, or if they'd put the tree somewhere else. A memory hit him hard and he slowed his pace. He'd shared his first kiss with Molly in front of their tree. The kiss had been secret and hurried so no one would catch them. He'd loved every second of it.

He stopped at the traffic light and checked his pace on his phone. *Not too bad.* Not his fastest run, but good after not running for a while. When the light changed, he crossed the street and started down the main drag.

He ran past the hotel. The rental car was still there. If he remembered correctly, Nick and Jill were headed back to California for Christmas festivities with his family. Good for them. He wished them well.

As he ran past the hardware store, Fynn waved. Alex grinned. He didn't get that kind of response in San Diego. He paused at another traffic light, but this time, two women stopped him. Both had copies of his books. A third woman joined the group, but handed him a piece of paper.

He autographed the books and paper, then waved. "I need to finish my run." He hurried away as the light changed. He ran straight to Molly's and into the store. Hopefully, Jill hadn't sent the media to find him again. Being spotted in public had never bothered him before, but he wasn't in the mood to sign books while in his running gear.

He welcomed the warmth in her store. Not great for his run, but good for a break. The scent of pumpkin spice curled around him. His stomach rumbled.

"What are you doing here?" Niecy strode up to him. "And what are you wearing? You shop in skin-tight pants? Don't get me wrong…it's attractive, but if you're here for a book…where are you going to put it?"

The clingy look worked for running, but not shopping. "I'm in the middle of a run."

"In the store?" She shook her head. "Do you want to see Molly? She'd like to know you're here."

"Would she?" *Nice.* He kept up with Niecy as she strode to the desk. Molly glanced up and her eyes widened. His heart skipped a beat. "Molly."

Molly crooked her brow, then swept her gaze over him. "Wow. Um…isn't it a little chilly for a run?"

"Nah." He turned the music off. "It's always a perfect, wonderful, great and awesome day for a run, no matter the weather. But yes, it's cold."

"Coach only said that so the team would run when they didn't want to and would work hard no matter what. It's snowing and has to be slippery." Molly rounded the desk. "Besides, you'll get sick."

"I'm hearty. I've run in colder weather." He tugged on the hem of his shirt. "How are you? Did you get a decent night's rest last night? We were out kind of late. You have your color back." Truth be told, she looked adorable in the fluffy red and green sweater. "You've certainly got your Christmas spirit back."

"I did." She grabbed his arm. "If you have a moment, I'd love to talk to you." She tugged him to the office.

"I've got lots of minutes for you." He wasn't about to argue with her. He'd go wherever she wanted, as long as he was with her.

She shut the door. "Thanks for the necklace. I know I told you that last night, but I wanted to say something." She sat on the edge of her desk. "I'm proud of you. All the work you're doing for the town is showing. You might as well run for mayor. You've spread a lot of good will."

"Molly." He beamed. She'd noticed and commended him. "I don't want to be the mayor, but I do love to spread cheer."

"I guess so." She pointed to the box of ornaments. "Did you send these? Or did Jill? They weren't cheap and I'd like to thank my secret Santa."

"I might have sent them. Then again, you might be right and Jill could've done it. She thinks the world of you."

"She wouldn't have signed the card in the same way. I remembered the note from high school. I still have it. Same corny wording, but the rhyme was a little better." She picked up the card. "How did you know I wanted them? Did Niecy tell you?"

He shrugged to hide his glee. "I wanted to surprise you. When I went to the hardware store, I saw the ornaments and knew my mother would like them. They made me think of you, too. I remembered your love of all things retro. Then Fynn mentioned you'd been eyeing them, so I got two sets. While I was there, I got Dad the tool chest he wanted. I figured if I had to finish my Christmas shopping, I'd do it in town."

"*I* was on your Christmas list?" Molly sagged in her seat. "Alex." She shook her head. "Well, thank you. I do like the ornaments and I'm sure the businesses in town appreciated the sales."

He spotted the necklace peeking out from under her collar. "Looks like you appreciated my other gift, too."

"The necklace? Or the gift certificate for the salon?" She waved the piece of paper in front of him. "Heather delivered it and swore my secret Santa insisted she bring it over. I assumed you were behind it, too."

He had to be honest. "I was and did. It's Christmas and you've been feeling low. Besides, you've always been on my Christmas list. I wanted to give you something nice. Don't you like a little girl time? A cut, some highlights maybe? Whatever you want."

"Alex." She sighed. "It's too much. I can't accept it."

"Sure, you can." He refused to take any of her gifts back. "The gifts are from me because you're my friend, just like I said." He rested his hands on his hips. "Will you reconsider coming to Christmas Eve? Alyssa can't wait to spend time with you, and the boys would love to see you."

"Alex." She opened the door. "Come on. You should go. Your family is probably waiting for you."

He followed her out of the office. "I need to talk to you about that."

"Oh my God." A woman rushed up to Alex. "I heard you were here." She grasped his arm. "I've been dying to meet you."

Alex tensed. He should've guessed someone would track him into the store. The women outside should've been a clue that someone had a bead on him. "How did you know I was here?"

"Your social media." She held up her phone. "See?" She pointed to an image—him running.

He groaned. He hadn't posted that. Jill was the only one, other than him, who had access to his social media accounts. "Oh."

"A bunch of us came through the line during your signing, but it was so impersonal," she said. "Girls. RR Taylor is in the house."

He met Molly's gaze. "I'm sorry." He signed the pieces of paper put in front of him and smiled for the photographs. Each time someone slid something that wasn't a book to him to sign, he checked to make sure it wasn't a legal document.

"Hi, everyone." Molly waved her hands. "Hi. Mr. Taylor needs to get to another appointment. If you can give him some room... I'm sorry. We'll set up a second author event in the new year. I'll keep you all informed on when the event will be." She touched Alex's arm. "If you'll come this way."

Alex waved. "Thank you. I'll be back. Promise." He ducked into the stockroom with Molly. Once out of the crush of people, he blew out a heavy breath. "Holy cow. Sorry about that. I try to keep a low profile on social media, but word must've gotten out."

"It's okay." She pulled her phone, then keys from her pocket. "Let me tell Niecy she's in charge for the next half hour. I'll take you home."

"Molly." He stilled her hands. "Thank you." She'd come through for him again. She'd known just what to do to help him and get him out of the jam. Yes, she was upset with him, but her heart had shown through.

"It's no big deal. You were out for a run and should be able to do so." She smiled. "Besides, you were sort of ambushed. What happened?"

"I don't know." He'd have to sort this out. "That usually doesn't happen."

"Well, you've got your phone. If we go through the back doors and take the car, they won't be expecting you. Come on." She strode over to the vehicle. "Ready?"

"Yeah." He climbed into the passenger side, then withdrew his phone. If a photo of him running was on social media, then Jill had to be behind it. He hated selfies. He swiped across his various pages and groaned. Whoever had photographed him had done it from a distance. Alex sent texts to his assistant. He'd get to the bottom of this.

"Have you found anything out?" Molly asked. She pulled out of the garage and drove down the alley. "Any answers?"

"Not yet." He glanced up and down the street. The fans hadn't left the store or they were searching for his location on social media. "Do you mind if I call Jill?"

"No, go ahead." She smiled. "I'm just driving the taxi."

"You're more than that. You saved my behind." He dialed his assistant. Hopefully, Jill would answer. After three rings, the call connected. "Jill, hey. It's Alex."

"I'm so glad you called me," Jill said. "I see you were out running. Was it enjoyable?"

Oh brother. "Yeah, I had fun until the fans showed up. I guess I can't go home and be invisible."

"You did have that signing. People in town recognize you, even if the fans don't," Jill said. "You need to spend more time with the fans, you know."

"I'm not wild about being followed," Alex said. He pinched the bridge of his nose. "I just wanted to go for a run. I feel like I have no control here in town."

"Actually, a fan posted it on your social media page, then to the fan group." Jill paused for a pregnant moment. "I'll bet they thought it was okay. I didn't even see it until a little bit ago."

He gritted his teeth, then blew out a breath. "When I plan my promotions and social media games, I always tell you first and you set them up."

"Forget the photo and worry about Molly," she said. "You belong together. Please let me help."

"It's not that easy," Alex said. "Trust me."

Molly pulled into the driveway at his parents' house and parked.

Alex smiled at her and held up his finger. He wanted this done first. "Just…take the photo down. Okay?"

"You've got it. I'm sorry, RR. I won't fail you again," Jill said. "I'm taking the images down as we speak. Have you spoken to Molly? Are things back on? I've kept my mouth shut, despite it nearly killing me to see you not with her."

"That part of my life isn't up for debate. I'm doing things on my own timeline. You worry about my social media presence and book sales. I'll worry about myself." He paused. "Wait. Why aren't you and Nick up to whatever it is you do? Has the shine worn off already?"

"No, but he's got to be at a meeting. We spent one day with his parents and the rest of the time he's been working. I'm bored," Jill said. "The luster isn't gone, but I want to be like we were in North Bend. It was like a dream or a romance book come to life."

"I told you North Bend is a magical place." He stole a glance at Molly. She'd been part of the magic all along. "I should get going. Thanks for removing the photo and please, if anyone tries to tag me in any others, don't accept the tag. If I want to be located, I'll let you know. Deal?"

"Yes, but I still want to get you together with Molly."

"Don't start." He sagged in his seat. "I'll see you after the holidays and we'll come up a few new promotions that don't involve my personal location. Oh, and thanks for all you've done to help me. I appreciate it. Merry Christmas, Jill. And Nick, too."

"Merry Christmas, Alex." Jill hung up.

Alex dropped his phone onto his lap and shifted in his seat to face Molly. He had so much he wanted to say and no idea where to start.

"That sounded positive." She picked at the stitching on the steering wheel. "No more dodging your public? You don't have to hide from fans or the media, do you?" She half-shrugged and smiled. "Makes for a truncated run, doesn't it?"

"I'm not going to get my exercise this way, no." He wanted to reach for her, but held back. "I'm sorry for the chaos at the store. I'll do two or more signings to make up for it. How about a monthly hour with the author?"

"You'll fly in from California just for an hour event?" She shook her head, despite smiling. "Don't worry about it. A little chaos never hurt anything and besides, it got people in the store. They might not have purchased anything today, but they'll be back. That's the wonder of a bookstore. You always find something there you didn't know you need, but you can't live without." She patted his leg. "Speaking of the store, I need to get back. Niecy's great, but I'd rather be there in case we have any other surprises. If I don't see you, Merry Christmas."

"You keep saying you might not see me." He cupped her jaw. Touching her would be the death of him, but he didn't care. "Consider coming to dinner. We'd all love it and I'd be happier knowing you weren't alone."

"I've got the dog."

"Bring him. The boys would love to have a dog to play with."

"I don't know if he'll handle kids."

"Molly. Now you're avoiding me." He rubbed her cheek with the pad of his thumb. He'd never get tired of her softness.

"I'll think about it." She moved his hand. "Get inside before your family starts worrying. Looks like your mother is watching us through the front window."

"Mom likes to keep an eye on me." He hadn't elicited the answer he'd wanted, but he'd deal. Eventually, he'd get a chance to get through to her.

"Bye, Alex." She gripped the steering wheel. "See you."

"Tomorrow," he said, finishing her sentence—he hoped. "I'm holding you to it." He left the car and closed the door. He had one more chance to win her over and a lot riding on the gamble. If anyone could make his plan happen, it was Alex. He stood in the driveway until she disappeared down the road. He'd worn her down a little more. Once he got the chance to tell her the rest of the truth, he'd get her to see they belonged together. "Merry Christmas, Molly. Until tomorrow."

Chapter Twelve

Alex woke to someone poking him in the stomach, then chest. He opened his eyes. His nephews sat on either side of him and both peered at him.

"I'm not dead or sleeping," Alex mumbled. He rubbed his face. He'd rather have a few more hours of sleep, but he didn't have many chances to play with the boys so he'd take what he was given.

The boys poked him again, then scurried off the bed. Both laughed. "We woke Uncle Alex up."

He grunted. They sure did. He flopped onto his side and checked the clock. Half past nine. How many days until Christmas? Two? Today was the dinner. *Good.* He'd slept in longer than he'd thought. Not too bad after overworking himself the night before. He could still see the longing and passion in Molly's eyes and the concern on her face. He'd change that today. Had to.

Alex got up, dressed but hesitated at his bureau. He noticed his notebook on the bureau. A few ideas formed in his mind. Ellie and Davin needed a proper love story. They'd worked together in over half of his books, but never had a true romance. He'd have to add more relationship problems to the next story. Too bad he didn't write romance. Maybe Davin and Ellie could have their first Christmas together, only to have something nefarious happen to bring them closer together. Davin was a lone wolf, but he'd need Ellie's unique help—for whatever trouble they got into. He left the smaller notebook on the dresser, but at the ready to bring along in case any other ideas for the story came to him.

He checked his phone. He doubted there would be any messages or texts from Molly, but a guy could hope since he'd given her his number. The only icons were for his social media accounts and one text from Jill.

Don't hate me. I'm the messenger. You're all over the Internet. Just…trust me. I've not posted anything to SM and whatever was put there by fans has been taken down.

Jill had added a link in the second text bubble.

Alex didn't bother to click the link. Instead, he went into his browser icon and searched his name. Four articles showed up just below his website and social media pages. Each of the articles were from trusted websites. Part of him wanted to leave well enough alone, but the rest of him needed to know what was being said. He tapped the first result.

Secret love for RR Taylor in North Bend? The author was spotted running through town and seeming carefree. Sources claim Taylor has been seen with a new woman on his arm. Could this be the woman to tame the author? The perpetual bachelor swears he'll never settle down, but at Christmas anything is possible.

He sighed. Sources claimed? If Jill hadn't started the media campaign, then a fan must've leaked information to the tabloids. Until he'd set foot in North Bend, his private life had been his own. Now, not so much. He closed the browser window and left his phone on the dresser before heading out to the living room.

"I made breakfast." His mother offered up a plate. "Your favorite."

His stomach rumbled. He hadn't overindulged in his mother's famous blueberry pancakes in forever. "Thanks, Mom."

"You're a sucker for pancakes," Alyssa said.

"When you've been eating green smoothies all this time, a little extravagance is worth the extra miles I'll have to run to burn it off." Alex sighed. "So, what's on the agenda for today?" He hadn't been around to celebrate with his family for the last few years and had no idea what new traditions they'd created.

"We're going to take the boys to see Santa at the Barn. Dad knows the guy who runs the place now and he got us a special visit this morning," Alyssa said. "Want to come along? The more the merrier and the boys would love it. Once I round them up, we'll go."

"Are you locked into that time? Like hardcore?" He'd call Glenn if it helped and explain why they wouldn't make it right away. "I'm not used to going on kid time." He still had to remind himself to be in kid mode and watch what he said. Little ears caught everything he uttered and his words tended to come out of little mouths, too.

"It takes some getting used to—kid time." She narrowed her eyes. "Big brother, what are you thinking?"

"Well..." He put his plate and silverware in the dishwasher, then headed to the living room.

"There's smoke coming out of your ears." Alyssa stood in the hallway. "The natives are beyond restless, but could be bribed if the price is right."

"Sorry." He sat on the arm of the sofa. "Where's Dad and Jeffery?"

"Dad is in the garage. He needed to fiddle with something," Kathy said. "He'll be in." She stood beside the couch. "Your brother-in-law is getting the boys dressed. Why?"

"I'd like everyone in here, if possible." He bobbed his knee. Nervous energy spiraled through his veins. "I have a suggestion that's more like a plan for today."

"If it means I don't have to put boots on the boys right away, I'm all in." Alyssa rubbed her belly. "You look happy. Like you found your Christmas spirit. Are you and Molly getting along? Maybe more than friends?"

"That's what I wanted to talk to you about." His hands shook. He'd never been so nervous.

Alyssa's eyes widened. "Oh my gosh. You're really getting back with Molly. I know you would. You're bringing her to dinner, right?"

"Not exactly." He had to act with care and concern. If he pushed too hard, Molly would freak out. If he kept his distance, he'd ruin the good will he'd created.

"What are you going to do? Some grand gesture to convince Molly to take you back? If that's it, I want to know," Alyssa said. "What is the plan? I see those wheels turning. Let me in."

Alex held up both hands. "That's where today's plan comes into being." He waited as Jeffery and Earl sat down.

"Where are the boys?" Alyssa asked.

"Watching a Christmas cartoon. I said they could be quiet and listen to Alex or watch a sponge. They elected for the sponge." Jeffery met Alex's gaze and chuckled. "Sorry, old man."

"Sponges are cool." Alex rubbed his hands on his pajama legs. He had to get on with this. "So...about today there are good points and bad ones. The yuck ones first. Part of being me involves being a public figure. You all knew that. Yesterday, it got more out of hand than I'm used to. Back in California, I can move about freely because no one really cares who I am. I spend a lot of time holed up at my condo and that is fine by everyone else. But yesterday, the fans decided to hunt me down. They made a point to find me for autographs and pictures. I'm not used to that much attention. Because the fans mobbed me, Molly had to give me a lift home. I only got halfway through my run before someone spotted me. I guess my location and picture were posted on my social media pages by readers. If I hadn't stopped at Molly's, I'd probably still be in the middle of town."

"You're *that* famous?" Jeffery asked.

He nodded. "Kind of. If I'm at the conventions or book signings, it's worse. Most of the time no one cares where I'm at, except when they're tipped off. That's what happened." He raked his fingers through his hair. "Don't be surprised if you're approached. The buzz should've worn off by now, but who knows. I thought you should know and be prepared."

"Is there anything we should or shouldn't say?" his father asked. "I'm kind of stunned. I knew you were popular, but I had no idea."

"Just be yourself. The press wants the scoop on whoever I'm dating because I've said so many times I want to stay a bachelor. It's not true, but it makes them happy. As for what you do or don't have to do—go about your business." He shrugged. "They'll ask, but if you don't react, they'll see they can't bait you and will go away. If they sense you're interested in spilling secrets, they won't let up."

"Will they bother Molly?" his mother asked.

"The media knows I've got someone I'm interested in. That's why there are so many stories about my secret love. There's no secret and no love right now. I'd have to get Molly to see me for more than a friend she once had first." He had no choice. The gossip sites didn't ask him for permission before posting anything. "If they get a sniff that she's possibly the girl I want to date, they'll mob that store."

"They want to solve the mystery of your secret love." Alyssa shook her head. "Why can't they let love happen when and how it's supposed to? Why intercede?"

"Part of being me is having restricted privacy. One day I can be anonymous and the next I'm surrounded. If nothing's happened to make me look interesting, it's a great day for me, but lousy for the tabloids. Then there are the fans. You'd be surprised what some fans will do. I've had a couple people want autographs when I went into the bathroom," Alex said. "I'd just rather know you're ready. I'll let Molly know what to expect. I'd hate for her to feel blindsided now that I'm back in North Bend."

"Wait." His mother put her hands up. "Did you just say you were back? You're coming home?"

"I am." His spirit renewed. Talking about being in North Bend and around Molly settled him. The muse liked being home and so did he. "For the last couple months, I've felt lost. I haven't wanted to write, and my muse went missing in action. I thought I'd lost my touch. I've got the deadline to turn in the outline for my fourteenth book looming, and until the other day, I had nothing. Then I came home. I realized I hadn't really wanted to go back to California."

"I don't want you to go." Earl nodded. "It's good having your around. Have you gotten anything accomplished on the outline?"

This he could talk about with ease. "I have thirty thousand words toward the story, but no outline. Normally, I just write and don't have a plan. This time around, I'm supposed to turn in an outline." He shook his head and laughed. "The thing is, I'm writing and the deadline isn't bothering me. It's huge. For the longest time, I thought I was missing something. Between volunteering here in town, shopping at the local merchants and seeing Molly, I realized the pieces were always there. But I had to go away to realize what was here all along. I belong here, even if I'm still leery of the fans chasing me down."

"You do." His mother hugged him. "Well, my Christmas wish has officially come true." She blotted away tears. "Fully."

He wanted to ask his mother what she meant, but Alyssa spoke first. "How does Molly feel?" Alyssa asked. "Did you tell her?"

"No and that's the good part of what I wanted to tell everyone," Alex said. "Every Christmas Eve, Mom makes so much food and we have a huge party. It's a fun tradition, but it's a lot of work. What if we opened up the festivities to others and Mom doesn't have to cook and it's two days earlier?"

Jeffery chuckled. "I don't know what you're planning, but it sounds interesting."

"Agreed," Earl said.

"What's this got to do with the Santa Barn?" Alyssa tipped her head. "I wanted to take the boys to see Santa since we didn't make it yesterday."

"They will." Alex straightened his back. Pride welled within him. "I talked to Mr. Martin the other day while I was volunteering. Actually, I set this all up two days ago, but the final parts fell into place yesterday. As of six tonight, the Santa Barn is ours. Kirk is catering supper. Mrs. Sandoval is providing the linens. Mr. Martin insisted the boys get a private audience with Santa and we'll all be together for Christmas." He balled his hands on his lap. "I might have also invited Heather and Tommy, plus Fynn and his family. All I've got to do is help clean up afterward."

"Wait." Alyssa narrowed her eyes again. "No Jill? You left your assistant out? And yes, I saw her. We chatted for a while and I'm amazed you helped her fiancé set up the engagement. You're full of surprises. Won't she be upset she's not invited?"

"She and Nick are home in California," Alex said. "If they'd stayed in town, they'd be included. But honestly, I did this without her. What I couldn't do was get the surprises set up without a lot of help from the people in North Bend. Kirk, Fynn and the others are our friends and Christmas is the time to be with the ones you love."

"What a wonderful idea," Kathy said. "Like a community dinner. I love it."

"Good job, son." Earl smiled. "I like it."

Jeffery crooked his brow. "That can't be cheap. Are you sure we can't help you?"

"Yeah," Alyssa said. "I saw part of what you bought the other day. You dropped some serious cash while you were shopping and donated a hefty sum to the shelter. I have no idea what you spent on us. Are you sure? We'd love to help."

"My credit card is crying and my savings took a hit, but this will be worth it. I had money squirrelled back and, plus I should make a pretty penny on the condo when I sell it."

"Are you serious?" Alyssa wobbled out of the chair. "You're coming home? You're going to be here in town and super close to Molly?"

"Sure am. I've been offered top dollar before on the condo if I want to sell and that was a year ago. That complex is popular so I have no doubt I'll be able to unload my unit." He shrugged again. "My place is here." And with Molly. "I'm going to make a few calls a little later, once my people in California are open for business."

"Are you going to tell Molly?" Jeffery asked. "I'll bet she'd like to know her ex will be back in town for good. She might be interested in finding out that her high school sweetheart wants a second chance. Am I wrong?"

"Nope and that's where I'll need some help. Mom? Lyss? Would you be interested in a visit to Heather's for a few hours at the salon?" Alex asked. He'd invested a lot in this plan and hoped the Christmas magic would be enough.

"Are you crazy? She loves the salon," Jeffery said. "I could go broke if she went as often as she wants."

Alyssa soft-punched Jeffery in the arm. "It's true, but you weren't supposed to have caught on so fast." She turned her attention to Alex. "I can't see my toes, but I'm game for a pedicure."

"Mom?" Alex asked. "I've already set it up with Heather. All you have to do is convince Molly to go, too. She won't go if she's not encouraged and if I do it, she'll get irritated. She thinks I've gone a little overboard for her." Maybe he had. He didn't care. "Convince her to come to dinner tonight, but don't tell her it's at the Santa Barn. I've got that part covered."

Alyssa poked Jeffery. "Looks like you and Dad are taking the boys to deliver cookies. I'm heading to the salon." She squealed. "Girl time. This so doesn't happen enough."

Jeffery shrugged. "That tends to happen when you're stuck smack in the middle of the testoster-ocean."

"I'm leveling the playing field when the baby comes," Alyssa said. "And if we ever get a dog, we're getting a girl."

"Alex, want to come with us?" Earl asked. "It'd help to have extra hands to wrangle the boys and keep them out of the cookies. I can't say we won't try to sneak a few samples, but you can pretend you guarded the boxes."

Alex nodded. "I'd be honored to come along, but I'm a horrible guard."

Alyssa wrapped her arms around him as best she could with her belly in the way. "I don't know what Mom's wish was for Christmas, but this will be the best one ever."

Good question… "What was your wish, Mom?" Alex asked.

"To have my family together for Christmas." Kathy blotted her face again. "All we need now is for Molly to join us and it'll be perfect."

"Well don't say anything to Molly about the party. I've got that under control," Alex said. "Hopefully it all works."

"When you set your mind to something, you don't give up until you've succeeded. I'm sure this will be the same." Kathy hugged him. "Let's get Molly dolled up and ready for this party."

"Works for me," Alex said. "Here's to a fantastic Christmas." And winning over the woman he loved.

Twenty minutes later, Alex climbed into the back seat of his sister's SUV between the car seats. While he waited for the rest of his family to get into the vehicle, he scribbled ideas concerning where Ellie and Davin would have their Christmas festivities. The more he wrote, the more his sister was right—he *had* found his holiday spirit. He might not have been the most popular person in North Bend until now, but he'd finally realized where he belonged—at home. Without Jill hanging on his arm and staring over his shoulder, he was free. He put the notebook away and listened to Christmas music and his nephews chatter while his father drove around the neighborhood.

His phone buzzed with a notification. Alex checked the icons, then retrieved the text. He groaned. From Jill…

I tried to head the media off at the pass. Sorry about the article. They assume so much. I'm still trying to get them to back off. As for Nick and me, he's been fibbing about working so late. Instead, he's taken a page from your book and set up the wedding for Christmas Eve right here in North Bend. Do you believe it? This has been the best Christmas ever. I owe you so much and can't thank you enough.

Talk about moving fast. Good for her and Nick. The man was a catch and exactly who Jill needed.

Alex: *I'm glad. You deserve what you've always wanted. Merry Christmas.*

He tucked his phone back in his pocket, then scrubbed both hands over his face. Despite the media being a little too intrusive, he'd solved most of his other problems. He refused to complain.

"You okay?" Earl asked. "Or did you have too many snack cookies?"

"I'm fine." *Focus on the future.* "My assistant is trying to keep the media from intruding on me here in town and she's getting married on Christmas day. I helped get her and her man together. How come I can get others together, but my love life is a mess?" He shook his head. "I'm here to spread some Christmas cheer." He held out his hands to his nephews. "Right?"

Both boys laughed.

"If they aren't, then we are," Earl said. "I told you those boys would cheer you up."

"Sure do." Alex sighed and focused on his family. He had complete control over his outlook and he refused to let her bring him down. He had plenty of fun planned for later. "Let's do this Christmas thing."

Chapter Thirteen

Molly stood before the picture window at the salon and watched the traffic. She still wasn't sure how she'd ended up at the hair salon, but when Alyssa and Kathy had shown up, she couldn't say no. She loved spending time with them. Alyssa had been her closest friend besides Alex, and Kathy had been the mother she needed after her own had passed.

"When's the last day you had girl time at the spa?" Alyssa plopped onto the chair in the waiting area. "I bet you can't remember."

She could. "July?" Embarrassment washed over her. She'd simply let her hair grow and pulled it away from her face instead of getting it cut. "I'm usually at the store." She should be there now. "You know what? I deserve this. I'm supposed to be Ms. Businesswoman and I'm not projecting the right image."

"You look fine, but I like the positive outlook. You should set aside money each month to make sure your image is the way you want. Plus, spa days are awesome." Alyssa grinned. "Boy, this kid is doing gymnastics today. All I did was get a haircut and style." She shook her head, then reached for Molly's hand. "I'm so glad you've found your confidence again. You glow when you're in your element."

"Thank you." Molly fidgeted with her phone. She'd expected texts from Niecy talking about all the minor disasters at the store. But Niecy hasn't texted. Molly wanted to think positive, but she knew the law of averages—it was a big day and things would go wrong. "I just can't stop thinking about what I left back at Turn the Page." God. If his sister only knew Molly and Alex had been making out in the rental car in front of the store...

"Because you put your heart into your work and want the best for your business." Alyssa patted Molly's hand. "But I'm serious. Stop worrying." When Molly didn't relax, Alyssa rubbed her belly and continued talking. "Okay, I'll change the subject. Did you get anything exciting for Christmas? I hear there might have been at least one gift given already."

She stared at her friend. Alyssa had to be up to something. She wouldn't ask about gifts completely out of the blue. She probably knew what Alex had given her, too. "I did. Your brother had some ornaments from the hardware store delivered to my store and he brought over a blue rhinestone necklace."

"Is it all vintage-y and awesome?" Alyssa brightened. "Did you wear it yet?"

"Yes, it's vintage. I think it's a mid-century piece and yes, I've worn it." Her cheeks burned from embarrassment. "Did he tell you about the gifts?" What else did he tell her?

"Nope." She held up both hands. "I can't even claim pregnancy brain for not knowing. He just plain didn't tell me, but they sound nice. I bet the ornaments are pretty and he put a lot of thought into that necklace."

At least he'd kept the secret of them making out. "I'm sure he did." She could swear she felt invisible hands pushing her toward Alex. "Did you know who the secret Santa is that sent me a cat and dog music box? Maybe you know about this gift certificate to get my hair done." She groaned. "Why is your brother trying so hard?" Because he'd nearly gotten in her pants twice and she'd put him off? She settled on the open chair. "He won't move back to Ohio and I'm not heading to California any time soon."

Alyssa blushed. "Who says we're trying hard?"

"I know you. Just like your brother, you go big or go home. There's no in-between." She rested her elbows on her knees. "I like him. Always have, but we're in two different orbits."

"Wait." Alyssa scooted to the edge of her chair. "Alex thinks the world of you. Full-on, *the world*. He could be on the moon and you'd be his first thought. You're very much in the same orbit."

"He doesn't have to spoil me to get my attention. I want to be friends. I've told him that." She sighed. "I'm not in the position to be in love. It's not my cards and probably not his either."

"You don't know what position he's in. If I'm not wrong, he's probably crammed in between the boys in the back seat of the SUV."

"Alyssa," Molly said. "That's not the point."

"You don't know what he's thinking. Maybe you should ask him. Strike that and talk to him. Use that confidence you've got and go for the man you want,"

Alyssa said. "I know he'd want you to. He's probably planning something to convince you this Christmas is going to be the best one ever."

Molly stared at Alyssa. She had to be kidding. Alex wanted to be friends. He'd be going home to California soon. Why would he want to give her a great Christmas only to rip it away again?

"Do you trust me?" Alyssa asked.

"Of course I do." She frowned, then massaged the lines between her eyes. "I've heard what you said. I know what I want, but what are the odds he'd want me, after all this time? We're different people than we were back then, but we're friends again. That's enough."

"Molly."

She faced Alyssa. "This Christmas has been magical. I finally adopted Boober, the best dog in the world and I love him. I got to see my two best friends, find out your baby is going to be named after me, and I've made peace with Alex. That's more than enough for me."

"But you're lonely. A dog only does so much." Alyssa struggled to her feet. "You know as well as I do, Christmas isn't about the getting, it's the giving. Alex is trying to give you tokens to show his appreciation because he's more into you than you're thinking. That said, sometimes, you've got to take what you want. He's trying to do that. Maybe you should, too."

She wanted to embrace the joy bubbling in her heart, but she hesitated. "How do you think I should do that?"

"When life hands you an opportunity, take it. You love Alex. Don't try to snow me, I'm not blind," Alyssa said. "You wouldn't be this upset if you didn't. Tell him how you feel and stop waiting for him to make that first move. Make it for him. Come to dinner tonight and say,

Alex, I love you and you needed to know. You might be surprised by the response."

"Alyssa." She wasn't sure she could accomplish any of what her friend wanted in the last days before Christmas—especially since she had to get back to the store. Did she love Alex? Yes. Was she ready to open her heart to him? Maybe. Christmas had a funny way of bringing out her sentimentality. She wanted what she and Alex had shared years ago...to be them again. Negative thoughts filled her head, but why? Alyssa was right. She needed to go for and embrace what she wanted—just like she had with her store.

"Just trust me." Alyssa gestured to the door. "I see Mom. Let's go." She glanced over her shoulder. "I bet Alex will love your new do."

"He might, but I wasn't planning on going to your family dinner. That's for your family." She fluffed her hair. The new look suited her face and added to her confidence. Why hadn't she opted for the updated style before?

"Wait." Alyssa stopped at the bottom of the stairs. "You're part of the family. I don't care how busy you are, you've got to leash up that dog and bring him over with you to dinner. I'm demanding it, so don't mess with the emotional pregnant lady."

"I'll think about it." She had good people working for her and trusted them with the store. If the West family wanted her to join them for a dinner tonight, she'd find the time. It might be the last one she'd have with Alex in a while.

"Good. We're eating at six." Alyssa opened the passenger door. "I'm holding you to it. I will see you tonight."

She climbed into the back seat of the car. "You've worn me down. Plan on me bringing the dog and being there."

"I told you we'd convince you to come to dinner," Kathy said. She met Molly's gaze in the rearview mirror. "Honey, you're one of us. We won't let you have Christmas alone — even if it's two days before."

"I've got Boober."

"And we have a big house that needs more people — and dogs — in it." Kathy sped away from the salon. "You look adorable. Those honey-colored highlights are very you."

"Thank you." Molly checked her makeup in her compact mirror. The more she looked at her hair, the more she liked the change. "This was what I needed to improve my mood — a new 'do and time with my friends."

"Told you," Alyssa murmured.

"You want me to drop you at the store?" Kathy asked. "How long do you think you'll need to get around tonight? I'll stall for you."

"Thanks, but you don't have to. I'll be there." Molly forced her attention to the scenery blurring by. "I've wasted enough time being alone, save for the dog, and I'm game to have one of your family Christmases."

"Then our work is done," Kathy said. "A chance to hang out with your friends doesn't come around often — especially when Lyss doesn't get home to Ohio all that much. I'm glad you're taking it."

"See? Mom does know best and so do you. You knew you needed to recharge," Alyssa said. "We're going to have a blast."

"We will." But the store was her livelihood and responsibility. "I'm sorry I can't take off my businesswoman hat more often. I will, though."

"And you're going to enjoy life for a few hours," Alyssa said. "With us."

"I will." She stared out of the window. When Kathy stopped at the traffic light, Molly noticed Jeffery, Earl, the boys and Alex on the sidewalk. Jeffery and Earl had the boys in order. Alex lugged a box. Molly sighed. Bits and pieces of the dream came to mind. She hadn't lied — she wanted Alex for Christmas. No, she wanted her own family. She wanted a life with Alex and Boober in it. She could almost imagine her and Alex being the ones dodging snowflakes and walking through town hand-in-hand with their children and dog in the lead.

Kathy drove forward. "We're almost to the store." She stopped in front of Turn the Page. "We had fun, Molly. This was a great way to spend the day and I think we should make it into a new tradition. Girls' morning for the day before Christmas Eve?"

"I love it." Alyssa clapped her hands. "And next year, we'll have a fourth."

"Fifth." Molly opened the car door. "If you're including me, the dog and the baby, you're going to have a full house. I'll see you later tonight." She scooted up to the front door. When Alyssa rolled down the window, Molly squeezed Alyssa's hand. "I'm glad I got to see you before you head home. If you have time before you leave, bring the boys to the store for books and cupcakes. If you can't make it, then keep me posted on the peanut. I'm pulling for an easy labor and perfect baby."

"Molly." Alyssa squeezed Molly's fingers. "You'll see me tonight. Besides, we're not heading back until the twenty-sixth. Jeffery's got to get back to work."

"Then we have plenty of time to hang out." Molly let go and waved. "See you later."

"At the day before Christmas Eve dinner," Alyssa said out of the window as Kathy pulled away. "We'll got a place for you."

Molly watched as the car disappeared down the road. When Alex had left years ago, she'd thought her world was over. She'd given up on a happy ending. Then she'd embraced her life as a businesswoman and allowed her surrogate family to pull her closer. The Wests, even without Alex, were some of her favorite people. Now she had Boober, too. Was there room for Alex? Maybe. Since he'd come back to town, her way of looking at her life had changed. Not because of him, but because she'd come to terms with how she felt about him. She wasn't just the store owner or the volunteer — but also a lover, fighter and woman with the big heart. Yeah, she'd meet them tonight for dinner and she'd have a great Christmas no matter what.

* * * *

At a quarter to six that night, Molly sat at her desk and finished filling out order forms. Boober had stretched out under her desk at her feet. She appreciated the warmth and companionship. Adopting Boober had been the smartest thing she could've done — even if it had taken her too long to come to the decision. Boober had always been her dog, although she hadn't thought so when she'd first met him. She thought he'd be snapped up shortly after he arrived at the shelter. He'd been house-trained, followed commands and stayed by her side. He hated loud noises and jumped when startled, but so did she. She had friends, but now she wouldn't be alone.

In fifteen or so minutes, she'd be heading to the West home for dinner. Part of her couldn't wait for the fellowship with her other family, but the rest of her was beyond excited to be in such proximity to Alex again. He'd intruded on her thoughts and even in her dreams the night before.

Niecy knocked on the door and crept into the room. "The doors are all locked and I've counted my drawer. The slip is under the twenties." She placed the container of money on the desk. "Thanks for closing early. We've had a good night with lots of sales and tons of traffic. The staff needed the early closing to recuperate for tomorrow."

"Then I'm glad I obliged." She gathered the cash into a money bag, then tucked the slip in before zipping it up. "Thank you for placing Doug's order the other day. I know you hate his guts."

"All but one of the books should be here on the twenty-seventh." Niecy rested her hands on Molly's desk. "His money is as good as anyone else's, even if he is a jerk."

"I know and thanks. We can use the business."

Niecy didn't move. "Um...Alex was here today, too."

"He's allowed." She shrugged. "I saw, remember? The fans found him and he needed an escape."

"He got stuff."

"Oh. I'm assuming he shopped for the boys." Or his parents or sister and brother-in-law. Maybe he wanted to put a few extra gifts under the tree. She wasn't sure when he'd been in to buy the items, but who was she to argue over a sale?

"He had four Giving Tree tags. If we carried items on those tags, he bought them. I know because I helped him find everything." Niecy tapped the doorframe. "He's dripping with goodwill toward everyone."

She looked up from her papers. "Wow." Good for him. "I heard he'd taken the remainders."

"Yes. Mr. Martin said Alex had whatever tags were left and fulfilled each of them — even the last-minute ones." Niecy tapped the desk. "He impressed me. Not the author part of him, but the human side. I didn't get the idea he'd done all that shopping to make points with anyone. I think he did it because he could help and people needed the assistance."

"I'm sure he did." Molly put her hand down for Boober. When he bumped his head into her fingers, she scratched him.

"Alex dropped off the money to the shelter, too. He showed me the photo. There wasn't a gigantic check or anything to show off, but he did give them money. I know because I called the shelter. They posted pictures on the social media pages, too. He gave them three thousand dollars."

"Niecy." His donation wasn't her business. "He's being a good person, but I knew that. He told me last night. Besides, you don't have to check up on him."

"At first, I didn't trust him. It felt like he'd done all these things to make you notice, but the more he talked about it, the more I realized he'd done it because, yeah, he's a good person."

"The problem is we see authors like him and assume they'll have a big ego. When they don't, then we don't know how to handle the difference. He's not the same person I remember, but that's a good thing. The guy I knew could be sweet and funny, but he ran from big problems. This guy seems to hit them head-on." Molly focused on the paperwork, but didn't see the numbers. In some ways, Alex was totally different, but still the same in others. "If he says he'll do something, he will."

"You still believe in him."

She shrugged to hide her true feelings. "I do." She'd never stopped loving him or caring, either, but people changed. Just because she loved him didn't mean he shared her feelings.

"You went to see your mom, didn't you?" Niecy asked.

Molly appreciated her changing the subject. "I did and I'll go tomorrow, too. I'm heading to the shelter tomorrow since they had enough people there tonight."

"What about going to the West family party?"

So much for the changed subject. "What about them? The party starts at six and it's almost time. I should get moving."

"You'd better. You won't have the same Christmas without them."

"You're right." Maybe she'd get another chance to see Alex. "So there. I'm going to put Boober on the leash and head out once I'm done with the paperwork."

"Good. I'd hoped you'd come around."

Molly closed her folder. "Don't tell me you're sticking your nose into my love life again. I won't get my heart broken. I promise."

"Who said anything about me butting in? I'd never do that." Niecy turned on her heel and walked out of the room, but she lingered in the doorway for a moment before finally going.

Molly counted and tallied the cash from the money bag, then added it to the main bag of cash in the safe. This was the part of Christmas Eve and Christmas Day that she hated — being alone. Now she had Boober, which helped, but she missed Alex's companionship. She finished her paperwork and put everything away for the night. Time to close the rest of the way down.

"Well, bud, we've got lights to turn off." She patted her hip and rolled away from her desk. "Ready to make the rounds?"

Molly stood. Boober trotted at her side as she made her way to the basement. She turned off the various twinkle lights and lamps, then ensured the security lights were on before she headed up to the second floor. She unplugged the Christmas lights and trees, then shut the overhead lamps off.

At the staircase, she sighed. She sat on the top step and thought about her life. She missed having family around. Her father wasn't going to budge — he had his new situation with Gertie. He wasn't coming back to North Bend. Neither was her mother. When everything had gone to pieces, she'd turned to her mom and Alex. Then he'd left, too. Her mother had stuck by her side, until she couldn't. Her mother was gone, but Alex had come back.

Molly missed having someone to talk to. Delia and Niecy were good, but they had their own lives. Loneliness set in. She had the dog, now and adopting him eased some of her heartache. He had a home now and she had a best friend. But Boober wasn't enough.

She left her spot on the stairs and went to the ground floor. She started turning off the Christmas lights. When she rounded the corner by the front door, she froze. Santa stood on the front steps.

Santa? This wasn't exactly like her dream — not even close — but the jolly old elf was in front of her store.

"Molly." Santa waved. "Hi."

Part of her didn't trust Santa. He could be a wisenheimer there to rob Turn the Page. Boober growled and the fur on his back stood on end. If he wasn't comfortable, then neither was she. Molly shook her head. "Sorry, we're closed."

"Molly?" Santa tugged his beard off. "It's Mr. Martin."

She exhaled as she recognized his voice. She unlocked the door. "Sorry. I wasn't sure if you were...legit. What's happening? Are you done for the night at the Barn? It's early." She ushered him inside. "Do you need help? Car trouble?"

"You've got such a big heart, Molly." He stepped into the store and brushed the snow off his hat. "But calm down. There isn't an emergency."

"Oh, okay. Did you need any last-minute items? I'll help." Molly petted Boober to calm him down. "Whatever you need, if I have it, I'll donate it."

"Molly, no. We had a donor provide items listed on the rest of the tags. We're fine," he said. "Isn't that wonderful?"

"Yeah. Sounds like the town came through." Alex probably had something to do with the last-minute generosity.

"They did," he said. "We closed at six and got everything to those who filled out the tags. We spread Christmas cheer all over North Bend, but I had to make one more stop. Since I was on my way around town, I thought I'd stop here and thank you for your donations and see how you're doing." He scratched Boober on the top of his head. "Hiya, buddy. You're such a good boy.

You're lucky that Molly finally realized she needed you."

Molly chuckled. "He won't leave my side." The tips of her ears burned. "Thanks for the compliment. I appreciate the kind words and you're right. I should've adopted him before now."

"You're welcome." He tucked his Santa hat in his coat. "With Boober, you'll always be safe. I can't imagine not having Boober." He toyed with the fur on his coat. "Did you hear RR Taylor donated three grand to the shelter?"

"I did. Niecy told me. She said he delivered it this afternoon." She paused. "Come to think of it, Alex said something about the donation, too. You know he's RR Taylor, right?"

"He mentioned that and about needing to follow through on that since the critters needed the funds."

"They do." She wouldn't argue that. "Santa should visit the critters. I bet if we did a calendar with you and the shelter animals, we'd not only raise funds for them, but a bunch would be adopted." Her respect for Alex grew each second.

"That's a great idea. Write it down or email it to me as well as Dave over at the shelter." He offered Boober a dog biscuit. "But I didn't come to your store for fund raising ideas. I, as Santa, have been dispatched to give you a message." Mr. Martin handed her a card. "This is for you."

She narrowed her eyes. "A letter *from* Santa? *Right*."

"Molly, just look at it, okay? I'm just an emissary. The real Santa went to a lot of trouble and the least I could do was deliver the message." Mr. Martin rubbed his belly. "I've had one too many cookies today. I need to head home. Read the card and have fun with it."

"Fine." She opened the flap, but before she could pull the card out of the envelope, Mr. Martin was gone. "He didn't waste time," she muttered. She tucked the card into her pocket, then locked the doors once again. With all the lights except for the security ones off, the place had a spooky feel. "Come on, Boober. Let's go." She nodded to her office. Once there, she retrieved her bag and phone. She sat on the edge of her desk, then pulled the card out of her pocket. "Mr. Martin said I've got to read the card." She glanced at the dog. "What do you think? I'm late for dinner with the Wests. Hope they wait for me."

Boober snorted, then scratched behind his ear. Not exactly a rousing endorsement either way.

"Thanks." Molly tucked everything but her keys and the card into her bag, then locked up the office. She headed to the stockroom, but paused on the loading dock. "From Santa." She tapped the envelope on her other hand, then pulled the card from its hiding spot. She sat on the loading dock steps and her breath lodged in her throat as she looked at the photo on the front of the card. Her and Alex at the Santa Barn during their freshman year of college. They'd had fun that season and spent half an hour that particular night after the barn closed just enjoying the light and quiet.

She finally opened the card.

Molly,

I've been told you can't go home again, except at Christmas. I wouldn't know – I'm from the North Pole and spend most of my time there.

You've been very good this year. So good, I wasn't sure what you'd like for Christmas – since you wouldn't tell me yourself.

I sent Glenn Martin to give you this card. It helps to have a few associates this time of year. Makes getting to everyone all the time a lot easier.

Now for the meaning of this card... Come to the Santa Barn tonight. Bring Boober. He's been a good boy, too. Come to the Barn because your gift won't fit down the chimney. Remember, Santa's watching.

Merry Christmas,
Santa

She read the note twice more, then stared at the dog. Part of her wasn't sure what to do. What if the note was something bad? If it was, then why would Mr. Martin have brought it over? She trusted him. But what about dinner with the Wests. Wasn't she supposed to go to their house?

She sighed. The security system was on and everything was locked up. If anyone wanted to rob the store, then she'd know.

Molly petted Boober's head. If she drove by the Santa Barn on the way to the West house, she'd be fashionably late, but she could text Alyssa when she left. She left the loading dock and crossed over to her car. When she opened the passenger door, Boober sailed onto the seat. He wagged his tail and rested his paws on the dash. He was ready to go. Was she?

She tucked her bag behind the seat, then closed the door and rounded the hood. Molly left the garage and closed the door. Christmas music played on the radio. The lights strung from light pole to pole shimmered and the new snow glittered on the ground. The spirit of the season wrapped around her.

She stopped at the traffic light and scratched Boober behind the ears. "If nothing else, we get to see the town set up for Christmas." Part of her wished her mother were there to enjoy the magic of the evening. She wished she could change so many things in the past—maybe warn her mother, go to wherever Alex was to try to change his mind…avoid him when he came back to North Bend or let him into her heart a second time. She couldn't change the past, but she could navigate her future and set it on her preferred course.

Chapter Fourteen

She turned the corner and drove to the Santa Barn. There were five vehicles in the lot. She recognized Kathy and Earl's car as well as Alyssa's SUV. She knew Kirk's van and Heather's periwinkle-colored hatchback. Fynn's massive dually truck was there, too. She didn't know the other cars. "Wonder what's going on. Must be a big party for the community? Maybe that's why I was invited—it's something for everyone and they didn't want me left out." That had to be it. Why would the Wests have a family dinner with everyone?

Molly parked, then clicked Boober's leash onto his collar. Her heart hammered and her stomach roiled. She hated surprises and being the center of attention. But there was no guarantee she was going to be singled out. Despite her misgivings, she headed into the Barn. People milled around the space. Glenn—now out of his Santa costume—stood with his wife, the owner of the grocery store. Kirk Jenkins stood with them. She noticed Sarah from the feed mill and Heather from the salon.

Alyssa strode up to her. "You made it." Her bright green and red sweater shimmered with twinkling lights. "I'm so glad you're here."

"Is this a party? Community thing?" She held tight to Boober's leash. "Lyss?"

"I've got a confession to make. This isn't exactly a community dinner or a meeting of the chamber of commerce. It's not really the West family Christmas, either. It's a little bit of everything rolled into one." Alyssa smiled. "We rented the Barn for the night, so Merry Christmas Eve...eve." She turned. "Let's eat since we're all here."

Molly wobbled forward. Tears welled in her eyes. Most of the people she cared the most about were there. This should be a grand time. Then why did she feel mildly sick to her stomach? Because she didn't see Alex.

Kathy hugged her. "I heard you finally took this guy home." Kathy knelt next to the dog and petted him. "I'm glad. You both deserve a good Christmas."

"We do." Molly ventured into the room and squared her shoulders. She liked being there, but part of her wanted to find Alex. This was a time to have fun. She'd earned a few hours of relaxation and joy. "Thank you. This is fantastic. I can't imagine how much work went into planning this—and you didn't let on when we were together earlier."

"Do you know how hard that was?" Kathy stood. She guided Molly to one of the chairs. "Honey, you do so much for everyone else and don't stop to do much for yourself. This night is so we can all be together at Christmas. Let us do this for you." She patted Molly's arm. "I'll get you and Boober a plate. I think Kirk brought a bone just for the dog."

Molly fidgeted with Boober's leash. No one stared at her, but she felt on the spot. Like everyone would turn at any moment to look at her. She didn't know why. She hadn't done anything greater than she normally did. She noticed one person wasn't there. Alex. Where was he? How could they have a family dinner without him?

"Want a Reuben or chicken soup? It's my treat."

She froze. Alex stood before her. He'd stuffed his hands in his pockets. The sweater clung to his body like a second skin and the jeans showcased the strength in his legs. The scent of his cologne wrapped around her. She wanted to reach for him, but didn't dare. "Alex? What are you doing here?"

Boober barked. He stood, but his fur wasn't up on his back. He wagged his tail instead. Was he enchanted with Alex, too? Everyone seemed to fall for Alex's charm.

"Molly." Alex sat beside her. He tipped his head to meet her gaze. "You look petrified."

"Just surprised." She'd figured he'd be on his way home or something. "This is great." Her cheeks burned. "I don't understand why I'm so nervous all of the sudden."

"Because I kind of maybe went a little overboard to make this a memorable night for everyone?" He tipped her chin, forcing her to look him in the eye. "This really isn't the place, but I want to talk about when we split. Want to tell me off? I deserve it."

"No." She shook her head. She needed a second to compose herself. "When you walked away, I was upset. Devastated. But the more I look at who we were and who we are now, I'm glad we didn't push. We've grown up since then. You're famous and I'm still here."

"But you're pretty special here." He bumped her knee with his own. "I still think you should give me a piece of your mind."

Finally, she met his gaze. She wasn't sure what to say. "I don't know what to say other than it's over and we've moved on. We're friends now and it's good." She tugged on her collar. "But it's warm in here. Aren't you warm?"

"Let's go into the foyer. It's cooler and a tad more private." He helped her to her feet and escorted her to the quiet and relative seclusion of the smaller room. "Better?"

Molly held Boober's leash. He sat at her feet and leaned against her leg. "Better." She eased away from Alex. "I don't know what happened."

"You're still recovering from your cold." Alex tipped his head. "Hang on." He opened the door and waved, then rejoined her. His mother appeared at the doorway.

"Why don't I take the dog?" Kathy said. "I'll keep a good eye on him and, besides, the boys are dying to pet him. Would that be okay?"

Molly hesitated. She didn't want to let her lifeline go, but the way Boober wiggled, he wanted to play. Kathy wouldn't let anything bad happen to him.

"What do you think?" Kathy asked. "Iron this out."

Her instincts told her to argue, but she gave in and handed the leash over to Kathy. There wasn't much more for Alex to explain—he'd left and now had come back. What else was there to say? "Thanks." She stood with Alex in the chilly foyer.

"First, Merry Christmas, Molly." Alex handed her a jewelry box. "I know I've gone overboard again and I should wait until Christmas, but I can't."

"Alex." She didn't accept the gift and instead sank onto the bench. "It's too much."

"I know, but I've screwed up enough. I want to do this right." Alex pushed the box into her hands. "I'm either making the most colossal mistake of my life, or the best choice."

She put the box on the seat, then placed her finger over his lips. "I don't know what you're talking about, but you don't have to buy me things to make up for walking away. I can handle it. Like I said, we've both matured in the last few years. I accept your apology and I like being friends."

"Molly, I'm not overcompensating." Alex paused. "I'm nervous because you make me that way." He sighed. "Let me say this."

"Okay." She wasn't sure where he was going with his line of reasoning, but she'd listen.

"When I went shopping for the things on the Giving Tree tags and for my family, I saw things that made me think of you. I thought, she'd like that necklace and those ornaments are the vintage style she prefers." He held her hand. "I'm making a mess of this."

"You're fine." She rubbed her thumb along his. "I appreciate the gifts. You know me well, even after all this time."

"That's just it. Years have passed and I never forgot you," he said. "My heroine, Ellie, is based on you. When I think about the happiest times in my life, they all come back to you." He shook his head. "For the longest time, I hated myself. I wanted to make things better between us, but I didn't know how. Then I found out about your store and the seed of an idea was planted. I had my path back to you."

"You did," she murmured. She leaned into him. Being this close to Alex set her nerve endings on fire. She wanted to kiss him.

The doors opened. Jill, a guy Molly didn't recognize and Kelly, one of the newspaper reporters, entered the Santa Barn. Jill tugged her leather gloves off and smiled. "Are we late?"

Molly jerked in her seat and inched away from Alex.

"Jill?" Alex stood. "Nick?" He paused and held his hand out to Molly, but spoke to the reporter. "Kelly. I thought you weren't going to make it until later."

Molly kept her expression as neutral as she could, but she didn't understand what was going on. Why was there a reporter at the Santa Barn? "Nice to see you, Kel."

"Hey, Molly." Kelly waved. "I finished my story for the day after Christmas and rushed down here. It's not every day we have something so special in town."

"See?" Jill opened her coat. "You told me to butt out, but you know I can't. I had to be here to nudge. It's Christmas and we should all have a fantastic holiday. Right?"

Molly clutched the back of Alex's shirt for stability. Nothing made sense, but she'd keep that to herself. "Hi, Jill, Nick. Good to see you. I thought you'd gone back to California."

"We came in for the night. We're getting married on Christmas Eve." Jill squealed. "I wish you could be there."

Alex grasped Molly's hand. "Congratulations, but I won't be able to get a flight in time."

Molly switched her gaze between Alex, Jill and Nick. She wasn't sure what to think. "Congratulations."

"Thank you." Jill hugged Molly. "It's time Christmas magic got to you, too."

Kelly waved and shrank backward. "I'm going to get something to eat if no one minds."

"Sure." Alex nodded. He turned his attention to Jill. "Why don't you and Nick head in? We'll be there in a moment."

Molly's heart lodged in her throat. She waited for the foyer to clear again. "Wow. I didn't expect to see them."

"I didn't either." Alex raked his fingers through his hair. "I wound up my courage, then everyone derailed me."

Kelly poked her head into the foyer. "Before I forget, I want to do a story on Boober's adoption, but I couldn't seem to catch Molly."

"A story about my dog?" Molly asked. "I don't understand."

"It's a love story. You took forever to adopt him, but you were meant to be together. It's a feel-good story we need in the paper." Kelly nodded. "Puppy love or fate or whatever, but the readers will eat it up in a good way. He was the old man in the shelter and now he's got a forever home."

"Well, then it fits. I'm the old lady of North Bend," Molly said. "We really were meant to be together."

"Then you'll let me do the story?" Kelly asked.

"Sure." Molly sighed. "I'd be glad to."

"Perfect." Kelly turned to Alex. "And you. I need to speak with you, too. Having RR Taylor in our very own town, a North Bend-er…that's huge. I don't want to make an issue of your fame. I want to write a story about how you've risen and become a great writer."

"I'm not great," Alex said. "Passable. I just got lucky."

"You're too humble. You're also pretty darn charitable. I'd love to have the volunteering angle included as well as the donation to the shelter," Kelly said. "You haven't just become a strong member of the community, but you've helped that community. Again, it's a feel-good story perfect for my reader base."

"Then count me in." Alex draped his arm around Molly's shoulders. "Just promise me you're not wanting to do these interviews tonight."

"Are you kidding? No way." Kelly laughed. "It's Christmas Eve. I'm here for the fun and friendship, not stories. I'll contact you after the holiday." She nodded to the door. "It's good to see both of you and to know I'm going to get those stories. Mostly, it's because I see Christmas magic all over and happy endings are possible. But enough of me rambling. Let's make a date for next week."

"Alex won't be here," Molly said. "He's heading back to California." She probably shouldn't have blurted that out, but too late now.

"No, I'm not." Alex rubbed Molly's shoulder. "That's what I wanted to talk to you about."

Kelly nodded. "That's my cue to head back to the party, but before I go, forget about the drama all around and focus on whatever is trying to happen here."

"Yes. If Alyssa hasn't found you, find her," Alex said. "She'll love seeing you."

"Done and done." Kelly headed back into the main room.

"Wow." Molly shrugged away from Alex. "I'm not sure what's going on, but there is a *lot* going on."

"I know." Alex stepped into her path and met her gaze. "First, let me apologize for Jill's interruption."

"Don't worry about it," Molly said. "She's a devoted assistant and you're lucky to have her. I bet she's been the biggest help to your career."

"She's a plus, but she's not the reason I wanted to talk to you."

"I'm sure, but you're fine. Things happen." She waved her hand. "Consider it a quirk of Christmas."

"Quirk? I keep trying to find time alone with you and I can't seem to get anywhere." Alex grasped her hands. "I'm sorry for leaving all those years ago, but I'm not sorry for moving back to North Bend."

"Moving back?" She didn't understand. "You want to be here in Ohio? I thought you hated snow. You aren't a fan of the cold or the nasty rainstorms we get."

"I changed my mind." He shrugged. "Ohio and North Bend have a lot of things going for them."

"Oh?" She wanted him to be happy. "But you live in California. Are you planning on having two homes? Or just coming here for a vacation? It'd be nice if you were around more, but you've got to live your life."

"I might live in California, but my heart's here. How can I exist all the way across the country when I'm in love with you and you're here?" Alex asked. "Did you miss that fact? The gifts, the nudges from my family, the party...what Kelly just said? I never forgot you. I wanted to sign books in North Bend so I'd have a reason to see you."

She stared at him. *In love with me? Never forgot me?* Impossible. He'd left her. She leaned against the wall for support.

"When I walked away, it was unforgiveable, but I got scared. I didn't think I'd find the woman I wanted for the rest of my life when I was nineteen. I got nervous that I'd keep you down or that I'd keep you from finding the man who could be the guy you needed. I put distance between us, but I was running from my feelings. I didn't want to be away from you because I never stopped loving you." Alex brushed a lock of her hair out of her eyes. "You've been the one all along."

"Then why not tell me?" she blurted. His touch seared her to her core and heated her skin. "Why did you leave that fact out all this time?"

"What? Did you want me to email all that? Send a text?" he asked. "You'd never have believed me."

"A letter might have worked." Did she sound cool? Detached? She hoped so.

"Okay, you got me on that." He paused. "But I needed to say this in person. No letter was good enough to admit how I felt. I've existed without you, but I haven't really lived."

"Alex." Her dreams were coming true. He'd said the words she'd wanted to hear for so long. His actions and the gifts made sense.

"Molly, I stayed away this long because I didn't know how to tell you I love you. If you told me to get lost...back then I couldn't have handled it." Alex's mouth quirked into a half-smile. "I was a mess."

"Now you can?" she asked. "You are more mature."

"Now I'm not giving up. I knew I was unhappy and that the other women in my life weren't right for me, but I thought I had to punish myself for my past. As soon as I saw you, I quit thinking about my mistakes because when we were together, everything feels right." He bridged the gap between them and held her hand tight. "I wasn't lying. Before the Barn closed to the public for the night, I just asked Santa for you for Christmas. I worked hard to create the right atmosphere and have the party tonight but Santa did the heavy lifting. He came through and you're here."

Everything he said made her heart sing, but her gut reaction was to keep some distance. He'd hurt her before and even though they'd fallen right back into the way things had been in the past, she couldn't help being wary. "Santa is Mr. Martin."

"The person who plays Santa has nothing to do with the magic of Christmas coming true," Alex said. "I see the wheels turning in your mind. You want me, too. I love you just as much as you love me."

He'd broken down her defenses and she couldn't lie. "I never stopped."

"Molly?" His eyes widened. "Tell me what I heard you say is true."

She knew he needed to hear the words — all of them. No more suspense. He'd poured his heart out, not it was her turn. "I love you, too."

"Molly?"

Were those tears in his eyes? She blew out a ragged breath. "When I got the first email from Jill wanting to schedule the signing, I thought I could handle it because I didn't know RR Taylor was you. I knew you'd written under your own name and tried to get those books in simply because I wanted to promote what you'd done. Then I saw you in the store and learned the truth about your pen name. You were so sweet to me. You took care of me when you didn't have to and the way you held me... I didn't know what to think. You came through, though. I felt the magic every time we kissed and touched, but I got scared, too." She let go of his fingers long enough to wipe her face with the back of her hand. "Did you think I'd turn you down?"

"For the signing? Yeah. I thought you'd hate me. After all these years and the separation, I knew I had to prove I could sell books for you. I also wanted to prove my feelings hadn't changed."

"Which possessed you to give me all those gifts?"

"Uh-huh." He picked up the present he'd left on the bench. "Want to open this?"

"No. I'm scared that if I do, the magic will fade, and this will all end up being a dream." She shook her head. The shiny paper on the gift looked nice, but it had to be part of the magic, too. "I don't want this to end again."

"I'm not giving up or going away. That's why I just told Kelly I'd do the interview. I'm sticking around." He kept the box in his hand, but tugged her into his arms. "Molly, I'm coming home to North Bend to stay—just like I said. There's no place like home, especially for Christmas, and nowhere else I'd rather be—except beside you." He kissed her. "I've needed you more than my next breath or my muse."

Her heart lightened. She'd gotten her wish for Christmas. She wound her arms around Alex and toyed with the hairs at the base of his skull. Both of her wishes had come to fruition. When he broke the kiss, she rested her hand over his heart again.

"I bet a lot on this working out. Until a moment ago, I wasn't sure you'd give me a second chance for anything beyond friendship." He chuckled, the sound light. "So, the details. This morning, I called my agent. She's giving me time to move before I have to start my next novel. Good, since I've already got the idea down and almost half of the general story written, but I do need time to bring my stuff home."

"Home?" She hadn't misunderstood him. "To North Bend?" She needed him to repeat the words once more.

"I've got a friend in real estate and I talked to him this afternoon. He'll get my condo sold. Says it won't take long and possibly already has a buyer lined up. It's a furnished condo in a popular neighborhood. I liked living there, but it's not here." He shrugged and kept her close. "I'll get a truck and bring my things home over the first week in January. I'm coming home to you — if you'll have me."

"Alex." She didn't know what else to say. Home to her. Christmas sure had a strange way of working out. "I can't wait," she murmured.

Boober broke free from Kathy and barked, then pushed between Molly and Alex.

Alex laughed and petted the dog. "I've tried to figure out what was missing all this time. Why Christmas wasn't Christmassy and life was boring. It was being here with you and our family. Spending time in the Santa Barn, being in town, seeing you, holding you…doing the things we've done and being together." He let go of her and knelt next to Boober. He scratched the dog behind the ears. "Now for the most important opinion — his." He rested his forehead on Boober's. "Am I allowed to be part of your family, big guy? Yes? No? I love your mistress a lot, but I need your approval."

Boober barked again and wagged his tail. He covered Alex's face with licks. Molly laughed and tears streamed down her cheeks. Her dog had accepted the man she loved. He must've known she needed them both in her life — no question.

"I'll take that as a yes." Alex tumbled to the floor. "Merry Christmas, Boober and Molly."

"Merry Christmas, Alex." Molly knelt next to him. "Thanks, Santa."

Kathy stood in the doorway and clasped her hands together. "I wondered where the dog had gone." She sighed. "I knew this Christmas would be magical. Now my family is complete. Tell me you're coming back to the house tonight and will be there tomorrow? The boys have been dying to play with Boober since they found out Aunt Molly got a dog and now they can't get enough of him. Do you mind?"

"Nope." Molly scratched Boober's head. "Go get the boys. Go play."

Kathy lingered another moment. "I want you there, too, Molly. You've always been part of the family and it hasn't been the same since...I just hope this is the start of something great and lasting."

"It is." Molly stood as the dog trotted out of the room.

"Good." Kathy smiled, then disappeared back into the main portion of the barn.

Alex dusted his jeans legs off. "I forgot how dirty the floor can be." He held his hand out to Molly. "Did you mean what you said? We're going to make this work?"

"We are. Christmas magic and fate are on our side." She threaded her arms around him again. "I love you. Always have."

"I love you, too." He kissed her, then snatched the gift from the bench. "I'm going to get you to open this before long."

"I'll open it on Christmas Day." With Alex beside her, she left the foyer in favor of the main room. Boober rubbed on Alyssa's legs and wagged his tail. She beamed. The boys took turns hugging and making silly faces at the dog. Jeffery sat on the floor and petted Boober.

Molly snuggled against Alex. He was right— Christmas came every year, but hadn't felt the same without him. Now they were together and in the place they'd shared so many fond memories. The tinsel glimmered, the lights shone brighter and the wonder of the season filled her heart. Her deepest desire for Christmas had come true.

Merry Christmas, indeed.

Once she and Alex left the Santa Barn for the night and parked in the warehouse portion of the store, she held tight to Alex and Boober as she practically ran to the elevator. She needed time alone with her man. She'd waited long enough.

Boober sat at her feet, but Alex caged her in his arms. The doors had barely shut before he kissed her. Molly didn't care. She loved the overwhelming, all-consuming feeling that came with being with him. He kissed her and slid his hands down her back to her butt. The bell dinged and the doors opened before he pulled away.

Boober yanked on the leash, tugging her into the apartment. Molly hustled through the doorway. "I should feed him," she said. He'd stolen bits and bites during dinner, but he needed real dog food. She unclipped the leash, freeing Boober.

"Can I help you?" Alex took her coat, then held her hand as she removed her shoes. "I want to be part of your family. Let me help."

Boober barked at her and Alex let go before he knelt with the dog. "You're a good boy, aren't you? Sorry boy. We should've given you more attention."

"Be careful. He'll knock you over." She poured a half-cup of dry food into the dog's bowl. Boober knocked Alex backward, making him laugh. Molly attempted to wrangle Boober off him. "Sorry."

"Honey, it's okay. He's still getting used to me and he's excited. I don't mind." Alex managed to sit up. "It could be worse. He could hate me."

"I suppose." She let Boober go. "Dinner, Boo."

The dog rushed over to his dish and scarfed the dry food. He wagged his tail at warp speed.

"That won't keep him busy for long." Molly rested her hands on her hips. "Why don't you start a bath? I could go for a nice soak. We can talk and I have eggnog."

"I'd like that." Alex stood, then kissed her. "But I should be taking care of you."

"You are, but Boober is my responsibility." She folded her arms. "Once he's done eating, he'll have to go to the roof to do his business."

"I'll take him."

She stared at Alex for a moment. He was serious about being part of her life." She handed him the leash. "The bags are in the squishy bag by the door. Just deposit his business in the little can up there."

"Deal." He bobbed his eyebrows. "Run the water and get stared. I'll join you when we're done."

She knelt next to Boober and ruffled his fur. "I really love this guy and he's going to stay in our life. Try not to get so goofy. Be cool, so he won't change his mind."

Alex helped her to her feet. "I love when you talk to the dog and I can assure you, I'm not going anywhere."

"Why do you like when I talk to the dog?"

"It shows you're tender-hearted." He slid his arm around her. "Anyone who loves a dog is my kind of person."

"Thanks." She handed over her keys. "Keep the key with you, just in case the door locks. It doesn't often, but I'd rather be safe than sorry. Just up the stairs. There's a grassy patch on the roof just for him. I planned on putting in a garden, but it never worked out."

"One day." He held on to the keys and leash.

"The switch in the hallway works for the lights on the roof." She pointed to the switch. "That one."

"Got it. Go start the water and we'll be fine." He patted his hip. "Come on, Boober." The dog led the way to the door. "We'll be right back," Alex said.

Molly hurried into the bathroom. She turned the water on. She lit candles along the backsplash and added bubble bath to the stream. The vanilla filled the room. While the tub filled, she stripped and twisted her hair into a bun on the top of her head. She abandoned her clothes in the hamper, then slid into the hot water. She needed the stress relief, but mostly she needed Alex. Her worries and stresses melted away. Heat seeped into her bones.

She played with the bubbles a bit before turning off the water. The clunk of the door closing echoed in the bathroom. Moments later, Boober sprinted into the bathroom. He barked at the bubbles.

"You're okay," she said. "Where's your chewy bone? Get your chewy."

Boober barked once more, then trotted from the room. When he returned, Alex followed. Alex held two glasses of eggnog. "Thought we could have a drink while we soak." He frowned. "That sounded silly."

"It sounded Christmassy." She blew the bubbles on her hand at him. "Join me."

"I need to catch up to you." He offered her the glasses, then kicked out of his shoes. He removed his sweater and undershirt, then unzipped.

Molly noticed the tattoo on his chest. "You've got your cross-country jersey number inked on you."

He flexed and his nipples beaded. "Like it?"

"I do." She swept her gaze over him as he dropped his jeans and boxer briefs. "You're shaved, too!" She longed to touch his smooth skin. "Still?"

"I hated how the hairs caught and rubbed when I ran." He wadded up his clothes, then joined her in the water. "Am I good enough?"

"What a silly question," she said. "You always have been."

"Same goes for me." He eased behind her in the tub and tucked her in the vee of his legs. "Lean into me."

She settled against him. He situated his cock between her ass cheeks and threaded his arms around her. "This is nice." She rested her head on his shoulder. A sigh bubbled in her throat.

"Just nice?" He offered her one of the cups.

"It's perfect." She sipped the drink. Boober returned to the bathroom and plopped on the rug with his chewy bone. The tips of her ears burned again. She closed her eyes and bit back the sigh. "Sorry. He likes to be close."

"He's fine. Remember when my folks had Casper, the nosy beagle? He had to be involved in everything and followed Mom everywhere," Alex murmured.

"He did." She laughed as her tension evaporated. She missed the West family dog. But she had the same kind of attachment to Boober. "Boo adopted me."

"He knows good when he sees it." He took the glass from her hands. He abandoned the eggnog and palmed her breasts. When she whimpered, he caressed her nipples.

She groaned. "Alex."

"Yes?" He continued to toy with her nipples, then slid one hand between her legs.

Tingles shot through her. She'd held back for so long. Why keep him at bay? She loved this man and how he played her body.

He stroked her clit and massaged her breast while he nibbled on her neck. "Have I mentioned I love how sensitive you are?"

"No." She bucked her hips and moaned. Heat centered in her core. She trembled and rocked into his touch. Her senses heightened. The lights were brighter, the suds softer, water warmer and the music more festive. She tipped her head back and kissed him. The taste of eggnog lingered on his lips and when she sucked on his tongue. Her body seemed to vibrate. The more he plucked and rubbed her clit, the more he nudged her to the edge. Her movements turned jerky and she dug her nails into his wrists. He knew how to tease her and refused to stop him.

A cry ripped from her throat. "Alex."

"Come for me," he whispered. His cock throbbed between her ass cheeks. "Do it. Come apart."

Her resistance shattered and she embraced the orgasm. She shuddered. Warmth rushed through her body. She cried out again and settled as the climax subsided. She slumped in his arms, thrilled he'd made her come.

"Beautiful," he said. "Love that."

She wanted to answer, but the words weren't there. She sighed instead.

"I love that sound." He raked his teeth over her throat. "You vibrate when you're satisfied."

"Yeah?" she managed. "You do that to me."

"Good." He held her tight.

"Make love to me," she said. She turned around as much as possible to face him. "I don't need sweet. I need you. All of you. Hot, heavy, crazy…"

"Anything you want." He kissed her hard. "I need you more than my next breath."

"Likewise." Her Christmas had come to life in brilliant color now that he'd come home and joined her.

"Her." He rinsed her off. "Why don't you crawl in between the sheets and I'll drain this for you?"

"You're too good to be truth." She stood and snagged a towel from the rack. Once she stepped out of the tub, she dried off. "Are you really home for good?"

"Yes, babe." He pulled the plug and the water gurgled. "I've never been truly happy unless I was here."

"In my bathroom?" She laughed to hide the nervous energy within her. He'd come home to stay and was her man forever.

"Maybe." A wild twinkle filled his eyes. He didn't dry off as he left the tub. Suds slid down his body, accentuating his muscular frame, as he chased her into the bedroom.

Molly tumbled onto the bed and continued to laugh as he collapsed on top of her. He pinned her to the mattress and covered her face in kisses. She draped her arms around his neck.

Alex tensed, then jerked off her.

"What?" She propped herself up on her elbows. "What's wrong?"

Alex blushed. "Boober licked my foot."

"He does that." Molly settled on the bed again. "Just push the bedroom door shut and he'll curl up on his doggy bed. He's got his chewy. He'll be fine."

Alex handed the bone to the dog. "Stay busy a while." He rejoined Molly on the bed and tucked her to his side. "I missed the way you smell."

"You did?"

"It's a comforting scent. Like being home." He rolled onto his side, facing her. "I'm me when I'm with you."

She had to agree. Her balance returned because she had him in her life.

Alex nuzzled her neck and palmed her breast. "I missed the way you taste, too." He worked his way down her throat to her upper chest. "Or how your nipples are the perfect pink."

"Oh?" She threaded her fingers in his hair. Why was he talking? She couldn't think straight.

He kissed along the upper swell of her breast, then bit her nipple. She shivered. Damn, he knew how to use her and how she loved to be touched. She tugged on his hair. In turn, he hummed around her nipple. She'd never survive this — he overwhelmed her too much.

Alex inched down her body and settled between her legs. He slid his hands over her thighs. A groan rumbled in her throat as he nuzzled her pussy lips. When he dragged his tongue across her folds, she cried out.

"Like that?" He eased one finger into her channel. "Christ, you're still tight." He smoothed his free hand up to her breast and squeezed.

Her thoughts blurred. The man knew how to use her up. She rocked against his face as he sucked hard on her clit. The combination of his mouth on her pussy, his finger within her and his other hand on her breast were more than she could take. She planted her feet on the bed. "Alex."

Instead of answering her, he pumped faster and added another finger to her pussy. "So wet. Pulling me in." He increased his pace. "Love it."

So did she. She tugged harder on his hair and rode the waves of pleasure. She couldn't think straight. "Alex."

He raked his teeth over her clit. "Yes?"

The orgasm rolled through her, sending a shudder down her limbs. She let go of his hair and moaned. "Oh my God." Molly sagged against the bed. She couldn't catch her breath and loved he'd made her this excited.

Alex released his light hold on her breast, then withdrew his fingers from her pussy. He flicked his tongue across her clit once more before he settled on his knees between her legs. He entered her in one thrust. "Damn." He gasped. "I'm home." He leaned over her and draped her legs on his. "Perfection." He kissed her hard and began to thrust. In and out. Within seconds, he sped up his rhythm. The sound of skin on skin echoed in the room. Passion sizzled in his eyes.

She threaded her arms around his neck and held on. Her body tingled. The orgasm continued as he pushed in and out of her pussy. She memorized every ripple and nuance of his cock. She loved being one heart, soul and body with him.

He slammed into her and his cock throbbed. She shivered as the delicious tingle of another orgasm crashed within her.

Alex cried out and shuddered. "Fuck." He added three more thrusts, then stilled. He panted. Tiny beads of perspiration sparkled on his temple.

Molly sagged beneath him. The lights in the room glittered a bit brighter and vanilla filled the air. She marveled at the power and thrill of finally getting what she needed — Alex for Christmas.

Alex stayed within her, but settled on top of her. He braced himself on his arms and knees. His breath warmed her skin. She toyed with the short hairs at the base of his skull.

"Whoa." He kissed her. "Better than ever."

"I never thought we'd get back to us," she said. "Never thought we'd find our way here."

"I knew we would." He pulled out and collapsed beside her on the bed.

"How?" She rolled onto her side and twined her legs with his. "You moved on and we grew up. The law of averages wasn't in our favor."

He dragged the blanket over them, then held her tight. "My heart was always right here." He kissed her palm. "You've had it."

A piece of her heart had always been with him, too.

"We needed the right timing and Christmas for us to find our way back to each other, but I knew we would." He rested his forehead against hers. "I had faith."

"And we have Christmas magic."

He laughed. "You did ask for me for Christmas. Remember?"

"I did and my wish came true." She splayed her hand over his tattoo. She'd never put much stock in Christmas magic, but now she knew it was real.

"I'm all yours." He kissed her. "Christmas made."

Molly closed her eyes. Nothing else mattered tonight—not presents or stress or even the store. She had the Christmas of her dreams with the man in her heart. Christmas definitely made.

Chapter Fifteen

Christmas morning, Alex left Molly to get ready for the day. Being with her renewed his spirit and convinced him he'd made the right decision to come back to North Bend. His heart lightened. He had his family around him and the love of his life where he wanted Molly — with him. Soon, Molly would be at the house and his life would be complete.

When he strolled out of his bedroom after his shower, his nephews were in front of the Christmas tree in the sunroom. Jeffery slept on the couch. The scent of coffee lingered in the air. Earl rounded the corner.

"I wondered where you were last night." Earl nodded to the kitchen. "Want some joe?"

"I'll get some water. Thanks." He filled a cup, then made his way back out to the sun room. "I guess they couldn't wait?"

"They couldn't," Earl said. "Jeff could." He laughed. "I remember doing that with you and your sister. You'd get up at four in the morning and your mother would beg for you to go back to bed."

"You'd come out here and sit with us while we picked through our stockings until Mom woke up." He sipped the water. "I loved that quiet time."

"It wasn't quiet."

"Okay, we might have gotten a bit rowdy."

"That's more like it." Earl widened his stance and put the coffee cup down. "I'm glad you made the decision to come home. Even more so that you sorted things out with Molly. You don't know how these last few years have worn her down. She smiles and works so hard for everyone in town, but it's been tough."

"I don't know all of it, but what I do know...I agree." He finished his water. "If you want to help Mom, I'll sit with the boys."

"And take my job?" Earl laughed again. "We'll both sit down here."

"Deal." Alex spotted Alyssa and his mother fiddling with one of the boxed toys. They seemed to have the situation in hand, so he sneaked over to the front window to look for Molly.

"Are you okay?" Alyssa stood beside him and bumped his shoulder. "She'll be here. Promise."

"I know." He'd wait forever for her, yet she couldn't get there fast enough.

"You both want this, so it'll work out," Alyssa said. "Besides, the boys are nearly climbing out of their skin to open presents. It'd be better if you were there."

"Okay." He turned but glanced out of the window once more. He spotted Molly's car. "Wait."

"What do you think I've been doing for the last nine months?" Alyssa rubbed her belly. "Molly's just about ready to make her appearance in the world."

"She's here." Alex paused. "Wait. You're naming the baby Molly?"

Alyssa nodded. "After one of my dearest friends."

"I had no idea, but I love it." He kissed his sister, then abandoned her in the living room and rushed outside to the driveway. Excitement zapped in his veins. He couldn't wait to have her in his arms again.

"Alex." Molly climbed out of the vehicle. Boober barked and steamed up the passenger-side window. Molly sighed. "He's excited. You'd think he was a kid. He got a new bone for Christmas, but all he wanted to do was put it in the car. I guess he knew we were coming over."

"I'm glad he did." Alex snagged her in his arms and kissed her. His world righted on its axis. Despite the chill in the air, she warmed him to his soul. "Merry Christmas."

"Merry Christmas. Help me get Boo out of the car. He's probably dying to see the boys." Molly shrugged away from him long enough to open the vehicle door. "Come on, you."

Boober bounded out of the car and across the lawn. He turned and his eyes flashed. Alex laughed. "Come here," Alex said. "Merry Christmas, big guy."

Boober jumped and dragged his dirty paws down Alex's jeans.

"Boober." Molly clapped her hands. "You know better than to jump."

"It's okay. It's Christmas and he's excited." Alex hurried over to the front door. He opened it for Boober. "Incoming," he shouted. "Dog in the house." He could've sworn he heard his nephews cheer. He closed the door, then ambled back over to Molly. "What can I help you carry?"

"The box in the back seat. Thanks. I had to put it back there so Boober wouldn't stomp on it. He forgets how big his paws are sometimes." Molly stepped out his way. "I got stuff for the boys and your family." She averted her gaze. "I've got something for you, but I wanted to wait until we're alone."

"Another kiss?" He bobbed his eyebrows. Another few hours alone with her to taste every inch of her body would be best. "I don't know if I can wait for that."

She smiled and tucked a lock of her hair behind her ear. "You can have a kiss any time."

"Perfect." Alex retrieved the box from the back of her car. "Then we'll wait. I've got one last thing for you, too."

"You've done too much." She swatted his arm. "But I'm not about to argue because you won't listen anyway."

"You're probably right." He held the box in one hand and her hand in the other.

She tucked the leash into her coat pocket. "Did you wonder if yesterday and the day before were real?"

He nodded. "Thought they might be a dream or a cruel joke because I wanted very much for my Christmas wish to be true."

"So did I." She kissed him. "Feels strange, us being together and you being home, but I wouldn't change a thing. I loved last night."

"So did I." He couldn't wait to make love to her again.

"I'm not used to being here for dinner with you around. I've done this for the past couple years with your parents, Alyssa and her family."

"Then that changes today. It's the start of our future—together." He kissed her temple. "And Christmas is the perfect day for that start."

"It is."

"We'll face the firing squad together." Alex escorted her into the house. "Now we can open presents."

"Were you waiting on me?" she murmured. "Alex." She paled. "You didn't have to."

"We were waiting on everyone over seven to wake up." He put the box down in beside the tree.

Boober licked and danced around the boys as they giggled. Molly folded her arms. "He's been looking forward to being around little people. I should've guessed he'd be a kid kind of dog."

Alex rubbed her shoulders. One day, he'd be doing this—accompanying her to Christmas with the family and being married. Molly would make a beautiful bride. Stunning, really. He didn't want to rush things too much, but he wanted to be her husband like yesterday.

"I got a phone call this morning," Molly said. She turned in his embrace and tipped her gaze to his. "Jill."

"She called?" he asked. "What for?"

"Well..." Molly slipped her phone from her pocket. "She and Nick just left North Bend this morning." She swiped the screen. "See? They got married at the village hall on Christmas Eve. She even apologized for not having us there as witnesses. I guess they wanted to keep it small."

He focused on the photo. Jill, in one of her favorite burgundy gowns, stood with Nick in front of the Christmas tree in the village hall. She clutched a bouquet of red roses and a poinsettia blossom had been tucked into her hair behind her ear. "Are those berries in her bouquet?"

"Probably." Molly tipped her head. "The flowers match her dress."

He draped his arm around Molly's shoulders. "Who is the officiant? I didn't know North Bend had anyone who could marry people."

"That's Judge McHenry and his wife, Estelle. She's a sucker for Christmas weddings and won't turn anyone away if they decide that's the day to tie the knot. I bet Estelle provided the flowers and played the organ. The songs tend to be a little wobbly, but her heart's in the right place." Molly shrugged. "I think it's romantic. Jill and Nick knew what they wanted and went for it. According to her text, they're on their way to Colorado. Denver, maybe?"

"She has family in Denver." Alex chuckled. He'd gotten Nick and Jill to take the next step and now they were married. Remarkable. He knew who he wanted too—and, if things went his way, he'd have his heart's desire by the end of the afternoon.

"She also said something about you being next." Molly crooked her eyebrow. "Want to let me in on what that means?"

"Jill," he mumbled. Trust Jill to keep gently pushing, even when he had everything under control.

Alyssa wobbled up to Molly, giving Alex a moment to consider what he wanted to say. "Thanks for bringing the dog over," Alyssa said. "The boys are excited. They want a dog and when we get home, we're getting one."

"We are?" Jeffery strolled over to where Molly, Alex and Alyssa stood. "I'm glad I knew and helped decide."

"You're not allowed to turn down a rescue pup—even if we haven't met him or her yet." Alyssa leaned into him. "You've wanted a dog all along. I'm just bringing the goal to life."

"That's what you do. That—and keep my life interesting." Jeffery sighed. "Um, your natives are restless and dying to get into the presents. A dog is great and all, but paper and toys are more exciting. Plus, it would appear Boober is trying to eat one of the presents."

"I wrapped a chew bone for him." Alex waved to his nephew. "Let the dog have the present."

"You'll be next," Alyssa said to the boys. She turned back to Molly and Alex and grasped Molly's hand. "Join the family. It's time for Christmas."

"Agreed." Alex stayed at the edge of the room with Molly. He wanted to push, but sensed her hesitation. "You don't have to hide," he murmured. "I know you hate attention—even if you are famous in this small town."

"I'm better out of the spotlight." She rested her back against his chest. "I'd rather observe."

"Looks like the boys like the gifts." He wasn't sure if they'd enjoy the blocks. "You got them books."

"What else would I bring?" Molly turned and caught his gaze. "It's a hazard of the job."

"Anyone who doesn't love books is no family of mine." He brushed his lips across her forehead. "The boys are still learning to read, but they love the books—just like they love you."

"And you." She paused. "You haven't answered me. What did Jill mean about you being next?"

"Give me a moment." He slid his hand into hers and tugged her out of the sunroom. "I want to talk to you about what she said and other things."

"Oh?" She tensed. "About? We've done a lot of talking."

"I know. Words are kind of my thing—kind of yours, too." He caged her in his arms in the living room. "I needed this. To hold you and know this moment was real."

"It is." She slid her palms over his chest. "Now about Jill's text…she meant…?"

"She meant she's thrilled to be married and wants everyone to be married, too."

"Well, I'm happy for her. It's not easy finding and keeping that special person in your life." Molly pursed her lips, then blew out a breath. "Why do I have the feeling she's been more than a little instrumental in your visit?"

"Her job is to be instrumental. Without her, I wouldn't have as much promotion done. Jill has a special talent for pushing when you don't want her to." He rubbed her back. "She's been trying to get you and I together since she found out you and I were something before."

"Something?" she asked. She crooked an eyebrow. "Wasn't it more than that?"

"Jill sensed you and I had a special relationship. Compound that with her Christmas spirit gone overboard and she decided to play matchmaker," he said. He thanked God, and anyone else out there listening, for putting Jill in his life. She might drive him crazy from time to time, but she had a big heart. Besides, he knew he'd find his way back to Molly, but Jill had been the extra nudge he'd needed.

"I'm glad," Molly said. Love shimmered in her eyes and she fixed the wrinkles in his shirt. "I love overzealous Christmas spirit, but speaking of over-the-top, I wanted to tell you how proud your father is. He comes into the store and tells me what you're up to. Your mother tells anyone who will listen just how high her opinion is of you and what you've done."

So they *had* kept her up to date? Score extra points for his mother and father. Molly deserved extra credit for paying attention, but he expected no less from her. "They're parents. They're supposed to feel that way. They think Alyssa is the best ever because she married Jeffery and had kids." Alex shrugged. "My parents are thrilled I've sorted myself out. That's the big thing. They wanted me to be happy and have direction."

"You've matured—as I said before." She picked lint off his shirt. "But you've always had direction."

He glanced out of the window. Snow fell and the lights on the houses across the street sparkled. The Christmas spirit wrapped around him. He couldn't stop this moment, even if he'd wanted to. Alex rested his forehead on hers. "I have matured. I know what direction I want in my life. I can write anywhere, but I need to put down roots. North Bend is the best place for those ties and you're the one I want in my life."

Molly smiled and didn't say anything.

"It's always been you. When the rest of the world is falling apart around me, I think of you. When I came back here, my first stop after a good night's sleep was to see you. That's something powerful." He rubbed his nose along hers. "I sneaked off this morning to this room because I needed a few moments alone with you. I don't want everyone to watch while I give you your gift."

"Alex?" Her eyes flashed.

"Here." He pulled the box out from behind the ceramic Christmas tree. "I hid this here earlier. Open it."

She hesitated, then tore the paper on the box. "At least you waited until today. I didn't think you would."

"Took everything I had to do that." He sat on the arm of the sofa. His heart beat double time as he waited for her to lift the lid on the box.

Molly gasped. She met his gaze and shook her head. "The pearls from the secondhand store."

"Like them?" His hands trembled. "No? When I saw them, I thought of you. Thought maybe you could wear them for the next book signing." *Or maybe at our wedding...* Boy, was he jumping the gun.

"I love them." She met his gaze. "Alex." Tears slipped down her cheeks. "I kept going back and looking at this strand, but never got around to buying them." She wiped her face with the back of her hand and smeared her eyeliner a bit. "The ornaments, necklaces...the gift certificate. You volunteered and gave so much back. You really did go all over town and helped everyone."

"I decided to spread a little Christmas cheer." He shrugged, then brushed her cheek with his thumb to remove the smudged makeup. "I wanted to be part of the community—like you."

"You are," she murmured.

"Then I did my job and based on your reaction, I made your Christmas." He tipped his head. "Yeah?"

"You did." She handed him the pearls. "Want to help me put them on?"

"I do." When she turned around, he draped the strand around her throat, then snapped the clasp in place. Alex kissed the back of her neck. "How about you wear those when we get married, too?"

She faced him again. "Married? Alex."

"If I'm taking the plunge, there's only one person I'm taking it with." He curled his fingers under her chin. "You and don't try to talk me out of it."

"Wouldn't dare." She sighed and pulled an envelope from her back pocket. "This isn't much, but it's your gift. Open it."

"A gift card for free books?" He grinned, then tore the seal. "Whatever it is, I'm sure I'll love it."

She blushed. "Just read it."

He worked the piece of paper free, then unfolded it.

Alex,

It's Christmas. This has always been our special time. You said something about the holiday being bleak without me. It's been shades of gray without you. I thought I'd moved on. Thought my heart was healed and you had no hold on me. I was wrong. I don't know who said this, but you never forget your first love. Not the puppy love kind, but the down-to-your-soul, can't-breathe-the-same-without-you kind. We proved we can live without each other, but I don't want to. You have always been the man in my heart. I love you.

Merry Christmas, Alex. The only thing I have to give you is my heart, but I'm sure you've known it was yours all along.

Love,
Molly

Alex refolded the paper and tucked it into the envelope. He met Molly's gaze. "Well, if you've got my heart and I've got yours...then I don't see any reason we need to postpone this. I don't have the ring and I'd rather pick one out with you, but I can't wait any longer." He dropped to one knee and grasped her hands. "Marry me, Molly."

Her smile wobbled, but love shone in her eyes. She nodded. "Yes."

"It's always been you," he said. He stood and snagged her in his arms. "Just you." He kissed her and the rest of the world melted away. He had the best Christmas gift ever.

"Wow." Molly's eyes widened as she seemed to look around him. "Oh."

Alex didn't bother to turn around. "My entire family is behind me, aren't they?"

She nodded. "They are," she murmured. "Your mom and sister are crying."

He rested his forehead on Molly's again. "Would you believe this is exactly how I'd planned on doing this?"

"Even with me?"

"Only with you." He kept her in his arms and faced his family. "I'm coming home and looks like we're planning a wedding. Merry Christmas everyone."

"Welcome to the family," Earl said. "Took you both long enough."

Alyssa held on to her belly and cried. "I've never seen anything so beautiful." She bobbed her head. "Except when Jeffery proposed to me."

Alex chuckled. Only his sister could get away with being so blunt, but he didn't care. He'd gotten what he wanted.

Kathy folded her hands in front of her mouth. "Now my Christmas wish has been granted."

Alex's dreams for Christmas had come true, too. Molly rested her head against his chest and rubbed his hand on her shoulder. The world seemed brighter and shinier now that he had his place. No matter what life threw at him, he had his partner beside him. He kissed the top of Molly's head. His Christmas in North Bend hadn't gone exactly how he'd wanted, but the result was worth the hassle. He had the woman of his heart in his arms and his life. He knew where he belonged and now he'd never have to leave.

Want to see more from this author? Here's a taster for you to enjoy!

Runaway Royal
Wendi Zwaduk

Excerpt

"I can do this." Princess Catherine shored up her courage. She was a royal. A princess. She could do anything she set her mind to—except stand up to the king and queen.

She stared at her reflection in the mirror. Her parents, the king and queen of Lysianna, wouldn't allow her to head to another country on her own. They insisted she be an advisor to her brother, the future king. Charlie could handle himself and he'd be a great king—whenever the time came.

If she didn't practice what she wanted to say, she'd flounder and this was not the time to lose her nerve. She tucked her hair behind her ears. "Mother, Father, I need to speak with you. I've completed two years of online schooling towards a degree in art history and I'm going to Kenton State College in the United States to finish it." Did she sound convincing enough?

She'd already completed her application for acceptance on campus, chosen her classes for the first semester and landed a good apartment in a building just across from the main portion of the campus. Her plane ticket had been paid for and she'd packed most of her things. All she needed to do was tell her parents she'd be leaving.

She abandoned her image in the mirror and resumed packing the last of her things—her brushes, photos and stuffed rabbit in her bag. She'd come back, but she wasn't sure when. Sadness filled her mind. Change would be hard—she'd only ever lived in the castle—but she needed to move forward with her life. She'd never be happy living as part of the court. Even if she did nothing more than teach an art class or run a portion of a museum back home, she'd be happy and doing something with her life.

Her lady-in-waiting, Corinne, hurried into the room. "I guess you're ready to go." She folded her arms. "Want me to go with you? I should."

She had plans for her lady and wasn't about to disclose them now. Corinne was terrible with secrets and would've told her parents before the point of no return. "It's handled."

Corinne sat on the bed. "What am I going to do with myself? I have nothing to do if you're not here. They might let me go."

"They won't." She closed her bag. "They like you. If my brother wasn't gay, they'd have married you off to him by now."

"But he *is* gay." Corinne groaned. "Sucks."

Her lady hadn't been shy about her crush on Charlie. In the whole of their time together, Corinne had insisted to Catherine she wanted to marry Charlie. The problem? Besides Charlie being gay, he wasn't going to marry Corinne simply to make an heir. He refused to change just for the royal line.

"Your parents would rather you marry Duke Elmore. He's handsome," Corinne said. "If you're into older guys."

Catherine shivered. "Older isn't the half of it. He's almost twenty years older than me, he's not handsome at all and I don't like him. I don't want to be married to someone who sees me as a ticket to the good life. He wants a title beyond duke." Her stepmother would never understand. She'd married the king, despite their ten-year age difference, just to have a title.

"So you're going to America to avoid him?"

"No." She simply refused to marry someone out of duty, not love. "I want to finish my degree. Art makes me happy. Him? Not so much."

"Well, it's time to talk to your parents." Corinne walked with her to the corridor. "Need me to do anything?"

"Nope. I've got this handled." Catherine gave her bag to the butler. "Thank you." She shored herself up again and headed down to the throne room. The car was ready and once she reached the airport, the plane would be waiting to whisk her to the States. Even if her parents said no, she'd left nothing to chance.

"Catherine." Her stepmother, Eloise, closed her book. "You look determined. Have you made a decision concerning the duke?"

"I have." She clasped her hands together. "I refuse to marry him." She stood tall. "I've made a choice about my future, too."

"Oh?" Her father finally looked up from his paperwork. "What have you decided?"

She sucked in a ragged breath, then sighed. "Mother, Father, I'm attending college."

Her father tipped his head and said nothing. Her stepmother gasped. "Why? You're a royal. You don't have to do *schooling*. Elmore will take care of you and you can play with your art all you want. Royals don't dirty their hands with studies."

Her stepmother spit the words out like sour candies. Catherine didn't care. She had to focus. "I want a degree in art history. I'd like to learn about the art here in Lysianna and around the world—like my mother used to know."

"Interesting," her father said. He tapped his pen on the table. "Why do you want to follow in your mother's footsteps?"

She'd prepared for this question. "I need to have something that's mine. I love art and I'm dying to continue my studies." She had to keep her explanation short and sweet. The more she talked, the greater the chance her parents would coerce her to change her mind. "I want something to hold on to that reminds me of my mother. I don't remember her and this is my private link."

"She's gone," her stepmother snapped.

"Let her have this, Queen. It's her choice," her father said. "She'll get bored after a year or she'll find this is the thing she wants to do. As for Elmore, he can wait. Or maybe he can't and he'll choose someone else. Doesn't matter to me. He's a pest."

She wasn't going to get bored, but if her father thought Elmore was a pest, then why try to palm her off on him?

"What about Charles?" her stepmother said. "He should be the one to go first. Yes, he deserves a degree."

"He already has one." Catherine gritted her teeth. Their parents didn't know Charlie well. He hated being referred to as Charles and he wasn't interested in going to college again. Charlie had attained a degree on his own and had his plan for making his own way without their parents to intervene. Now was her chance to do the same.

"Anyway, I'm leaving." She turned on her heel and left the room. If she looked back, she risked changing her mind. Only forward now.

"You're what?" Her stepmother chased after her. "You cannot. We need to arrange lodgings and security and everything else. You'll need handlers and Elmore should accompany you for protection. Or he should set up a security detail so he can keep you safe, but stay here to run his businesses."

God, no. Catherine headed through the foyer to the waiting car. "Goodbye, Mother." The idea of calling her stepmother Mother annoyed her. She'd had a mother and the queen wasn't a very good substitute.

"Catherine." Her stepmother caught up to her. "We'll summon Elmore. You cannot make the flight unprotected."

She sighed. "He's old enough to be my father and he's not attractive, so no." She tossed her bag onto the seat. "I'll be fine. No one in the United States knows me, so I won't need the huge protection you're planning." She'd have her roommate in her new apartment and a few transplanted palace security guards around, but out of sight.

"Take Corinne, please?" Her stepmother pushed Corinne at her. "You can't go alone. And don't forget, you need to have an approved consort by the time of your official portrait reveal."

"Fine." Catherine nodded to her lady-in-waiting. "Let's go." She ducked into the car without bothering for hugs or kisses from her stepmother. That wasn't her stepmother's style. Her father hadn't left the throne room. Her stepmother glared at her, but didn't otherwise show emotion. She wouldn't dare. Any bit of cracking might show she was human and the people of Lysianna didn't think she had emotions. She wanted to say goodbye to her brother, but he wasn't even in the country.

Catherine settled on the seat and sighed. "That worked out exactly as I planned."

"What about me?" Corinne asked. "You said I'd stay here."

"I lied." She winked. "I couldn't go totally alone. They're right. I do need someone with me that I can trust." Well, mostly trust. "I packed you a bag and added your name to the charter. You're flying with me."

Corinne's eyes widened. "My princess." She grinned. "Naughty."

She sighed again. "I've never been naughty a day in my life. Crafty, maybe, but never naughty."

"You've lived in your brother's shadow for too long."

"He'll be king and I won't hold the throne. Even if something happens to him, they won't let me be queen, so why not have something that's mine?" Catherine asked. "I don't mind." She didn't. "This way I'm out from under their thumb and can experience life." She couldn't wait for the next Chapter to start. There was a great big world out there just waiting for her to explore it.

There was the tricky thing about her needing a consort, but she had plenty of time. The portrait reveal wasn't for another year. The world wouldn't wait a year—not when her consort might be out there somewhere.

About the Author

Wendi Zwaduk is a multi-published, award-winning author of more than one hundred short stories and novels. She's been writing since 2008 and published since 2009. Her stories range from the contemporary and paranormal to BDSM and LGBTQ themes. No matter what the length, her works are always hot, but with a lot of heart. She enjoys giving her characters a second chance at love, no matter what the form. She's been the runner up in the Kink Category at Love Romances Café as well as nominated at the LRC for best contemporary, best ménage and best anthology. Her books have made it to the bestseller lists on Amazon.com and the former AllRomance Ebooks. She also writes under the name of Megan Slayer.

When she's not writing, she spends time with her husband and son as well as three dogs and three cats. She enjoys art, music and racing, but football is her sport of choice.

Wendi loves to hear from readers. You can find her contact information, website details and author profile page at https://www.totallybound.com

Home of Erotic Romance

Sign up for our newsletter and find out about all our romance book releases, eBook sales and promotions, sneak peeks and FREE romance books!